D0952446

# GABRIEL FINLEY

# FINLEY

## & the Raven's Riddle

# GABRIEL FINLEY

# FINLEY

## & the Raven's Riddle

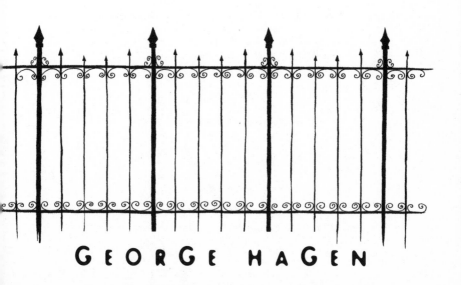

# GEORGE HAGEN

schwartz & wade books · new york

Text copyright © 2014 by George Hagen
Jacket art and interior illustrations copyright © 2014 by Scott Bakal
Frontispiece illustration copyright © 2014 by Jake Parker

All rights reserved. Published in the United States by Schwartz & Wade Books,
an imprint of Random House Children's Books, a division of Random House LLC,
a Penguin Random House Company, New York.

Schwartz & Wade Books and the colophon are trademarks of Random House LLC.

Visit us on the Web! randomhouse.com/kids

Educators and librarians, for a variety of teaching tools, visit us at RHTeachersLibrarians.com

*Library of Congress Cataloging-in-Publication Data*
Hagen, George.
Gabriel Finley and the raven's riddle / George Hagen. — First edition.
pages cm
Summary: Eleven-year-old Gabriel, with the help of the young raven Paladin, with whom he has a magical bond, travels to the foreboding land of Aviopolis, where he must face challenges and unanswerable riddles to rescue his long-missing father.
ISBN 978-0-385-37103-2 (hc) —ISBN 978-0-385-37104-9 (glb) —
ISBN 978-0-385-37105-6 (ebook)
[1. Adventure and adventurers—Fiction. 2. Voyages and travels—Fiction. 3. Magic—Fiction.
4. Missing persons—Fiction. 5. Ravens—Fiction.] I. Title.
PZ7.H12346Gab 2014
[Fic]—dc23
2013032533

The text of this book is set in 12-point Weiss.
Book design by Rachael Cole

Printed in the United States of America
2 4 6 8 10 9 7 5 3 1
First Edition

This raven tale is written for a soul whom I adore.
To spell her name correctly, please first solve these
riddles four:

> Let's go back to the Romans, who,
> When writing 50, always drew
> This letter for a numeral, too.

> Oh, the shame and dreadful woe
> Expressed by poets long ago
> (This very rhyme's a clue, y'know).

> Letter three can best be found
> Upon the banknote of a pound
> Before the number, safe and sound.

> At last, the fourth, a note played clear
> For all in an orchestra to hear
> Before the maestro may appear.

> —G.H.

*Solution to dedication: The answer to the first riddle is the letter *L*, which is the Roman numeral for 50. The second answer is *O*, which rhymes with *woe*, *ago*, and *know*. The third answer is *L* again, the symbol for the British pound. The fourth answer is *A*, the note always played by the first violinist to get an orchestra in tune before a performance. Sharp eyes may have noticed that each riddle begins with its answer!

PART ONE

# ❊ Ravens and Riddles ❊

Ravens love riddles.

In fact, ravens greet other ravens by telling a riddle. When one meets another, he'll introduce himself by asking something like: "Can a raven and owl be friends?"

The other might shift from one foot to the other, puzzled, because ravens and owls are mortal enemies. But then he'll think of an answer like:

"Yes, if the owl is stuffed and mounted on the wall!"

Then both ravens will start laughing in a coarse, throaty way that sounds rather painful, but it is just raven laughter.

A good many raven jokes are about owls. This is because ravens fear owls. Owls prey on ravens and eat their young; they swoop down upon their victims soundlessly; they are cold-hearted killers. Ravens consider owls to be stupid and dangerous, which is why they get so upset when they hear people use the expression "as wise as an owl." There isn't an owl alive who is as clever as a raven.

The most popular riddle ravens tell is the one about owls and sparrows.

"How stupid is a sparrow?" the first will say.

"As stupid as two owls!" the second will reply.

After this, they will cackle with laughter and become fast friends.


Why do ravens greet each other with a riddle?

It is to tell the good ravens from the bad.

This may surprise you, but long ago, ravens were our best friends. Ravens talked to us as easily as we talk to each other; they traded jokes and sang to babies to amuse them; they flew high above the fields and watched over our sheep; they led our fishing boats toward great schools of fish in the ocean. Out on the battlefields, as knights and soldiers lay wounded or dying, their faithful ravens would tend their wounds, give them medicine, or carry messages home for help.

After one tragic battle long ago, a grim phantom of a bird appeared. It looked like a raven—the same beak, silky feathers, and dark talons—but its eyes glowed a sickly yellow that pierced the mist of death around the fallen soldiers. This phantom asked each raven a question:

"How would you like to live forever?"

"Live forever? Impossible! How can any raven live forever?" each replied.

"It is simple," continued the phantom. "Eat the flesh of your master."

Many ravens were disgusted and flew away; but one raven listened. He had stood by his master for hours, offering words of comfort as the soldier's last mortal breaths faded in the chill air. Death was a horrible thing, he told himself. Feeling terribly alone and helpless, he considered the grim bird's promise.

"Could I truly live forever?" he replied.

The phantom nodded. "One bite."

The raven leaned over the body of his fallen companion and took the tiniest peck of flesh. First he felt ashamed; then a queasiness filled his belly, followed by an icy sensation that trickled into his heart. Suddenly, his heart began to race so fast that he thought it would burst from his chest.

In the same instant, time began to move faster for him: the grass wriggled out of the ground in a hurry to reach the sky; the sun crossed from east to west as quickly as a second hand sweeping around a clock. Then the terrible part—he felt hunger: a nagging, gnawing, craven ache in his belly. He ate more to make the hunger disappear, but it grew worse. When his master was nothing but a pile of bones, he became horrified. Had *he* done this? A cold, wretched bitterness engulfed his soul.

The hole in his belly would be there forever.

"You are a valraven now," said the phantom to his new disciple. "Come, help me. We shall make more of our kind!"

Soldiers couldn't tell the difference between ravens and valravens. When they saw one bird eating the flesh of a soldier they blamed all ravens and swatted them away with their swords and told their families, "Don't trust ravens anymore; they'll eat you."

It saddened the ravens to be shunned by men, for they were loyal creatures who loved jokes, laughter, and life. Afraid of being stoned or caged, they dared not speak to humans anymore. Instead, they spoke only to each other and kept company with their own kind.

As for valravens, they were vicious, spiteful creatures. If a raven refused to join them, he would be killed or blinded. Perpetually hungry, valravens never lost their taste for human flesh.

That is why ravens use riddles to tell the good ones from the bad.

No riddle is funny to a valraven.

That is always the first clue that you are in trouble.

So if a valraven asks *you* a riddle, what should you do?

Run for your life.

# ❋ The Book of Ravens ❋

Gabriel Finley didn't know anything about ravens, but he loved riddles.

He loved them the way other kids love baseball or computer games or mystery books. Riddles were like locks to Gabriel. He liked to pry them open and figure out what made them work. He liked the tricky ones that forced you to think about double meanings in words:

*When is a door not a door?*

*When it's ajar.*

He liked riddles that used unfamiliar words, like *ajar*, which means a door that is slightly open, but he also liked riddles that stretched your imagination, like this one:

*You'll always see me in first place in a running race, third in a marathon, fourth in a tear, yet never in a dash! Who am I?*

He spent a day puzzling over it, until, finally, he wrote it down and realized that the letter "r" comes first in *running race*, third in *marathon*, and fourth in the word *tear*.

Of course, Gabriel had another reason for loving riddles. His father had been a master of riddles. He'd told Gabriel a riddle every day, every single day—that is, until the day that he disappeared.

The Finleys' house was nestled in the old part of Brooklyn, where all the houses were brownstones with flickering lamps in the front yards, curved glass windows, and wrought-iron gates. It had once belonged to Gabriel's grandparents; the front door was cracked and weathered, its stairs were creaky, and its furniture was peculiar—lumpy armchairs of faded silk and velvet tasseled pillows, locked desks and cabinets with carved animal feet, a chandelier with candleholders made of antique pistols, and odd paintings of relatives (all very strange people, from the look of them).

The oddest painting hung in the study over a black desk. It depicted a boy of about twelve. Most of his features were in shadow, but the visible parts were very disturbing: his mouth was so small you might think he didn't have one; his hair was black and iridescent, like the rainbow of colors in an oil slick. And the nose? It was more like a raven's beak—strong, curved, and sharp at the tip. His eyes watched you with a cold, heartless stare and followed you wherever you stood in the room.

A single word was printed on the bottom of the portrait's frame. It didn't sound like a boy's name, but it suited the figure in the picture. *Corax.* Someone solitary, mysterious, and terrible.

"Did he really grow up to be my uncle?" Gabriel asked his aunt one late-summer evening during dinner.

Aunt Jaz had looked after Gabriel for the three years since his father went away. They were eating mu shu pork from a cardboard container (Aunt Jaz rarely cooked because the ancient kitchen stove made creepy bonking noises).

"Who, dear?"

"The boy in that weird painting upstairs."

When she didn't want to talk about something, Aunt Jaz's eyebrows rose high into her forehead. They weren't really her eyebrows; she had bright red hair and such faint eyebrows that she used a pencil to darken them into two little black boomerangs. When the boomerangs reached her hairline, Gabriel knew he had asked a difficult question.

*"Painting?"*

"Yes. The one in the study."

"Oh, yes, that's Uncle Corax Finley."

"Is there a grown-up painting of him?" asked Gabriel.

His aunt's expression darkened. "No, dear. He hasn't been seen since he was twelve. Corax is the black sheep of our family."

"Why? Where is he?"

"I haven't a clue." Aunt Jaz gave a shudder as if she didn't even want to know.

When Gabriel's inquiring stare persisted, her boomerang eyebrows wilted in surrender. "Your father probably knows."

At the mention of his father, Gabriel dropped his

chopsticks. "Aunt Jaz? Are you *sure* you don't know where my dad is?"

His aunt shook her head, rose from the table, and distractedly emptied her food into the sink and her plate into the trash can. Gabriel had seen her make this mistake many times before. He fished the plate out of the trash and wondered if there was any other way to find out about his father.

Jasmine Finley was a schoolteacher, a very eccentric sort. She could speak Chinese and write her own name in Egyptian hieroglyphs but was ignorant of the simplest things. For example, she became terribly alarmed when Gabriel outgrew his clothes. Looking him up and down one morning, she had fretted, "Dear me, how did this happen? Do you need to see a doctor?" She had been teaching for so many years that she assumed children came in one size: fourth grade.

Gabriel was never sure if she was hiding something or just confused. But he knew she loved him.

The next morning at breakfast, as they finished the Chinese-food leftovers, Gabriel tried another question.

"Aunt Jaz, you remember telling me that my mother disappeared when I was a baby?"

"Yes, dear, of course I do!"

"Did something happen to her?"

"Oh, no. Nothing happened. As I think I've said before, it was just a sudden disappearance."

Any child would have been upset to lose a parent this way, but Gabriel lost his mother when he was too young to remember her. Finleys seemed to disappear in unexplainable ways.

"Aunt Jaz?" Gabriel turned a piece of pork thoughtfully between his chopsticks. "Do you think she could . . . reappear?"

"I certainly hope so. Anything is possible."

"And my dad?"

This time, her boomerang eyebrows tilted kindly. "Yes, Gabriel, I'm quite sure he will."

"I miss him," Gabriel said. "I really miss him. Tell me something more. . . ."

Aunt Jaz's eyes became misty. "My poor Gabriel," she said. "There are so many things you must know, but every answer is like a fruit."

"A *fruit?*"

"Yes, dear," she replied. "Answers have a correct time, just as fruit is ripe at a certain time. I want my answers to be sweet rather than bitter. Do you understand?"

"I guess," said Gabriel, although her answer just made him more curious.

A few weeks after seventh grade began, Gabriel did find out something remarkable about his father. Oddly, it happened because of a new boy who had joined the class.

His name was Somes Grindle. When the teacher first pronounced his name like *sums*, he raised his hand and explained that it rhymed with *roams*.

"What an interesting name, Somes!" said Ms. Cumacho. "Where does it come from?"

"My mother's from Maine. There's a big gap of water there. . . ." The boy's voice trailed off as he became aware that everyone was staring at him. He exhaled sadly, his large dark eyes retreating to his hands, which were also unusually large.

That was the most Gabriel ever heard the boy say, at least until a week later. Somes was seated directly behind him. During a quiz, Gabriel could feel the boy's breath on his neck as he uttered deep, unhappy sighs.

When the quiz was returned, Somes saw that he'd failed. Gabriel didn't do very well, either. Once they were out in the corridor, Somes lifted him with his enormous hands.

"I thought you were smart," he growled. "Every answer I copied from you was wrong!"

"Sorry," said Gabriel nervously. "I guess you picked the wrong person to cheat off of."

With a look of gloomy disappointment, Somes dropped Gabriel back onto his feet and shuffled away.

As he walked home after school, Gabriel heard Somes's low voice calling after him. "Hey! Tell me the answers to the homework!"

When Gabriel refused, Somes reached out and raised Gabriel against a fence so that his feet dangled off the ground.

Helpless in the boy's grip, Gabriel shared his answers. But he had another reason for doing this—there was something pitiful about Somes. He felt a little sorry for him.

Now, before we go any further, I must warn you that this is not a story about a bully; it is a story about riddles, ravens, and a remarkable adventure. Still, it is important for you to know how adventures can sometimes begin with the people we least expect.

That evening, Aunt Jaz noticed a rip in Gabriel's jacket. When he explained about being hung from the fence, she peered at him over her horn-rimmed glasses. "Gabriel? You must never give that bully your answers again!"

"Well, he was pretty desperate," Gabriel explained.

"You must stand up for yourself!"

His aunt made a small fist, which amused Gabriel. He explained that he couldn't *stand up* against a bully if his feet were already off the ground.

Aunt Jaz shook her head. "Your father never had such problems when he was a boy."

"What kind of problems *did* he have?" Gabriel replied curiously.

His aunt's boomerang eyebrows converged suddenly,

and Gabriel knew he had stumbled upon a very important secret.

"Oh, nothing really," she said, her eyes doing a little scramble, as if looking for somewhere to escape.

"Aunt Jaz? Won't you tell me *anything* about him?" Gabriel asked.

Now her painted eyebrows tilted in a look of obvious sympathy.

"Oh, Gabriel, I'm a terrible aunt," she confessed. "You deserve so much better than me!"


Later that evening, in bed with the lights out, Gabriel became aware of his aunt's presence. She kneeled by his bed and patted him. He didn't open his eyes because she was only affectionate this way when she thought he was asleep.

The next morning, he realized she had placed something on his bedside table. It was a small notebook, bound in black leather. If he had opened it, he would have seen that the first page said *The Book of Ravens*, and it was signed in child's lettering—*Adam Finley*—with a small but carefully rendered drawing of a raven beside it.

Adam Finley, of course, was Gabriel's father.

And if Gabriel had started reading it right then and there, he might have forgotten about breakfast, or perhaps even to go to school; but since Gabriel had overslept, he gave the notebook a quick glance, then stuffed it in his school back-pack, planning to take a closer look at it later.

Instead, it was the notebook that was forgotten. It lay in the bottom of his backpack among a pocket pack of tissues, twelve gum wrappers, a worn eraser, and several very short pencils—a place where something might be lost for a long time.

# ❀ Breakfast ❀

"**C**lass? Today, we're going to talk about nutrition and the importance of a good breakfast," said Ms. Cumacho. "I want each of you to tell us what you ate this morning."

Somes emitted a deep, unhappy groan. Then he poked a pencil sharply into Gabriel's back. "Gabriel," he whispered. "Tell me—what did *you* have for breakfast?"

"Oh, Somes," Gabriel whispered back. "It's not a hard question!"

Somes sniffed. "I never eat breakfast. Tell me what you ate!"

Somes jabbed him, harder, so hard that Gabriel arched his back in pain. "Ouch! Chicken fried rice!" he muttered.

Ms. Cumacho, who had been pulling up the window blinds, turned back to the class. "Somes?" she said. "What did you eat?"

The bully's lips quivered. "Um, chicken fried rice."

"Chicken fried rice. How unusual!"

Ms. Cumacho wrote this on the blackboard. "Now," she said, scanning the students before her. "Who else? Gabriel, how about you? What was your breakfast?"

Gabriel paused, faced with a fresh problem. How would it sound if he also said *chicken fried rice?* Then he felt a surge of outrage that he even had to worry about his answer.

"I had chicken fried rice, too."

Ms. Cumacho's smile faded. "If you can't take this discussion seriously, Gabriel, you can leave."

"I'm *being* serious," he said. "That's what I had. It's Somes who—"

Somes uttered a roar and punched Gabriel sharply in the arm. "He's lying, Ms. Cumacho!"

A large purple bruise appeared on Gabriel's arm that afternoon. On the walk home from school, his friend Addison Sandoval gazed at it with admiration.

"Wow." He whistled. "Looks painful."

"You have no idea," muttered Gabriel.

"Well, look on the bright side. Ms. Cumacho saw Somes hit you. He's got detention."

Gabriel didn't get much satisfaction from this.

"You could have just said scrambled eggs or oatmeal or anything," suggested Addison.

"Why should I lie about breakfast?" Gabriel replied.

It was an uphill walk from school to their houses on Fifth Street. In the fall, acorns dropped from the tall oaks that lined the street, bouncing on car roofs and crunching under the boys' feet. Gabriel noticed a large black bird watching them from a nest of twigs and leaves overhead. He pointed it out to Addison.

"That's a raven," said Addison. "You can tell by the beak and the iridescent feathers—they change colors as it turns, see? Ravens are the largest of the corvids, which are a bird family that include crows, ravens, and rooks."

"I didn't know you knew so much about ravens," said Gabriel.

"I have to be an expert on these things," Addison explained. He wanted to run a natural history museum when he grew up.

"I'm an expert on riddles," said Gabriel as he looked up at the raven.

"What job requires a riddle expert?" said Addison. "It doesn't seem very useful."

Gabriel remembered his father telling him that riddles were good for the brain. "Athletes have flexible bodies," he'd said. "But great thinkers have flexible minds."

Meanwhile, the raven's eyes rested curiously on Gabriel, as if waiting for a reply to Addison's question. When Gabriel remained silent, the raven settled its gaze on an apple core on the sidewalk.

Addison waved his hand at the bird. "Shoo, off you go!" he cried.

"Wait," said Gabriel. "I think it wants that apple core for its chick."

The moment he said this, the raven flew down and seized

the core with its curved black beak. It placed one claw forward toward Gabriel, dipping its head graciously, then flew back to its nest.

Addison regarded his friend curiously. "How do you know that's why the raven wants it?"

Gabriel gave him a firm stare. "I just knew what it was thinking."

"Impossible," said Addison. "Totally impossible!"

"You have to admit that it seemed to thank me."

Addison frowned and shook his head. "I doubt it," he said. "Ravens are mimics, like parrots, but they don't have much intelligence."

Gabriel stared up at the tree. He was sure the raven had bowed to him.

## ❀ Paravolating ❀

The raven carried her apple core up to the edge of a big nest of twigs and sticks. She was a large, dignified bird—her feathers had a stunning blue sheen to them; her beak was dark and polished, with an elegant curve. She checked the skyline for danger before peering deep into her nest. Then, anxiously, she began rocking from one foot to the other.

"Paladin? My darling, where are you?" she said.

Nothing stirred. The mother raven began to poke about in a panic. "Paladin?" she repeated. "Oh, this can't be! Paladin!"

Out of the sticks, twigs, and gray fluff at the very bottom of the nest, a small dark beak poked through. Pinfeathered and very clumsy, a raven chick wobbled out of its burrow and opened its beak with eyes shut. It would still be a few days before he would be able to see.

"I was hiding, Mother. Just as you told me!"

"Oh, Paladin," sighed the raven. "Thank the heavens!" She gently caressed the baby with her enormous beak. "I thought I'd lost you."

She began chewing pieces of the apple core and offered

the pulp to the fledgling, who immediately opened his beak and swallowed in great gulps. When his belly was full he swooned, tipsy with satisfaction, and rested his head against the side of the nest.

"I thought you'd never come," he said. "I heard wings, so I hid."

"Very good," she replied. "You did exactly the right thing."

"Mother? Must I be afraid of all birds?"

"Not all, my love. Just owls and their kind—eagles, hawks."

She considered mentioning valravens but decided that her chick was too young to learn about them.

"What about people? I hear them walking below the nest," asked the fledgling.

The mother raven cast a cautious glance down.

"Most people leave us alone. They fear us, which is a pity, because we were once their best friends."

"Their best friends?"

"Yes. We even talked to them, but that was a very long time ago. Now only a few humans ever become friends with ravens. Still, when they do, amazing things happen."

"Like what?" asked Paladin, curious.

"Well, a raven's human friend is called an *amicus*. Once they meet, the raven and his amicus can share thoughts. They can merge as one, and fly as one, which is called *paravolating*. It is a very special bond, Paladin. Your grandfather Baldasarre had an amicus."

The fledgling felt a sudden tremor of excitement. "Is there an amicus for me, Mother?"

"Perhaps, my love." The mother raven became thoughtful. She watched the two boys she had just encountered make their way into a house across the street. "If you meet the rare kind of human who appreciates riddles."

# ❃ Moving ❃

Gabriel often spent the afternoon at the Sandoval house. It had the same brownstone facade, tall windows, and iron gates as his own. Inside, however, the furniture was new and modern.

When Gabriel went to Addison's, they often wound up playing computer games, which Addison always won. This afternoon, Gabriel became tired of losing and suggested they tell riddles instead.

"Here's one," Gabriel said. "What lies at the end of forever?"

Addison chewed his lip and stared up at the ceiling. "That's an impossible question," he replied. "Forever is infinite. It never stops."

"Yes it does." Gabriel smiled. "If you give up, I'll tell you."

"Fine. I give up," said Addison.

"Okay. The letter 'r' lies at the end of forever."

Addison slapped his hand against his forehead. "That's not a fair question."

"It's a riddle!" Gabriel grinned. "You have to stretch your mind!"

Just then, there was a knock at the door. It was Aunt Jaz with a bag of take-out food from the Chinese restaurant. If his aunt didn't find Gabriel at home, she knew he would be at Addison's. After talking to Mrs. Sandoval for a moment, she turned to Addison and said, "How do you feel about moving to a new city?"

Gabriel looked at his friend with surprise. "You're moving? Why didn't you tell me?"

Addison shrugged, thrusting his hands in his pockets. "My dad got a job somewhere else, but I was hoping he might not take it—"

"Not take it? Oh, Addison," sighed Mrs. Sandoval. "It's a wonderful opportunity! He's going to open a new restaurant in Los Angeles. You'll have a great time there."

"Whatever," replied Addison glumly.

As they left the Sandovals' house, Gabriel's mood sank. He thought about his friend being far away, which reminded him of his father's absence.

"Aunt Jaz?" he said as they trudged up their stoop.

"Yes, dear?"

"Where exactly is my dad?"

"Oh, goodness, Gabriel, not again!" said his aunt. "I only wish I knew. About three years ago—I remember it so well—

your father remarked that he might disappear quite suddenly. I laughed at the time, because it was such an odd thing to say. . . ." Aunt Jaz put her hand to her cheek with a look of regret. "But a few days later, on a fall evening, like this one, I brought you home from the playground. The house felt cold and strangely empty, so I hurried upstairs to the study and found the curtains blowing freely from the wide-open window. Everything was tidy in the room—unusual for your father—but there was a note with instructions saying that if I should find the window open, I should take care of you until he returned."

Gabriel studied his aunt's expression. "When a person is missing, shouldn't you call the police?"

"I don't believe your father is in a place where the police *could* find him," replied Aunt Jaz. "Gabriel, he promised me he would return as soon as it was earthly possible. Did you take a look at that book I gave you? It explains a lot of things."

"Oh," said Gabriel. "I forgot about that old leather book!"

Aunt Jaz glanced around nervously, as if the very trees might be listening. "My dear, it was his *diary*." Then she hurriedly fumbled with the lock to the front door.

As soon as he got to his room, Gabriel fished the notebook out of his backpack. He opened it up and squinted at the very small handwriting. It was difficult to get past the first page or two; but slowly, Gabriel grew accustomed to the scrawled lettering, and it became easier and easier to understand, until he was racing along faster than he had read anything in his life.

# ❀ Baldasarre ❀

The things I am going to write in this book will seem unbelievable, but I can promise you that they are true. Each and every thing I describe really happened to me.

April 1: Today, as I was walking home from school, a big black bird landed right in front of me on the sidewalk. It had a large, blunt beak and black eyes and a strange oily sheen to its wings. It sat at my feet, wobbling unsteadily.

"Shoo," I said, and I stepped forward, expecting it to hop away, the way pigeons do.

Surprisingly, it didn't move. And then, even more surprisingly, I heard a voice in my head say very clearly:

*I have one eye but cannot see,*
*A long tail always follows me,*
*I'm a doctor and a cobbler's friend,*
*Your button I will gladly mend.*
*What am I?*

Now, I don't believe magical stories with animals that talk. But this was amazing. This voice was as clear as could be, in my head, and the bird had a look—very serious—as if it was waiting for my answer.

"Well, what has an eye, a long tail, and mends a button. It must be . . . a needle!" I said aloud.

The bird made a sound like a laugh, as if it was pleased with my answer. It limped forward.

*My leg is broken,* said the voice in my head.

I opened my mouth, but I couldn't speak from surprise. I could understand the bird's thoughts so clearly, and it seemed to understand me!

"If you show me to your father, he can mend it," said the bird. "My name is Baldasarre," he added, dipping his head in a bow.

Now I was really astonished. A bird talking like a person! Then his voice became desperate. "Please help me," he begged. "I am in grave danger."

How could I leave this amazing bird? I gently picked him up in my jacket and carried him to my house.

My father was in the kitchen. I told him the bird had a broken leg. He said I should have left it outside.

"I swear it spoke to me," I said. "It told me a riddle."

My father looked confused, but then he smiled.

"Oh, I understand, it's April Fools' Day, and you think this is a funny joke!" he said.

"No. It's true."

I was ready for him to laugh again, but he didn't. After a careful look at the bird, he cleaned the wound with some things from the medicine cabinet and bound the leg with a pair of chopstick splints.

Now came many entries in the diary describing the raven's recovery; but what most fascinated Gabriel was an entry farther along. . . .

April 10: Watching my father take care of this bird, you might think he was a veterinarian, not a family doctor. He seemed to know exactly what was best to feed it, and he was very tender, as if he understood, somehow, what it was feeling. When I asked how he knew so much, he took a deep breath and let the question vanish into silence.

April 15: Today, after examining the bird's leg (it's a raven, I've learned), my father turned to me and said, "So, Adam, tell me what our patient has been saying to you."

I explained that the bird had told me that he had enemies. And that he was in grave danger.

"In grave danger from what?" my father asked.

The raven stopped eating, tilted his head, and looked at me. Then he looked at my father most carefully, as if weighing a very serious decision.

"I am in danger from Corax," the raven said.

My father's expression changed quite suddenly.

"Who is Corax?" I asked him.

My father said nothing.

The raven spoke again.

"Your father knows exactly who he is."

When I questioned my father about this, he let out a long sigh.

"Corax is my son. Your older brother," he replied.

"What? I have an older brother? Where is he? Why haven't I ever met him?"

"Because . . ." And here, my father's expression darkened. "He is a disgrace to our family."

# ❈ Valravens on the Move ❈

In the oak tree near Gabriel's house, the raven mother was feeding her chick with scraps found in the neighborhood. Between mouthfuls, she asked questions:

"Now," she said, "what's smarter than a raven?"

"Nothing is smarter than a raven," he replied.

The mother uttered a small, appreciative throk—a clicking sound that ravens like to make. "And why are ravens so smart?"

"We watch and listen and learn," replied the chick.

"Very good. And when a raven sees another raven, what does he do?"

"He tells a riddle."

Nodding, the mother raven replied, "Very well. Tell me a riddle."

The chick buried his beak in his chest to think, then raised his head with an enthusiastic blink. His eyesight was still weak, but he could make his mother out more clearly now. "What flies but has no wings?"

This seemed to surprise the chick's mother. She cocked her head.

"*Flies but has no wings?* What?"

"Time," said the chick.

"Time!" His mother collapsed into a peal of throks. "I'm so proud of you, Paladin!" she said. "Now it is time to talk about a raven's greatest danger."

"Owls!" said the raven chick. "Eagles? Hawks?"

"No, my love. Valravens."

The young raven noticed fear in his mother's expression. He trembled slightly. "What are . . . valravens?"

"They look like us, but they are nothing like us. Doomed to live forever, they are wretched, bitter creatures. Nothing is funny to a valraven. That is why we greet each other with a riddle. A valraven will not delight in the answer. It is the best way to tell them apart from us."

"But why do they hate us, Mother?"

His mother looked deeply into Paladin's eyes, wondering if he was ready for such a dark tale. Then she decided that it was important for his own safety.

"It is all because of a riddle," she explained. "Long ago, when ravens were man's best friend, a furious battle erupted between creatures called dwarfs and humans. Each wanted to live on the earth's surface and banish the other underground. The dwarfs lost this battle, and were imprisoned in a dark cavern far beneath the earth's surface. Desperate for sunlight and freedom, they offered a gift to the human king in return for their liberty—a silver necklace called a *torc*, which granted wishes. The king was wary of this gift, however, and asked his two ravens, Huginn and Muninn, for advice. Huginn, the bolder of the two, urged the king to accept the torc and use its power to rule, but Muninn, the wiser bird, reminded the king that the dwarfs were mischievous silversmiths who wove black magic into such gifts. The torc was sure to bring misery and despair, and Muninn advised him not to accept it.

"So the king refused the necklace and kept the dwarfs deep beneath the earth. Twenty years later, however, when he arrived to release them, he found a surprise."

"What kind of surprise?" asked Paladin.

"The dwarfs' underground dungeon, a maze of caves and holes, had been transformed into a marvelous city of carved marble, granite, obsidian, and quartz. They had fashioned rock and rubble into glittering floors, vaulted ceilings, and towering marble columns veined with gold and silver. Their craftsmanship was so fine that they could sculpt furniture out of granite. Delicate beds and armchairs and sofas were carved to feel as soft to the touch as a quilted blanket or cushioned seat. A magnificent tower stood in the center of the cavern, tethered by a slender bridge, and every chamber in the surrounding cavern walls had windows shuttered with alabaster or jade and stately doors, and behind them more fantastic furniture wrought by the dwarfs' skill and ingenuity.

"Amazed, the king called out to his prisoners. 'You have all earned your freedom!' His voice echoed through the cavern, but not a soul answered. It seemed that the dwarfs had tunneled an escape of their own, long ago, and left this extraordinary city to a few birds nesting in the cavern walls. 'It belongs to the birds now,' declared the king, and he named the city *Aviopolis*. 'Come, Huginn and Muninn,' he said to his raven companions. 'Let us go back to sunlight and forget this place.'"

"But why would birds live in an underground city?" said Paladin.

"It was far away from humans," his mother explained. "It was a huge safe haven, especially for birds that most feared humans, like the dodoes."

"But what does Aviopolis have to do with the riddle?" Paladin asked.

"I'm getting to that," said his mother. "As the king departed from Aviopolis, Muninn, the wiser bird, rode with him on his shoulder, but Huginn hung back. Some dark, enticing power drew him from room to room in this dark, magnificent cavern, until finally, he arrived in a chamber at the very top of Aviopolis. There, in a room grander and more exquisite than any other, laid upon a table of brilliant green marble, was the magic silver necklace the dwarfs had fashioned for the king. Huginn took it and placed it around his neck.

"It was many hours later, in the cold early light of dawn, that Muninn awoke from his perch in the king's bedchamber.

He felt an eerie sense of discomfort and opened his eyes to see a most horrible sight.

"The king looked deathly pale and lay rigid in his bed. The bold raven Huginn, wearing the glittering silver torc around his neck, stood upon his master's chest, eating his flesh.

"'Brother! What have you done?' cried Muninn.

"His beak shiny with blood, Huginn glanced up with a sullen, cowardly look in his eyes. 'I found it, brother,' he whispered. 'The necklace that grants wishes. I wished to live forever, and it compelled me to eat the flesh of my amicus.' He looked regretfully at the dead king. 'I feel sick, sick and wretched. But changed.'

"Then his eyes danced wickedly. 'Time passes differently for me now. I am immortal and fearless! Join me, brother. Become a valraven, as I have! One bite of flesh is all it takes!'

"Muninn shuddered. 'Join you? Never! That torc has twisted your soul, Huginn. Give it to me, before it does more harm!'

"'Be off!' The scornful raven laughed. 'You're no match for me now!'

"Muninn tipped his head craftily at Huginn. 'No match? Prove me wrong. Answer a simple riddle, and if I win, the torc is mine. If you win, do as you wish with your new power.'

"No raven or valraven can resist a riddle," his mother reminded Paladin.

"Yes, I know, but what was the riddle, and who won?" asked the baby raven anxiously.

"Muninn's riddle was simple," she continued. "A raven has one, a valraven has two, and a man has none. What is it?"

"Hmm," said Paladin, thinking. "My first guess would be a life, but a valraven doesn't exactly have two lives."

"And men have lives just as ravens do," added his mother.

"It's a very hard riddle." Paladin frowned.

"The answer is simple," said his mother. "It's the letter 'v.'"

"Oh!" said Paladin.

"When Huginn couldn't guess the answer, the torc flew from his neck onto Muninn's neck. Bitter and furious, Huginn promised to get it back by force. 'I'll raise an army of valravens,' he vowed. From then on, he haunted the battlefields, where it was possible to tempt other ravens to eat the flesh of their fallen comrades. Soon, there were thousands of valravens, all seeking the torc."

"But what happened to it?"

"Well, my understanding is . . . ," she began, but then she gasped.

A large bird had landed on the rim of the nest. Its neck feathers were splayed out in fury, its wings raised as if prepared to attack, and one leg brandished three black talons. In a deep, foreboding voice, it spoke:

*"Every house has one of me,*
*I will not let you in, you see,*
*Unless you feed me with a meal*
*Of jagged brass or hardened steel."*

Without showing any doubt, Paladin's mother replied. "I believe that would be a lock. You *feed* it with a key!"

The visitor's proud neck feathers deflated very suddenly. It uttered a broad, raspy laugh that was as merry as it was loud.

"Oh, good show, Endora! Good show indeed!"

"Bertolt!" exclaimed Paladin's mother. "You almost scared the wits out of little Paladin. How dare you creep up on us like that?"

Bertolt buried his beak in his chest for a moment. "My dear Endora, one has to be careful. I come with a warning."

Paladin had stopped shaking. He was interested to hear his mother's name spoken: *Endora*. He had never heard it before. Being so young he had assumed that she was called "Mother" by everybody.

"A warning? About what?"

Bertolt looked around, then whispered the word:

"Valravens. Three of them. Sent from below. They're on the move, Endora. One of them attacked Argus when he couldn't answer a riddle."

"What was the riddle?"

"A very unpleasant one," said Bertolt, shaking his neck feathers. "What do owls taste like?"

"What a disgusting question!" replied Endora. "As if any raven would want to know what owls taste like."

"The valraven went for Argus's eyes. That's what they do, you know. They blind their victims when they don't get what they want. This one was looking specifically for a young raven with a boy amicus."

"I thought they were looking for the torc!" said Paladin.

Bertolt looked down at Paladin with a stern frown. "Oh, you know about the torc, do you?"

Paladin trembled under the bird's wise stare.

"Um, yes."

"Are you ready to fly?"

"He needs a month or two," said Endora, putting her wing protectively over Paladin.

Bertolt looked at Endora. "Does he know any riddles?"

"Oh, yes, he's already learned a few."

Bertolt cast a thoughtful glance at Paladin. "Guard him well, Endora. A lot may depend on this young raven."

Then, raising his wings and uttering a cheery farewell *throk!* Bertolt flew off into the sky.

"What did he mean by a lot may depend on me, Mother?"

Endora gently nuzzled her sleepy chick. "That is a story for another day, my dear," she whispered.

# ❈ The Raven's Amicus ❈

Gabriel couldn't wait to get back to the diary. The next entry described how Gabriel's grandfather brought a portrait of Adam's missing brother, Corax, down from the attic to show him. Adam was very upset by his resemblance to his brother.

We have the same shape face, the same small mouth, but I don't think my eyes are as cold or ruthless—at least, I hope not!

But the most interesting entries were about Adam's conversations with his raven, Baldasarre.

April 29: Today I asked Baldasarre why, if ravens can talk, they don't talk to most people. This is what he told me: "Ravens used to talk to humans, long ago, but they grew afraid. If a raven spoke, he might be put in a cage to be shown around as a kind of performing animal. Every raven cherishes his freedom."

"Then why did you speak to my father and me?" I asked.

"You are different, Adam," said Baldasarre. "I knew I could trust you. You see, you were already able to understand my thoughts. At age twelve, a few children—like you—acquire this special power. It is very rare. You are what is called a raven's amicus."

I was flabbergasted. And I still am.

May 6: Baldasarre told me he is almost ready to fly again. I'm very sad about this. When I told my father that I wished I could keep him, he said that a raven is not a pet. "Healing his leg doesn't give you the right to own him," he said. "You owe him his freedom."

I don't want him to go. For the next few days, I will give Baldasarre all his favorite foods, hoping he'll decide to stay.

May 10: Baldasarre asked me to let him out. I was upset, but I remembered my father's words and pulled up the window and let the breeze blow the curtains aside. It was a gorgeous evening, clear and cloudless. Baldasarre hopped to the ledge, flexing his healed leg.

"Goodbye, friend," I choked out.

Baldasarre tipped his head at me, surprised, and spoke in my head.

*This is not a farewell, Adam.*

"It's not?" I replied out loud, forgetting that I could answer him without speaking.

*We're going to fly together, Adam. First, imagine jumping toward me, but do not move your legs. Think about flying, and when you do, you will leave yourself behind and become part of me.*

*How can I leave myself behind?* I thought.

*I know it seems impossible,* the raven replied. *But that is what you must do. Look at your feet, and just* imagine *jumping.*

I tried to concentrate as hard as I could, and then, staring at my bare feet on the floorboards, I imagined a jump.

Nothing happened.

*Adam*, said Baldasarre. *Try to believe it will happen.*

Looking back down, I focused my thoughts. This time I imagined how wondrous it would be if I could actually fly like a bird.

In the next instant, I felt my limbs shake violently. My bones appeared to be rearranging themselves. My arms trembled and seemed to roll to where my shoulder blades would be, my legs felt shorter, and I saw claws where my feet had been. I looked around, confused—I wasn't standing on the floor anymore!

*Where am I?* I wondered. Then I realized I was on the windowsill where Baldasarre had been. But where was he?

*We are one,* came the reply.

*Baldasarre? Where is my body?*

*Don't worry; you have no need of it. It will return when we part. Now be quiet. We're going to fly.*

Before I could answer, I tumbled through the open window. I was about to scream, but in the next instant I felt my wings beating powerfully against the air and (this was the strangest thing) the air around me seemed to press back, thick and sluggish as water. Yet my wings could slice through it, grasp it, or glide over it like a surfer on a wave.

Oh, the joy I felt! So high above the buildings, high above everyone in the city. The streetlamps were brilliant little points far below. I was free in a way I had never imagined before. So this was what flying felt like!

I laughed, and the most extraordinary sound came from my throat—the croak of a raven, rough as sandpaper, so loud that it echoed across the chimneys, roofs, and water towers of Brooklyn.

*Did I do that?* I wondered.

*It was both of us,* came Baldasarre's reply. *We are paravolating.*

# ❧ The Truth About Corax ❧

A huge thunderstorm swept over Brooklyn on Addison's moving day. The moving men worked quickly, running boxes up and down a ramp to an enormous truck. Gabriel kept Addison company, planning to tell him about the amazing things he had discovered in his father's diary. He wanted the right moment to explain about magic and talking ravens, but it never seemed to come. The hours moved quickly, and soon the moving truck was loaded and pulling away.

Gabriel and Addison stood under an umbrella next to the taxi as Addison's mother and father stowed their baggage.

"I'm sorry you're going," Gabriel said.

"Me too," said Addison, glancing up at the trees. "Gabriel? I have this weird feeling, like I'm leaving just when something awesome is going to happen."

"Really?" said Gabriel. "Like what?"

"I don't know," Addison replied. "Do you remember when you saw that raven? Well, I looked up ravens. I was wrong. They're very intelligent birds."

Gabriel nodded. "Yes! I meant to tell you about my dad's—"

Mrs. Sandoval interrupted. "Let's go, honey. We're late for the airport."

Addison sighed. "Gotta go."

The boys bumped knuckles, and Addison joined his parents inside the taxi. Then his head appeared through the window. "Hey, I just remembered something!"

"What?"

"I met your new neighbors. *Girls.* One of them is our age. The other two are older, I think."

"Oh. Girls? Really?" said Gabriel, trying to sound enthusiastic.

The taxi pulled away as a fresh downpour enveloped the street.

As the rain pattered down outside, Gabriel curled up by the window and opened the diary. The next entries were so carefully described that he felt as if his father wasn't just writing, but was talking directly to him.

May 15: Baldasarre and I fly every evening. Each time, it gets easier to merge with him—all I have to do is tighten my muscles and we become one. In the air, I have to remember to be slack. Last night I tried to point out the sunset, and we fell into a spin in midflight because I had taken control of Baldasarre's wing. He was furious.

*Do you want to kill us both?* he muttered. *Let me do the flying!*

May 17: We tried something different today. Baldasarre leaped into *my* body! We walked into a supermarket. He had never seen so many fruits and vegetables in one place. Suddenly, I felt my head dart down and my mouth grab a grape.

*Baldasarre?* I said. *Humans don't eat like birds. Control yourself!*

May 19: Baldasarre doesn't like glass. Like most birds, he finds it very confusing. We went to get ice cream today in my body, but he got scared by the glass door and tried to fly away. I felt my arms flapping wildly, but there was nothing I could do until he calmed down.

May 20: This evening we flew around the whole city and landed on the crown of the Statue of Liberty. There is nothing more amazing than looking over the harbor with the city in the distance, thousands of lights from the Verrazano Bridge glittering all the way to the Empire State Building.

*I feel so happy,* I told Baldasarre.

He told me not to get too comfortable. *One owl attack can wipe that smile off your face.*

*But you said ravens are smarter than owls.*

*Yes, but we're no match for cold-blooded killers.*

May 22: Tonight was terrifying. We were flying across the bay and happened to circle the buildings around Battery Park. There's an excellent air current there; Baldasarre loves to glide over the trees and let the breeze lift us up over the city like the smoothest roller-coaster ride. But this time, just as we crested over the skyscrapers, I felt his muscles stiffen.

He looked down behind us and I saw it, moving with us almost like our shadow. It had a huge wingspan, maybe three times that of a raven's.

*What is it?* I asked.

*That's an owl. Worse—a great horned owl.*

We rolled over toward the river, but the owl gained on us without even trying. Baldasarre began flapping frantically to go higher, but the owl matched our climb with barely an effort.

*What are we going to do?*

*The only thing we can: find a place an owl can't go.*

I could feel Baldasarre's fear all through me. My heart was thumping like crazy, my wings were sore, and a grim ache in my belly told me this creature would kill us. The great brown-flecked predator swallowed the distance between us in about three heartbeats.

We swooped down between tree limbs in the darkness, but the owl dodged every branch, stem, and bush with the slightest tilt of his power-ful wings. We weaved through a row of pillars, and so did the owl, with identical precision. Silent. Deadly. Ever closer.

Finally, Baldasarre spoke in a weary, tragic tone.

*Adam?*

*Yes.*

*This may be our last minute alive.*

Ahead, I could see an enormous construction site. It was a building about a hundred floors high, just a framework of iron girders with a skin of netting to keep the workers safe as they toiled on the edges of the structure.

*Let's fly there!* I cried. *Into one of those upper floors. Weave in and out, but be careful to avoid the netting!*

Baldasarre did as I said, and we streaked into the skeleton framework of the structure, barely avoiding pillars, wires, and pipes.

The great horned owl had no problem with these new obstacles. I could sense his merciless eyes upon us, getting nearer and nearer.

Baldasarre dodged and careered past the beams, then suddenly dropped down a shaft.

The owl wasn't fooled for a second. It followed us, claws extended for the kill.

I screamed—which came out as a raven's anxious croak.

Abruptly, Baldasarre spun in a tight circle.

The owl kept going, struck a curtain of netting, and fell, down and down, to the ground floor, where it tossed like some great fish caught at sea.

Baldasarre let out a giddy series of throks, gloating at the owl's mistake. We landed on a heap of bricks and watched the creature flop around in front of us, helplessly snagged.

"Ho ho ho!" Baldasarre said. "Look who's in trouble now!"

I jumped apart from him and caught my breath. I felt exhausted, and my legs trembled.

Meanwhile, Baldasarre strutted around the owl, his neck feathers spread out in a cocky display of victory.

"What's stupider than a sparrow?" he taunted. "Two owls!"

The owl struggled against the netting, twisting to escape as it wound itself tighter and tighter. It was a magnificent-looking bird with great brown feathers, huge talons, and large hornlike ears just above its enormous yellow eyes, but it began wheezing now, the netting tightening around its throat.

"He'll never get out of there," chuckled Baldasarre.

Although I was relieved to be alive, I couldn't look at this extraordinary bird without feeling some respect for it. To see it struggle this way was heartbreaking. I kneeled beside it.

*Be careful, Adam. He's a killer,* warned Baldasarre.

"This is an awful way to die," I replied out loud.

The owl's great amber eyes batted at me through the mesh. They seemed desperate and fearful now.

"If I free you, will you return the favor?" I whispered.

*Adam, don't ever trust an owl,* said Baldasarre. *Let's go!*

"On your honor?" I asked.

*Owls have no honor!* cried Baldasarre.

The owl blinked at me very slowly. I couldn't tell if this was a signal that it had agreed, or if it was just slowly dying.

"It doesn't seem honorable to let it die," I argued, then reached out and pulled at the mesh around the owl's neck with my fingers. I had to pull strand by strand because the mesh was so tight. The owl's breathing improved. Then I unraveled the mesh from its wings. It didn't stir, but lay on the concrete floor, its feathered chest heaving slowly. It could have pounced on Baldasarre in a split second, but it didn't. Its enormous eyes flickered at me.

Baldasarre was furious. *Adam, we must go!* he cried.

"Remember," I whispered to the owl, and then I jumped. Instantly we were flying back toward Brooklyn.

All the way, Baldasarre ranted. *Of all the stupid things to do! An owl! Never help an owl! They're all fluff, stupidity, and ruthlessness! We'll never get home! He's probably following with his gang of friends. They'll have us for breakfast and lunch and spit our bones into the river!*

The sky was empty, but Baldasarre kept looking back for our assailant.

The city dozed quietly as dawn lit up the eastern sky with a faint purple glow.

By the time we reached my window, I wasn't sure which would have been worse—being an owl's breakfast or having to keep listening to Baldasarre complain about what I'd done.

No sooner had I jumped free of him and dusted myself off than a voice spoke out of the darkness.

"Adam?"

My father was seated in a worn green velvet armchair with a blanket pulled up to his neck. His glasses had fallen onto his chest. He had seen us separate, but instead of looking amazed, his eyes were wide with concern.

The entry stopped there. Gabriel quickly turned to the next entry and found the pages wrinkled, as if they had been wet with water or, perhaps, tears.

May 23: I was too upset last night, but I have to explain why my father was not surprised by what he saw.

First, he took me downstairs and cooked us breakfast.

It was the only meal my father cooked, and he did it very well; he fried eggs so that they were crispy on the edges but runny in the center. He made potato hash in the skillet, browned all over and flavored with pepper and a little cumin and plenty of butter. We ate together while I told him about our adventure, and when I had finished, he folded his hands and looked at me.

"Adam," he said. "Your older brother also found a raven. He was twelve when it happened, exactly your age. Like you, he became the raven's amicus, and like you, he learned to talk to it in his head. Like you, he could . . ."

Here, my father looked upward, as if following a bird's flight.

"Paravolate?" I said.

He nodded sadly. "Paravolate. Yes, I remember, that's what he called it, too."

"You make it sound like a bad thing," I said. "If you could only try it yourself, you'd understand that it's the most amazing—"

My father interrupted by raising his hand. "Like you, Adam, Corax was an adventurous and clever boy. He loved to fly, and told his secret to a friend, an unfortunate fellow named Thomas, who did not believe him. To prove it, Corax spied on him as a bird, listened to his arguments with his mother, watched from the sky as Thomas stole an apple from an outdoor grocery and ignored an elderly woman who asked him for help picking up her spectacles. When Corax revealed all he had seen, Thomas still could not believe Corax could fly, but he looked terrified and ashamed. This pleased Corax more than anything, for it was power.

"This boy's mother told me he began complaining of hearing voices where there were no people." My father's voice became low and grave. "Then, about a week later, he was seen, screaming, as he ran in front of a bus. He was killed. Corax promised me he had nothing to do with it, but I saw no sorrow at the loss of his friend—only a defiant, cruel glint in his eyes."

I shook my head. "I don't want to become—"

"Let me finish," he insisted. "In just a few months of doing what you have been doing"—here, he pointed angrily at me, then at Baldasarre—

"Corax became a wretched and heartless boy. That picture downstairs? It doesn't begin to show the terrible transformation. His soul was slipping away, leaving a cruel spirit in its place.

"One evening I realized I had to protect him from himself, so I took a hammer and nails and sealed Corax's window so that he couldn't go out on his flight. I locked his door and told him it was for his own good. In the morning, we planned to take him to see a doctor.

"Corax wept that night," said my father. "The most awful sounds came from his room, monstrous cries like an animal in torment. When they stopped very suddenly, your mother and I felt relieved; but then there was a crash, and we ran upstairs to find that his window had been shattered. He was gone. I stayed up many nights waiting for him, as I did for you tonight, but I never saw him again."

Although it was late, Gabriel turned the page, desperate to find out what happened next, but the entry stopped there. The pages that followed were entirely blank except for a small note that said *See Book 2*.

# ❊ A Key Without a Lock ❊

"I don't know anything about Book Two," said Aunt Jaz. "How strange. Your father never mentioned a second volume."

"But it must be somewhere," said Gabriel. "Do *you* know what happened to Corax?"

She shook her head. "No, Gabriel, I'm afraid not. But to be honest, this was a much happier house after he left. I was eight and your father was only two. We never spoke of him, and Adam was too young to remember him." Aunt Jaz sighed. "I had one childhood friend who had a big crush on Corax. She was quite heartbroken when he left home, but we . . . the rest of us were all relieved."

It was a dead end. Gabriel had so many unanswered questions. Perhaps that explained the unusual dream he kept having over the next few nights. It was always set in the same place, with the same thing happening. He found himself back in the study, standing before the painting of the eerie-looking boy with the beaklike nose, but then something would change—a small, almost imperceptible movement in the background of the picture. Behind the raven boy's black velvet suit, an enormous pair of silken wings would appear and flex slightly. Then both eyes would look Gabriel up and down. Gabriel would back away, but the raven boy would step out of the portrait, beckoning to him with one black-taloned claw and repeating a short phrase over and over. Gabriel couldn't understand the words; they were muddy—it was like hearing someone talk when you're at the bottom of a full bathtub. But eventually, they became clearer. Two words. Two awful words:

"You're next."

Jerking awake, Gabriel would catch his breath in the darkness, wondering what it meant. *You're next.* Each time, he closed his eyes and clamped his pillow over his head to shut out the nightmare, but Corax would reappear. *You're next.* His birdlike eyes became a sickly yellow, and he would transform into a raven with tattered feathers and a jagged beak.

Next for what?

After one of these unsettling dreams, Gabriel woke up to find it was a bright November morning and time for school. Relieved, he stumbled downstairs to the kitchen. Aunt Jaz was wearing her coat, and her cheeks were pink from being outside; she removed two steaming muffins from a white paper bag.

"Good morning, birthday boy!" she said breathlessly.

Gabriel was momentarily confused. "It's my birthday?"

"Yes, did you forget? You're twelve today."

"Twelve?" Gabriel repeated. "How could I forget that?" He recalled the line in his father's diary:

*He was twelve when it happened, exactly your age.*

A dreadful thought crossed his mind. Could turning twelve be the reason Corax kept repeating "You're next"?

"Gabriel?" said Aunt Jaz. "Open your present!"

"Present?"

She pointed to a small brown box wrapped in a green bow beside his plate.

"Before your father left, he asked me to keep this very safe. He said that I was to give it to you on your twelfth birthday if he had not returned."

Quickly, Gabriel pulled the bow apart and opened the box, expecting to see another notebook. Instead, there was a small brass key. It was an old-fashioned sort, smaller than a house key or a car key—the sort that might open a tiny chest or a cabinet.

"What's it for?" he asked.

"I have no idea."

"A key without a lock?"

"Yes." Aunt Jaz's smile turned mysterious. "I believe you'll have to solve that riddle yourself. But it must be very important. Your father wouldn't have asked me to give it to you now unless he had a good reason."

"Why is twelve so important?"

His aunt's dark boomerang eyebrows trembled slightly. "Well, your father began to notice things he'd never noticed before. Perhaps that will happen to you."

Gabriel nodded. "I have noticed some things—"

Aunt Jaz drew in a breath. "What, exactly?"

"Just . . . things you say."

Aunt Jaz blushed. "What have I said, exactly?"

"Actually, it's not what you say," Gabriel admitted. "It's what you *don't* say."

She sighed. "Gabriel, if there's anything I haven't told you, it's for a very good reason."

"Like what?"

"I can't say." Then she looked flustered. "Oh, listen to me, I've done it *again!*"

"You're just trying to protect me, I guess."

His aunt pressed her lips together and nodded vigorously.

"Because answers are like fruit—they have to be ripe?" said Gabriel with a faint smile.

Aunt Jaz raised a finger toward him. "Gabriel, I must tell you one thing: you should be paying attention to other voices besides those of grown-ups."

"*Other* voices? What do you mean?"

"I think you know, my dear."

\* \* \*

That morning at school, Ms. Cumacho introduced a new student. Her name was Abigail Chastain. Although the fall weather was still warm, Abigail wore two layers of cardigans; a thick, patchwork corduroy skirt; woolen tights; and rubber boots—one red, one blue. Her eyeglasses were old-fashioned cat's-eye glasses with blue frames, and her eyes moved quickly around the room, regarding her new classmates with inquisitive confidence. Her hair had been divided in tiny squares across her scalp, tapering into small braids of different colors that rose into the air in all directions.

Gabriel noticed that Somes stared at Abigail for the longest time. Passing her desk later in the day, he touched one of her braids. Abigail reacted by brushing his hand away, as if shooing a fly.

This didn't stop Somes from watching her. In art class, Gabriel grew so irritated on her behalf that he said, "Somes, quit staring. You're being weird!"

Mortified, Somes dropped his eyes. Abigail gave Gabriel a fleeting glance but said nothing.

Later, in gym, Somes slammed Gabriel in the face with a volleyball, giving him a bloody nose.

"I am not weird!" he shouted, and stalked out of class.

Gabriel spent the rest of the day with a wad of tissues clamped to his nose. Somes's desk was empty. He had been sent home early.

On his walk home, Gabriel saw the new girl marching

ahead of him along Fifth Street. He was going to say hello, but he felt his nosebleed start up again. He watched her enter Addison's old gate. So, Abigail Chastain was his new neighbor.

It was only when he got to his stoop that he remembered it was his birthday. He recalled the brass key and wondered again about where he could find the lock that belonged to it.

But this thought swiftly disappeared when he saw what was waiting inside.

## ❉ The Visitors ❉

Two very large suitcases rested on the landing. Battered and smelling of smoke, they appeared to have come a long distance. Gabriel was puzzled. Then a delicious thought struck him—a hopeful, glorious, wonderful thought. His one wish at every birthday, more than anything else in the world, was that his father might come home. Was his loneliness finally at an end?

He realized he was wasting time staring at the suitcases. His father must be downstairs, catching up on everything with Aunt Jaz. Almost tripping with excitement, Gabriel hurried down to the kitchen.

The sight that met his eyes was not what he expected. Two figures were seated at the large wooden table with Aunt Jaz: a dour woman and a pale girl.

"Ah, Gabriel, there you are!" said Aunt Jaz brightly. "This is Mrs. Baskin and her daughter, Pamela. Mrs. Baskin and I were childhood friends."

The woman was small, with short-cropped gray hair. Her eyes were blue and flinty; she smiled and nodded at Aunt Jaz.

"Yes, I remember those days so well," she said. "You had such a good-looking brother. . . ."

"Well, this is Adam's son, Gabriel," explained Aunt Jaz.

"Hi," said Gabriel, offering his hand politely.

"Oh?" Mrs. Baskin's smile vanished. "Adam?" she repeated. "The baby brother with the runny nose who was always crying? I thought you might have been the son of the handsome one who went away."

"Handsome?" murmured Gabriel, thinking of Corax's strange portrait.

Mrs. Baskin's eyes narrowed. Ignoring Gabriel's hand, which was still extended, she turned to her daughter, a slender girl with long dark hair and an anxious expression. "Pamela is twelve." She tipped her head at Gabriel. "He must be younger, Jasmine."

"I just turned twelve," interjected Gabriel.

Mrs. Baskin shrugged. "Anyway, most boys are less mature than girls."

Aunt Jaz ignored this remark. "Gabriel, Mrs. Baskin's apartment building had a fire yesterday. Almost everything was destroyed. While it's being renovated, she and her daughter will be staying with us."

"That's too bad," said Gabriel.

Mrs. Baskin glanced at him sharply.

"I meant, about the fire—" he added.

"Pamela will need her own room," Mrs. Baskin interrupted. "She practices violin for ninety minutes a night. She must not be disturbed."

Pamela held a violin case in her lap, cradling it as a mother might hold a baby.

"Of course she won't be disturbed," Aunt Jaz assured her friend. "She may have the room beside Gabriel's on the third floor."

"Can he carry Pamela's bag to her room?" said Mrs. Baskin.

Gabriel lumbered up the stairs with the bag, hoping Mrs. Baskin's apartment could be fixed up in a weekend—the sooner the better.

The bag was so heavy that he needed to pause to catch his breath on the first landing. "What's *in* here?" he asked Pamela, who was following him.

"I don't know," she replied. "My mom packed it." She offered to help, but Gabriel refused, and huffed and puffed his way up the next set of stairs.

Meanwhile, Aunt Jaz led Mrs. Baskin along the parlor floor. "Now, Trudy," she said, "I thought I'd give you the third bedroom on the top floor."

Mrs. Baskin happened to glance into the study; her eyes immediately settled on the boyhood portrait of Corax. She uttered a sentimental sigh. "This room will do," she said.

"Oh, you don't want to sleep here," said Aunt Jaz. "It's gloomy, and it doesn't have a proper bed."

"Nonsense! I'll be fine on that couch."

Puzzled, Aunt Jaz nodded. "Very well," she said. "If you're sure."

By the time Gabriel got Pamela's suitcase to the top floor, he was dizzy and had to steady himself. He dragged it into the bedroom and let it fall with a colossal thump. Pamela unzipped the suitcase; instead of clothes, a huge pile of music books fell out, reeking of smoke.

"Do you really practice for an hour and a half every night?" asked Gabriel.

Pamela nodded. "My mom says if you want to be any good at anything, you have to practice all the time."

"I practice riddles," Gabriel said, hoping this sounded impressive.

The girl looked up. "Riddles. How weird."

Gabriel tried to explain. "You see, riddles stretch your brain. They force you to look at problems in a completely different way. At least, that's what my father told me."

"I don't have a father," she replied. "And you don't have a mother, isn't that right?"

"Yes." Then he added, "My dad's coming back. . . . I just don't know when."

"My father died when I was a baby," Pamela continued. "Is that what happened to your mother?"

Gabriel paused. "Not exactly. She disappeared." When

he realized how strange this sounded, he added, "It's kind of a mystery."

"No wonder you like riddles," replied the girl. "So, tell me one."

He tried a simple one:

*"Everyone catches me,*

*Strangers share me,*

*Yet nobody wants me."*

Pamela thought for a moment, then shook her head. "I give up."

"You have to give it a try," insisted Gabriel. "What can you catch?"

"A ball."

"What else?"

"Another ball."

"No," said Gabriel, frowning. "Think of *other* things people catch."

"Smaller balls?" suggested Pamela.

"Forget about balls. Think of catching as an *expression*. If you're sick, for example, what have you caught?"

"Oh, like a cold?"

"Exactly!" said Gabriel. "Strangers share me, yet nobody wants me!"

Pamela smiled faintly. "Yes, I get it, but I don't see the point."

Gabriel tried to explain. "It's funny. Don't you see?"

Pamela gave him an apologetic glance. "I'd better get

started or I'll be up all night." She removed her violin, her bow, and a small windup timer from the violin case.

That night as he lay in bed, Gabriel heard the girl practicing her violin. The sound carried clearly through the wall. The music was both jubilant and terribly sad. Gabriel never imagined these two feelings could go together, but they did with a violin. Then he remembered that his birthday had been forgotten with the arrival of these visitors. He wondered again if he would ever solve any of the riddles on his mind: the riddle of his mother's disappearance, the riddle of his father's return, and the riddle of the key.

In the dark, he grasped the key tightly in his hand.

# ❈ The First Valraven ❈

A dark bird was perched on a branch above Paladin's nest. Its voice was as rough as a rasp on a rusty gate.

*"Everyone looks up to me,*
*For I am always true,*
*And yet the slightest gust of wind*
*Can change my point of view.*
*What am I?"*

Paladin squinted at the cold, unkind silhouette. He could see perfectly well now, but he couldn't fly or defend himself. His mother protected him, wings raised, sharp talons flexing.

"That is a very hard riddle," she replied.

"Do you give up?" said the bird, and its powerful beak opened threateningly.

"I didn't say that I couldn't answer it," said Endora.

Paladin trembled, old enough to know how his mother's voice sounded when danger was near. The strange bird had a chip on its enormous beak, and its feathers were bedraggled and oily, like a city puddle. "What is your answer, then?"

"A weathervane," replied Endora.

The bird looked surprised. It blinked.

"You're not laughing," said Endora. "Only valravens can not laugh at riddles."

With a hiss and a screech—hardly a raven sound at all, but something unearthly and ghoulish—the bird sprang toward Endora with talons extended. Terrified, Paladin buried his head in the bottom of the nest. He could hear a furious fight above—beaks snapping, a violent beating of wings, then a taunting cry that chilled him. The nest shuddered as something toppled off and fell to the street.

Timidly, the baby bird peered through the tight mesh of twigs to look.

Lying way down on the pavement was a bird twisted so violently by its fall that its head was reversed to face its tail. To Paladin's horror, the creature suddenly jerked upright, flapped its crooked wings, and did a somersault. No normal creature could have survived such a perilous drop. With a ghastly squawk, it looked up, snapped its beak at Paladin, then waddled on broken wings nearer the tree. It was the creepiest sight to behold, and Paladin wondered what the valraven had done to his mother.

"Mama?" wept Paladin. "Oh, please! Mama, answer!"

There was no reply.

Paladin peered upward. The sky was a dismal gray shroud.

Then the branch supporting the nest began to shake. Something was climbing up the limb toward Paladin. He felt a shudder of panic. Was it that ghoul, returning for him? He squirmed his way to the edge of the nest, trying to see. How could he defend himself against something that wouldn't die? Perhaps he should just jump before the hideous bird captured him. Balancing on the rim, he looked out over the dark city and raised his tiny wings.

"Where do you think you're going?" said a warm, weary voice.

Endora appeared at the side of the nest, her collar feathers ruffled and untidy, one eyelid bruised and swollen.

"Oh, Mama!" cried Paladin. "I thought you were . . ."

"I'm fine," said Endora, climbing inside and gently nuzzling him with her beak.

"What happened?" he asked.

"That was a valraven. He won't do us any harm now. I just dropped him down a storm drain to keep him from telling his cronies about you."

"Me? Why me?" asked Paladin.

Endora hesitated. What she had to say was important, but she wasn't sure Paladin was ready to hear it yet. Still, she felt she had no choice.

"You remember the story I told you about Muninn?"

"The bird who won the riddle and took the torc?"

"Exactly. Well, for over a thousand years the valravens have been looking for that torc. Now they seem to think they are close, and if they can only find a certain raven and his boy amicus, the torc will be theirs."

"But I don't have an amicus or the torc. I can't even fly!"

"Yes, my love, that is true. But your grandfather Baldasarre had an amicus named Adam Finley. Finley came into possession of the torc and asked Baldasarre to hide it. Your grandfather did this right before he died. Finley's boy lives in that house."

"I've seen a boy come out of there," murmured Paladin.

"It is rare for a raven to meet a human worthy of being an amicus, but the Finleys appear to be a rare family. I only wish . . ."

"What, Mother?"

"I wish that your sisters had survived, my love. They were hatched last spring, but—" Endora paused, and a tear glittered in her eye. "Valravens killed them while searching for the torc—which means they are even more determined to find you—"

"But I don't know where it is!"

"Yes, that is true for the time being," his mother replied. "But Adam Finley, wherever he is, knows where it is hidden. You and his son may be its next defenders."

# ❀ The Wandering Desk ❀

**W**ith the birthday key strung on a ribbon around his neck, Gabriel began his search for the mysterious lock that might reveal his father's whereabouts. First, he tried a cabinet in the dining room. The key wiggled loosely in the lock; it didn't fit.

As Gabriel pulled it out, he became aware of a silhouette in the kitchen doorway. Mrs. Baskin was standing there. She was a cookbook editor, and Aunt Jaz had invited her to test new recipes on the noisy old stove in the kitchen. Her flinty eyes narrowed at him.

"What are you poking around with that key for?" she said.

"Just curious," Gabriel replied, startled.

"I remember your father being very nosy, too," she said. "Always crawling about, getting into things when he was a baby."

Gabriel thought for a moment. "Isn't that what babies *do*? Crawl around, I mean."

"His older brother was so smart, so elegant." A misty look

appeared in Trudy Baskin's eyes as she said this, and her voice softened. "Such a pity he ran away from home. I was the only one who really understood him."

Gabriel felt a cold shiver. He remembered Aunt Jaz saying she had a childhood friend who had had a big crush on Corax. Was it Trudy Baskin? He tried to imagine the gray-haired woman as an eight-year-old girl, but it was difficult. Mrs. Baskin looked as if she had been old forever.

"That must have been a *very* long time ago," he said.

Trudy's smile vanished. "Don't you have homework to do?" she snapped.

Gabriel trudged up to his bedroom, deciding that he would continue his search if Trudy went out shopping.

An hour later, he heard the front door shut. Immediately, Gabriel began looking for keyholes in the spare bedroom beside Pamela's. It was small, with a four-poster bed, a blanket trunk, and a bureau with glittering crystal knobs. There was also a desk in the darkest corner. The bureau's keyholes were too small, so Gabriel moved on to the trunk. As he pressed the key into its lock, he heard a thump. Looking up, he saw no one. Almost as soon as his eyes dropped, however, he was aware of a shadow on the carpet.

Perhaps it was a squirrel crossing the skylight. Gabriel wiggled the key, but it was obviously the wrong shape for the trunk.

He continued around the room, settling on the end table. He tried this lock, but it was too small. He turned to the last item—the writing desk—but the dark corner was empty. This puzzled him.

Since Pamela attended a music school in Manhattan, and wouldn't be back for another hour, Gabriel decided to try her room. There was a captain's bed with three drawers, and a simple mahogany dresser. Oddly, the missing desk was *here*, sitting in the corner near the window.

Beginning with the captain's bed, he tried the key in each drawer, but the locks were much too large. He tried the dresser, but the locks were too small. He turned to the desk.

It was missing.

Gabriel surveyed the room. There was no sign of the desk anywhere. Had he imagined it?

Then he heard footsteps on the stairs. Stepping out of Pamela's room, Gabriel peered through the balusters at the landing below. He saw nothing unusual. Nothing, except for the same desk standing against the wall.

Gabriel stared at it for a few moments. It was old and black, with a drop lid that appeared to be locked; small wings were carved into the sides; and the two front legs were shaped like the talons of a bird. Suddenly, one of the legs twitched slightly and scratched the other one.

Gabriel hurried downstairs, but when he reached the landing he found nothing but a shiny brass wastebasket.

The desk had disappeared.

Gabriel tried to make sense of this puzzle. Had the desk moved? *How* could a desk move? Why would it move? Was it going from room to room to escape being discovered? He fingered the key around his neck thoughtfully.

A bathroom faced the staircase; there wasn't space for a desk there. Aunt Jaz's bedroom came next, a room Gabriel knew very well. He peered inside. Everything was as it should be: a double bed, a rolltop desk, a dresser, and a closet. He didn't need to check the locks—none of them had keyholes. Anyway, he had a hunch now—a very strong hunch—that the key belonged to that black desk.

He proceeded to the study, which was now Trudy's bedroom. The door was shut, but he opened it just a crack and peered in.

The bizarre portrait stared grimly back at him. Beneath it stood the black wooden writing desk.

"Gabriel?" said a voice. "What are you doing?"

Trudy Baskin was at the bottom of the staircase, holding a shopping bag full of groceries.

"Um. Nothing," he said.

"Why are you in my room?"

"Oh, I just . . . Nothing, really."

He hurried out and trudged back upstairs to his bedroom to finish his homework. One thing was clear, though. He would be back.


"Trudy, dear?" said Aunt Jaz the next morning. "Is there any salt or sugar in these pancakes?"

"Not a speck!" replied Trudy. "I'm testing a salt-free, sugar-free cookbook. Aren't they delicious?"

"Well," said Aunt Jaz, after a taste. "They certainly are salt-free and sugar-free."

"No salt, no sugar, and *very* good for you!" said Trudy triumphantly. "These are healthier than any pancake you've had in your life."

"And they're disgusting," murmured Gabriel to himself.

Aunt Jaz went to the fridge.

"What are you looking for?" asked Trudy.

"Just wondering where the maple syrup is," replied Aunt Jaz.

"Oh, I cleaned your fridge for you," said Trudy. "I threw out lots of things. The syrup went with everything else."

"You threw it *out*?" said Aunt Jaz, her penciled eyebrows quivering at the top of her forehead. "All of it?"

"And the sugar, the honey, and the salt. They're all terribly unhealthy, dear. You'll get used to it! Look at Pamela. She never even asks for salt or sugar anymore."

Pamela was eating her pancakes the way a reluctant patient takes medicine—in small bites, chewing vigorously to make it seem as if she were eating a lot.

Gabriel wondered if there was any mu shu pork left.

Aunt Jaz must have been thinking the same thing, because she asked Trudy what happened to the Chinese food cartons in the fridge.

"Tossed in the trash," Trudy replied smugly.

Later, Gabriel asked Pamela how she felt about not having sugar or salt.

"You can't miss what you've never had," she replied.

It seemed to Gabriel that the least he could do was introduce Pamela to ice cream, chocolate bars, and pretzels.

The next day, Gabriel returned from school to find Trudy in the kitchen stirring a bubbling gray mixture that smelled like sweaty socks. Gabriel felt a pang of concern that this might be dinner.

"Hmm. What's this?" he asked, keeping his fingers crossed that Trudy was just boiling her laundry on the stove.

"Bouillabaisse," she replied. "It's a French dish."

"Bouillabaisse?" he repeated. "Is that French for *socks*?"

"No," she snapped. "Fish soup. We're having it for dinner."

As Gabriel retreated upstairs, it occurred to him that with Trudy busy in the kitchen, this was an ideal time to have a look at that desk. He peered into the study, but the place beneath the portrait was vacant.

"Gabriel, you need to start your homework," cried Trudy from downstairs.

"I'm . . . I'm going to do it on the stoop," he explained, quickly stepping out of the study.

Outside, Gabriel began sifting through the papers stuffed in his notebook, when he heard footsteps. It was Somes. A purposeful look appeared on the big boy's face.

"Hey!" he said. "You're going to help me prepare my geography report!"

Gabriel regarded Somes warily. "How'd you find out where I live?"

"The class directory, of course," the boy replied with a grin.

"No, Somes, I have my own report to do," said Gabriel. "Ask somebody else."

Somes ignored this remark, taking Gabriel's notebook out of his hands and replacing it with his own geography book. "Concentrate. I have to compare and contrast Paraguay and Argentina."

"Did you hear me, Somes?" Gabriel replied, raising his voice. "I said no."

"Well, I can't do it," insisted Somes, this time in a pleading tone. "Reading drives me crazy. I can't make sense of what I'm looking at!"

"So look at a map," Gabriel replied, taking back his notebook.

Somes threw Gabriel's notebook off the stoop so that the papers scattered in the breeze. Then he flung his arm around Gabriel's neck and tightened his grip.

"What's the difference between Paraguay and Argentina? Tell me," said Somes through gritted teeth.

"Get off!" shouted Gabriel helplessly.

At that moment, a girl's voice rang out.

"I'll tell you the difference."

Abigail Chastain was standing at the bottom of the stoop. She was a blizzard of color—hair in an orange band, three colorful bandannas around her neck, one yellow sneaker, one purple.

"But first you have to let him go," she said.

Somes immediately lowered his arm.

"Okay," she said. "For starters, they're both South American countries below the equator."

"Below the equator," repeated Somes.

"One is landlocked, one is not. Now, Paraguay is like the hat on the head of Argentina, can you remember that?" she said.

"I think so," said Somes. "A hat."

"While Argentina has a long, long coast."

"A long, long coat?" said Somes.

"*Coast*," Abigail replied.

"Coast," repeated Somes.

"Now, this is the tricky part. The capital city of Paraguay begins with an 'A'—Asunción. But the capital of Argentina begins with 'B'—Buenos Aires."

This seemed to please Somes. He repeated the words to himself, then paused. "A hat and a coat, and A and B."

"That's it," said Abigail. "Now, Argentina's natural resources are . . ."

"That's enough." Somes winced, as if more information might burst his brain. Taking back his book, he walked off, shooting Gabriel one last glance.

Although he wasn't too pleased to have been rescued by someone so small, Gabriel felt he owed her some gratitude. "Thank you, Abigail," he said, gathering his scattered papers.

"*De nada*," she replied. "Call me Abby. Abigail sounds so old and *normal*." She grimaced at the last word.

"Abby," he repeated. "Okay."

Abby narrowed her eyes at him.

"Quick, what's the longest, thinnest cat in the world?" she asked.

"I—I don't know anything about cats."

"That's okay. It's a riddle. I just made it up."

Gabriel gaped at her. "You like riddles?"

"Of course. Now hurry up," she said impatiently.

"Okay, longest, thinnest cat . . ." Gabriel set to work, thinking about names for cats, and crossed them with names for long, thin things. "I've got it," he laughed. "A polecat!"

"That was too easy," she said.

"Try this," he replied. "What goes up and down the stairs but never moves?"

Her expression became very thoughtful. "Up and down the stairs . . . I know what it is. It's a *banister*! How many sides does an egg have?"

"Two," replied Gabriel. "Inside and outside!"

They went back and forth, telling riddles for several minutes until it became obvious that they had something remarkable in common. Both of them began to laugh as they challenged each other.

"Do you know my favorite riddle of all time?" asked Abby. "'Why is a raven like a writing desk?'"

"Oh, that's from *Alice in Wonderland*," Gabriel remembered. "But there's no answer to it, I think."

"Well, I've made up my own answers." She had a mischievous look in her eye.

"Really?" he replied, impressed.

"First, they both produce notes. Although," she admitted, "a raven's are rather hoarse and out of tune." She ticked off other possibilities. "Both of them have *quills*." She made a motion as if she were writing with a feather. "And they both have *bills*, though a raven's bill can't be paid."

A thought popped into Gabriel's mind. "Hey, have you ever heard of a writing desk that could move by itself from room to room?"

The minute he said this, he expected Abby to look at him as if he were crazy; instead, she removed her glasses, breathed on them, then polished the lenses with her shirt hem. "Well, if you've got one, I'd love to see it."

Gabriel grinned.

Abby dug into her pocket and produced a handful of brown sweets wrapped in wax paper. "Want a caramel?" She held one out. "My sister, Viv, makes them. She loves candy. She wants to make candy for a living, like Willy Wonka in that book!"

Gabriel took one and popped it into his mouth. It had a

soft, buttery flavor and melted gently on his tongue. "Do you think anyone makes a living out of riddles?" he asked.

"Oh, I hope so," said Abby anxiously. "It's the only thing I can do well."

"Really? Me too!" he admitted. "Sometimes I think it must be for a special reason, but that's crazy, because why would anybody *need* to be good at riddles?"

All at once, Gabriel decided to tell Abby about his father's disappearance. He expected her to react like Pamela, who didn't think much of it, but Abby's eyes lit up. "He *vanished*?" she marveled. "That's incredible! Tell me everything!"

So Gabriel explained about his father's notebook, Corax, the key, and the elusive writing desk. Abby listened very intently, her eyes wide, interrupting sometimes to ask a question. Before long, the sun settled below the rooftops, and the children were whispering in the twilight when a shrill voice called from inside the house.

"Gabriel, are you finished with your homework?"

"I have to go," Gabriel said to Abby. "We're having fish stew tonight."

Abby wrinkled her nose with sympathy. "Here!" she said, emptying a fistful of caramels into his hand. Gabriel stuffed the candies into his pocket and waved as she skipped across the street in her mismatched shoes.

\*    \*    \*

Trudy Baskin's dinner had to be eaten. Aunt Jaz gave Gabriel a look across the table that made that very clear. He followed Pamela's example, taking little nibbles and spreading his food around the plate to make it look less full.

Finally, he excused himself to empty his plate in the kitchen. Pamela followed him. They shared a smile as they tipped their food into the trash can.

"Want a caramel?" he whispered.

"What's that?"

Gabriel pulled one of the sweets rolled in wax paper out of his pocket and handed it to her. "Just put this in your mouth, and don't tell your mother."

Cautiously, Pamela unwrapped the paper and slipped the caramel between her lips.

Gabriel watched her eyes slowly widen. She'd obviously never tasted anything so wonderful before in her life. When she asked him if he had more, he dropped six of them into her hand.

# ❀ Corax Is Plotting ❀

In a tree outside the Finley house, the baby raven huddled in a nest rebuilt of sticks, string, linen, and fluff. He had poked a spyhole in the nest's lining to watch a boy named Gabriel emerge from his house every morning and walk to school. Paladin guessed this was Adam Finley's son. He had seen him threatened by a bigger boy and immediately felt concern for him. He wondered if he might even *almost* understand what the boy was thinking.

Paladin's beak was more ravenlike now. Its curved tip resembled his mother's. His feathered coat was as dark and shiny as coal. He wished he could fly, but his wings were still small and weak. This worried him because there were more valravens around. The sparrows and finches often traded gossip about them. When he told his mother what he heard them saying, she warned Paladin not to listen to little birds.

"*Anything* a sparrow or a finch says is probably nonsense," she said. "They will say whatever will make themselves feel important. Then there are the pigeons, also notorious liars, but they only talk about money."

"What's money?" asked Paladin.

"The scraps of metal and paper that people exchange with one another. Haven't you ever wondered why pigeons are constantly staring at the ground?"

"I thought they were looking for food."

"Oh, there's plenty to eat on a city street," his mother said. "Pigeons hoard money. That's why they're always pecking between the cracks in the sidewalks. They gather coins and stack them where they roost, then boast about how much they have."

"But why?"

Paladin's mother shook her head. "It makes no sense; pigeons are dull, witless creatures."

Endora flew off to find more food, but she was gone longer than usual. Paladin became scared and poked his head up to look for her. A small brown finch named Twit landed on a branch above his nest.

"We're done for! Finished! Doomed!" she cried.

"Why?" asked Paladin.

The finch looked down at Paladin. "Valravens. Calamity! Corax!"

Paladin became alert. "Who?" he said. "Who is *Corax*?"

Always delighted to share gossip, the finch proceeded to explain. "Corax is the leader of the valravens," she said. "Part human and part raven. A demon!"

Trembling, Paladin wanted to know more. "Have *you* seen him?" he asked.

"Oh"—the finch puffed up her chest—"seen him? Oh—
*hundreds* of times!"

"What does he look like?"

"Bigger than a buzzard, louder than a lark, meaner than a
merlin," bluffed the bird.

"Where did you see him?" asked Paladin. "Near here?"

Twit glanced around. "He lives under the ground in a
scary place called Aviopolis. Miles down under. Last place
I'd ever go!"

Paladin cocked his head, confused. "If it's the last place
you'd ever go, how did you see him hundreds of times?"

A finch's brain is so small that it can't remember all the
lies it tells. She ignored the question and continued to spin
more incredible stories for the young raven; but we shall
move on to one piece of information that was true. This came
at the end of the conversation, when Twit grew tired, and her
imagination ran out.

"I hear from my friends that Corax is plotting his return
to the land above. He's captured the torc's last owner, but
not the torc. When he wraps his talons around *that*, he could
wish for . . ." The bird blinked her foolish little eyes. "All the
worms he could ever want! Or a cage for every cat in the
world! It's black magic, you know."

At this moment, a shadow swooped overhead; the finch
uttered a frantic cry and took off.

Endora landed, holding a peach slice in her beak.

"Oh, Mother!" said Paladin, eager to share his news. "Twit

told me about that valraven, Corax. He's plotting his return from Aviopolis."

If there was any proof needed that the finch was speaking the truth, it lay in Endora's expression. "Yes, my darling," she replied. "It is why I guard you so carefully. If he found you . . ."

Trembling, the young raven replied, "I'd be done for? Finished? Doomed?"

Endora smiled, recognizing the wild remarks of a finch. But then her expression turned serious. "Remember, Paladin, you're a raven, not a finch. Your grandfather was brave and cunning and hid the torc so well that no valraven has found it. You will follow in his path."

"Me? But I can't even fly!"

"It's almost time for you to learn," his mother replied.

# ❁ The Telltale Caramel ❁

The next day at school, Gabriel watched Somes try to explain the difference between Paraguay and Argentina. Unfortunately, everything Abby had told him had become jumbled in his head.

"One's a hat, the other's a coat," Somes explained.

"One's a *hat*?" repeated Ms. Cumacho, her eyes narrowing. "Somes, exactly what do you mean?"

"I m-mean, one's a hat on the other," stammered Somes. "Argentina's a long coat and its capital begins with a 'B,' or is it an 'A'? I'm not sure. But they're very different."

"Hats? Coats?" The teacher put a mark in her grade book and shook her head. "You need to dig into that textbook and stop giving me silly answers, do you understand, young man?"

The boy's eyes surveyed the classroom, looking for someone to blame for his disgrace. They rested on Gabriel.

Later, as Gabriel headed down the corridor, he felt Somes's enormous fist thump against his back.

"Look, I didn't tell you what to say!" protested Gabriel.

"But if you had given me the right answers, I wouldn't be

in trouble!" thundered Somes, pressing Gabriel against the lockers so hard that he knocked the air out of the smaller boy's lungs.

"If you did your own work," Gabriel gasped, "you wouldn't be in trouble."

"After school you're going to help me!" Somes said. "You'll tell me everything I need to know, or—" Just then, the bell rang, and Somes had to release Gabriel.

When the teacher dismissed the class that afternoon, Somes was on his feet before Gabriel had even thrown his books together.

"Somes, you want some taffy?" said a voice. "My sister Viv made a ton of it!"

Somes's eyes turned to Abby, who beckoned to him with a paper bag stuffed with the salty candies. Abby looked at Gabriel and silently mouthed the word *run!*

"Here, Somes," she said. "I've got three flavors. . . ."

As Gabriel sprinted home, he thought about Abby's ploy. She was so cunning—the perfect person to help him catch the writing desk.

He slowed down at the steps to his house, and all of a sudden, he felt as if he was being watched. The feeling wasn't scary; it was warm and comforting. Gabriel looked up at the nearby oak tree, to the nest on the high branch, and saw the small head of a raven chick. Their eyes met briefly. Gabriel smiled, feeling a strange hint of kinship.

\*   \*   \*

Trouble was waiting for Gabriel when he stepped into the kitchen.

"Ah, there he is!" said a furious voice.

Trudy Baskin stood beside a pot on the ancient stove (which made loud knocks of protest). Judging from the colors bubbling around the lid, the evening's dinner was a brown sweater. There was no sign of Aunt Jaz; Gabriel remembered that she had an event at school that evening. Pamela faced her mother, looking scared.

"Mom, can I just explain?" she began.

"Now, dear, I'm sure *you* had nothing to do with this!" Trudy said softly, her fierce stare directed at Gabriel. "It isn't the sort of thing you would *ever* do by yourself. You go up and practice the violin while we sort out this foolishness."

"Mom," Pamela pleaded. "It's not his fault!"

"Go practice," snapped her mother.

Shooting Gabriel an apologetic glance, Pamela picked up her violin case and hurried up the stairs.

"Have you seen this before? I found it in my daughter's coat pocket!"

Trudy held a small object between her trembling thumb and forefinger—as if it might suddenly explode.

"Oh! That's just a caramel," said Gabriel.

"I know very well what it is," she snapped. "It's also a

dentist's best friend. A few of these and Pamela's beautiful teeth will be ruined. *Utterly ruined, thanks to you!*"

"Every kid should know what a caramel tastes like," Gabriel replied.

"Every kid?" sputtered Trudy. "Don't you *dare* give my daughter these horrible things to eat again. Do you understand me? I've kept her healthy since the day she was born!"

By this time she was shouting and red-faced. Gabriel had backed away, his knees buckling.

"Go to your room and don't come down until I call you for dinner!" she said.

Gabriel glared at the bubbling pot. "No thanks," he replied. "I'll just go straight to bed."

Lying there, Gabriel could hear his stomach rumbling with hunger. Still, he was determined not to go back downstairs.

About twenty minutes later, he heard footsteps, and his aunt's silhouette appeared at the doorway. She was still wearing her coat and held a shopping bag in one hand.

"Good heavens!" she said. "What on earth happened in this house tonight? I came home and Trudy was in the most furious temper. She says you poisoned Pamela?"

"It was a caramel," he replied.

Aunt Jaz gave a half laugh and sighed. "Oh, how ridiculous."

She reached into the bag and produced a small white carton of chicken lo mein and a pair of chopsticks.

"Hungry?"

"Starving," he replied.

"Eat," she said.

Gabriel sat up and began gobbling golden lumps of chicken and snow peas from the carton. When he was full, he cast a thoughtful look at his aunt.

"She liked your brother Corax, didn't she?"

Aunt Jaz nodded. "Oh, yes, she fell head over heels for him."

"She doesn't like me."

Aunt Jaz sighed. "It's because of your father, Gabriel. Corax was very jealous when his brother was born. He felt ignored by our parents. Trudy took his side. When he left, she was sure it was because of Adam. She didn't know about ravens, or any of that business."

"So, how long does she have to stay?"

"Oh, I think it will be many months. I could never turn her out. They have no home."

Gabriel nodded glumly. "Thanks for dinner."

After his aunt wished him a good night, Gabriel's thoughts returned to the writing desk. How could he possibly catch this piece of furniture if it insisted on hiding in Trudy Baskin's bedroom?

# ❋ How to Capture a Writing Desk ❋

"**W**hat an amazing house!" Abby said as she looked around Gabriel's hallway. She patted the gargoyle carved on the front of a dresser and made a monkey face at a big oval mirror.

"Wait until you see the desk," whispered Gabriel. "It has legs like a bird's talons."

"Do you really think it *runs* around?" said Abby. "I'm just wondering *how* to catch it, you know?"

"We could tackle it," Gabriel suggested.

"Maybe lassoing it with rope would be better," Abby replied.

Pleased to have Abby's help, Gabriel asked her to wait in the hall while he tiptoed down to the kitchen to see if Trudy was there. When he saw no sign of her, he remembered that she always went to Pamela's Wednesday violin lesson. This meant that they had at least an hour to track down the desk. He took a clothesline from the basement and returned to the landing.

"We'll trip its legs with this," he said.

Abby frowned. "I thought you said it had wings, too."

"Yeah, but they're shrimpy—too small to fly."

"Excellent," said Abby. "So, last time it was in the study?"

Gabriel led her toward the study door. "Maybe we can surprise it," he whispered.

As they entered, Abby gasped at the painting of Corax. "Wow! How can she sleep with that gross picture staring at her all night?"

"She called him handsome," said Gabriel.

"No way!"

An ironing board stood in the center of the room, skirts were draped on the furniture, underwear was stacked in a pile on the armchair, and socks fringed the laundry basket. They were startled by Trudy's nightgown, which hung in the corner. In spite of its rose pattern and lacy collar, its attitude seemed hostile, as if it wanted to shoo them off.

"Well, I don't see the desk," whispered Gabriel. "Let's start on the top floor and work our way down. One of us will search while the other watches the hall in case it—"

"Runs away?" giggled Abby.

They tiptoed upstairs and Abby readied herself in the hall while Gabriel searched.

"Nothing," he told Abby when he came out of the last bedroom.

Confused, they went down the stairs.

"Let's check the study again," suggested Abby.

There was still no sign of the writing desk. But something *had* changed.

"Gabriel," whispered Abby. "That nightgown with the roses. It's missing."

She removed her glasses and polished the lenses, something she always did when she was thinking. Suddenly, she smacked her forehead with her hand. "I know. It disguised itself!"

"The *desk* disguised itself?" said Gabriel skeptically.

"Well, wouldn't you if you were trying to hide?" she replied.

So, looking for a desk wearing a nightgown, Gabriel checked his aunt's bedroom. Abby peered into the bathroom, then immediately darted out and waved for Gabriel's attention.

"What?"

Abby pointed emphatically inside. Gabriel tiptoed to the bathroom doorway and spied a dark shadow standing behind the pale blue shower curtain.

Should he turn on the cold water? This seemed like an unfair thing to do, even to a desk. So Gabriel counted to three and drew the shower curtain back.

The nightgowned desk leaped out of the tub and butted Gabriel square in the chest. He collapsed backward. Abby let out a scream. Flapping its pink sleeves, the desk vaulted over her and galloped down the hall. At the base of the staircase, it skidded to a halt, whirled around the banister, and thundered upstairs.

Stunned, the two helped each other up.

"That was close!" said Abby. "It almost stomped us to death."

"Yeah," agreed Gabriel.

"Do you think it'll give up if we keep chasing it?"

"I hope so."

The two shared a wary glance, then advanced up the stairs. Gabriel made a lasso of the laundry line, holding it ready.

Gabriel's bedroom door was closed; they padded toward it. Then they heard the sound of coat hangers bumping together in his closet. The children braced themselves. *Bang!* The door burst open, but this time the desk wore a yellow rain slicker. Waving its arms, it charged toward them.

"It changed its disguise!" said Abby.

Gabriel threw the lasso, snagging the desk around its middle. Struggling like a roped steer, the desk dragged Gabriel along the hall on his elbows. He ducked as one taloned leg tried to kick him.

"Hold on tight!" cried Abby.

The desk suddenly stopped, pivoted on its clawed feet, and pulled the rope, sending Gabriel clear over the banister.

Abby let out a cry. "Gabriel!"

There was a terrifying silence. Abby peered over the banister.

Gabriel was dangling between the floors, holding on to the rope for dear life.

"Are you okay?" she cried.

"Fine," he said weakly. "Just tie the desk's legs together so it can't run. Then I'll swing onto the staircase."

Since the desk was held tight against the banister by Gabriel's weight, Abby quickly fastened its legs together with twine. Gabriel clambered nervously to safety. His palms were raw from clutching the rope. He wondered what his aunt would have written on his tombstone if he had died from the fall: HERE LIES GABRIEL FINLEY, KILLED BY A DESK.

With its feet bound, the desk wriggled helplessly before the children.

"Poor thing," said Abby. "It looks like it wants to roam free across the open range."

"Poor thing?" Gabriel grumbled. "It almost killed me."

Its keyhole looked just right for Gabriel's key. When he touched the desk, it shook violently and fluttered its small wings.

"It's okay, Deskie," Abby whispered soothingly, but the black wings still responded with small, frantic motions. "You must have a very important secret tucked in here."

It was only when Gabriel drew the key from the string

around his neck that the desk appeared to relax. The wings settled. The taloned feet stopped flexing and seemed to stiffen.

"Look at that!" said Abby. "It *knows*."

Gabriel put the key in the lock and opened the lid.

# ❊ Ask ❊

"**I** don't believe it!" said Abby.

"After all that fuss?" murmured Gabriel.

The four compartments inside the desk were completely empty.

"If it wasn't hiding anything," Abby said, "why would it be running away from us?"

Gabriel stuck in his fingers and wiggled them.

"It's a dead end."

"It can't be," replied Abby. "Your father gave you that key for a reason." She breathed on her glasses and rubbed them again. "I'm thinking," she said. "I'm thinking as hard as I can. Gabriel, lock the lid again!"

He closed the lid and turned the key.

"Now open it," she said.

He opened it again. There was still nothing inside.

"Wait!" cried Abigail, raising a finger. "Close the lid."

When he closed it, she pointed to the dull black wooden surface. In its very center, there was a small indentation, which she traced with her finger.

"It's a word."

Gabriel peered closer. Carved into the wood with small decorative swirls and just barely visible was one word: *Ask*.

Abby looked at Gabriel. "What are you waiting for? Ask it something!"

Gabriel tried to think, but what kind of a question could a desk answer? And then he realized that there was only one question to ask.

"Okay," he said. "Where's Book Two?"

Holding his breath, Gabriel raised the lid.

A black leather notebook sat in one of the compartments.

Abby let out a joyous laugh. "Aha!"

Gabriel turned the cover. In handwriting more legible than the writing in *The Book of Ravens*, the first page read *Book Two*. There was also a small note tucked inside.

*My dear Gabriel*, it read. *If you have found this book, then your twelfth birthday must have passed. It was my wish to be there to watch you grow up. Only the most terrible circumstances have prevented me from doing so, and it is my great regret. I hope you can find answers to your questions in these pages.*

*With love,*

*Dad*

Before they read any further, Abby placed her hand on Gabriel's. "Would you like to read the rest yourself?" she asked. "I mean, I can go, if you want."

"Are you kidding?" Gabriel replied. "You're part of this now."

Abby's face lit up. "Well, what are we waiting for?" she said impatiently. "Turn the page!"

June 6: Baldasarre has gone to find out about Corax. I have so many questions about this older brother I never knew. What happened to him after he flew out of that window? Is he alive? Where did he go? Before he left, Baldasarre told me he knew some ravens who might have some information.

August 10: Still no news of Baldasarre. I took the picture of my brother into my room; the painting seems to stare back in the dark. Sometimes it looks very angry to me.

August 13: I woke up after a nightmare. It seemed so real. I was flying with Baldasarre when an enormous raven swooped down on us. Its eyes were a sickly yellow color and its breath smelled of rotted meat.

"Who are you?" I said to it.

"Your brother," the raven replied, and he grabbed me with his talons so tightly that I couldn't breathe.

My father and mother found me screaming in bed.

August 29: I woke up in the middle of the night because of a tapping noise at my window. When I opened it, Baldasarre flew in. He had been flying all night to get home. After I took him downstairs for something to eat, he told me that he had some news.

"It's about your brother," he said.

I sat down at the kitchen table and Baldasarre hopped on my arm, lowering his voice so that I would be the only one to hear.

"I met some ravens who told me what happened to Corax. This is what they said: Many months after he left home, Corax arrived in the wild frozen reaches of the north with his amicus, Silverwing. He was miserable from days spent worrying about finding food and from sleepless nights tossing with sorrow about having run away from home. One day he saw a flock of unusual ravens land on a mountain peak. They were fearless and crafty; one pretended to be wounded, luring an eagle away from his nest while the other stole the food hidden there. Silverwing explained that these birds were called valravens and pointed out the feeble yellow hue of their vicious eyes. Cursed to live forever, they roamed the earth in search of the torc stolen from the first valraven.

" 'What's so special about this torc thing?' asked Corax.

" 'It grants any wish,' Silverwing explained.

" 'Any wish?' repeated Corax, intrigued. 'And how did the birds become cursed?'

"The raven shuddered. 'Each one ate the flesh of his dearest comrade. His amicus. Each is cursed to live forever.'

"Living forever didn't sound like a curse to Corax, but he didn't say this to Silverwing.

"As his friend slept that night, Corax plotted a solution to his troubles. He would become a valraven and never again have to worry about surviving. He would find the torc and grant any wish his family asked, and they would welcome him back home.

"Just before dawn, eyes wide with horror at what he was about to do, Corax throttled the last friend he had in the world—poor Silverwing. As he bit into his flesh, shame gripped him, followed by a sickening ache in his stomach; then his heart turned ice cold. As it began to beat faster than ever before, Corax noticed the sky changing with every breath he drew and realized time was slowing down. His body quivered violently. Feathers sprouted from his skin; his pores bled; black wings pierced through the skin of his shoulder blades. The sudden transformation was painful and terrifying. His smooth hands became gnarled talons. Corax realized he was neither human nor raven but a savage combination of the two. Worst of all, his head was full of bitter and furious thoughts. He'd lost all interest in returning to his family. All he wanted was the power to rule over men and birds, or to crush them if they defied him."

"That's horrible," murmured Abby.
"Keep reading," said Gabriel.

"The valraven flock had a strange visitor the next day—a demon with a human face but raven wings. He was enormous, and even the valravens felt afraid of him; they had never seen such a hideous creature. He promised to lead them to find the torc, and in return demanded their undivided loyalty. It was, of course, Corax."

October 17: I've been thinking about my brother. What would become of us all if he found this terrible torc? A creature that eats the flesh of his last friend in the world has no soul. What would stop him from wishing the death of anyone who resisted him? Baldasarre thinks the torc can never be found, but he also tells me that ravens are especially good at finding precious objects. With an army of valravens, who knows what is possible?

November 2: In the Norse mythology book I'm reading, there are two ravens, Huginn and Muninn. Could these be the same ravens who dueled for the torc?

November 22: Tonight I told my father I'm going to become an archaeologist. I'm going to find this torc. Somebody has to make sure that it is kept out of my brother's hands!

Just then, Gabriel and Abby heard a noise downstairs, followed by sharp footsteps on the staircase.

"Gabriel?" said a voice. "What are you doing? Who is with you?"

Sitting on the top landing, the two peeked cautiously through the balusters. Trudy Baskin's face was staring up from the first floor.

"Oh, hi, Mrs. Baskin," Gabriel said. "This is my friend Abby."

Trudy noticed Abby's feet first: the green clog on her left foot and the red one on the right. She grimaced. "Come downstairs this instant!"

"So nice to meet you, Mrs. Baskin!" Abby gave Gabriel a sympathetic look.

The desk slammed shut with a loud *bang*. Gabriel caught the key in his hand just before it tumbled over the banister.

He whispered to Abby, "Where's the book?"

"Vanished inside the desk!"

The desk began marching away from Gabriel and Abby

with sharp, defiant steps. (It had been slyly unraveling its bindings as they were reading.)

"Hey! Come back!" shouted Gabriel.

The desk leaped down to the landing with a crash and scuttled into the study.

From the floor below, Trudy's head reappeared through the balusters. "What happened?"

"Mice!" said Abby.

"*Mice?* You're telling *mice* to come back?" said Trudy with horror.

Abby and Gabriel scrambled downstairs, but the desk slammed the study door. They continued down to the kitchen, where Pamela was seated at the table, taking cautious sips of a steaming carrot-colored drink. She looked up at them enviously.

Gabriel introduced Abby to Pamela while Trudy squinted doubtfully at Abby's different-colored clogs. "They don't match," she said.

"Oh, yes, they do," Abby replied. "I always wear green on the left and red on the right."

For once, Trudy was speechless.

"Well," said Abby, "I'd better go home. Viv's making Turkish delight tonight."

"I'll walk you out," said Gabriel.

\*   \*   \*

The October night air was brisk and crisp. Gabriel and Abby shivered outside the front door.

"There's a lot more to find out," Abby gushed, rubbing her glasses vigorously. "Did your mother talk to ravens, too?"

"I don't know—"

"We've got to get more info from that desk," she continued. "This is so exciting! I always get into trouble for trying to make things more exciting at home. The other day I painted the toilet with glow-in-the-dark paint; my sister woke everyone up screaming when she went to pee in the middle of the night."

Abby replaced her glasses, now hopelessly smudged, and uttered a high-pitched *yippee* into the sky before skipping down the steps.

When Gabriel stepped back inside, Trudy blocked his way. "Every time I come back to my room, I find the furniture rearranged!"

"It's not me."

"A desk doesn't move *itself* from one side of the floor to the other, does it?"

*Are you kidding?* Gabriel wanted to say. *A desk threw me over the staircase!*

"Young man," said Trudy impatiently, "I want an explanation."

"I don't have one."

Trudy stared at him and snatched the desk key dangling from his fingers.

"Very well," she said. "I'll take this until you explain why you were going through my personal belongings."

"Give that back!" Gabriel cried. "That's mine!"

Her eyes glittered as she held the key out of his reach. The wickedness in her expression seemed strangely familiar.

"Please, that's a birthday present from my—" Gabriel was going to mention his father, but it seemed that this might only encourage her unkindness. "I need it. It's really important," he said.

"Oh? Then perhaps you can explain how *this* wound up in your room?" Trudy's other hand held up her pink nightgown with the little roses. "And why it's been ruined?"

The nightgown had been stretched horribly from fitting over the corners of the writing desk. Gabriel looked at it and chose his words carefully, "I didn't touch your nightgown—" He reached for the key.

"Liar!" snapped Trudy, holding the key just out of his reach.

"Why would I want your stupid nightgown?" Gabriel shouted.

A voice interrupted from the staircase. "It was *me*, Mother," said Pamela.

Trudy turned to her daughter with surprise. "You took my nightgown?"

Pamela shrugged. "I was cold on my way upstairs, so I put it on. I went into Gabriel's room to borrow a pencil, and I must have left it there."

Trudy looked utterly dismayed. Gabriel quickly snatched the key from her and stalked past her upstairs.

Later, as Pamela took out her violin to practice, Gabriel appeared at her doorway.

"Thanks," he said.

"For what?" Pamela began tuning her strings.

"Saving my butt, before."

"No problem," she replied. "My mother would never believe that a desk could walk, let alone wear clothing."

Gabriel tilted his head at her. "*You've* seen it do that?"

Pamela nodded. "A couple of nights ago, I couldn't sleep. Sometimes playing helps, so I took out my violin and put the mute on."

"Mute?" repeated Gabriel.

She pointed to a small black rubber disk that sat on the bridge of the violin. "It dulls the sound on the strings so that I can play without anyone hearing me. Anyway, I was playing for a minute or two when I noticed this strange desk in the corner of my room tapping its feet. Then it began to dance—"

"Seriously?"

"Yeah, it likes lively tunes like jigs and reels. Its feet are pretty strong."

"I know," Gabriel muttered. "But why didn't you tell me?"

"Why didn't you tell *me*?" she replied. "I'm not like my

mother, you know. I can see that this house has secrets. You can trust me. I won't tell."

So Gabriel told Pamela about his father's diary, Baldasarre, valravens, and the torc. When he got to the part about Corax becoming a valraven, she interrupted.

"Wait . . . are you saying my mom had a *crush* on a flesh-eating demon?"

"Almost definitely," Gabriel replied, expecting Pamela to be upset.

"That's cool," she said with a shrug. "All this time I thought she was boring."

# ❋ Trying to Fly ❋

**B**y mid-November, the trees on the block were bare. The mornings were crisp as children walked to school blowing billows of steam below Endora's nest. Paladin's feathers had grown in thickly, spurred by the cold. It was time to learn to fly.

Endora gave Paladin all kinds of instructions beforehand, coaxing him to perch on the edge of the nest and flap his wings to test his balance and strength.

"You need to *feel* the air," she said.

The poor chick did as he was told, but he tottered unsteadily. He didn't trust his wings' ability to bear him aloft. Terrified, he uttered a few hopeless clicks to his mother.

"Try, Paladin!" she urged.

"But I'm afraid I'll drop to the ground! Then someone will find me and put me in a cage forever."

"Of course you'll fly, my darling," Endora assured him, but there was an anxious edge to her voice. Her eyes traced the rooftops. She felt danger in the air and saw silhouettes that seemed to vanish moments later.

*　*　*

Just a few blocks south of Gabriel's house there stood a cemetery on a hill. Its grand view of Brooklyn stretched far to the north, south, east, and west. Among the stark monuments and solemn gravestones was a row of small mausoleums with marble pillars on the outside and carved names above their stained-glass doors. Inside each lay the caskets of a family.

An anxious mockingbird stood upon a mausoleum marked FINLEY, crying its lonely song in the darkness. This mausoleum had a row of ravens carved deeply into the marble— like an army—with jagged beaks and glowing eyes. It had no stained-glass door, just a tarnished metal gate with a dark hole in the center, large enough for a raven (or valraven) to squeeze through.

As an eerie mist spread over the graveyard, the mockingbird smelled something terrible—an odor of rot and dread. In the next instant, a large black bird emerged from the gate's dark hole. Its eyes glowed with a ghoulish yellow light. It was followed by several others, each one shabbier and more foul than the last.

The murderous group assembled around the headstones. One bird spoke.

"I'm hungry."

"Me too," said another.

"Terribly hungry," said a third.

"Wretchedly hungry," said a fourth.

The fifth bird's yellow eyes focused on the terrified mockingbird.

"I smell flesh," it remarked, and dove at the little creature with its beak open wide.

The mockingbird vanished in a swift, voracious gulp. The valraven spat out a few feathers and hissed. His name was Hookeye, and he must have been hundreds of years old, for he had streaks of gray in his feathers and a bony socket where his right eye should have been.

"I'm *still* hungry," he complained.

As the sun rose over the city, the sickly glow in their eyes faded, and they began to look more like common ravens. They clustered together, shivering at the fresh breeze and puffy white clouds sailing over the city. The pleasant view irritated them, and the glittering river offended them most.

"How long must we wait here?" said another.

"Stop your blathering!" said Hookeye. "Follow me. We have much to do!.

The old valraven took to the sky and the others followed him over the rooftops to a tree-lined street of brownstone houses with tall windows and flickering gas lamps in the front yards. Coming to rest in a tall oak, Hookeye waited for the others to land beside him.

"Who are we to kill?" asked the first.

"You will do no killing unless I say," said Hookeye, glaring fiercely at the group. "In that tree"—he pointed with his beak to Endora's repaired nest—"we seek the young raven descended from Baldasarre. He must be taken alive. Be warned, he is protected by his mother."

"A raven chick? Why can't we just kill him now?" asked a cross-eyed valraven.

"Silence! Do as you're told!" snapped Hookeye. "Just follow orders and everything will be explained." The birds reluctantly huddled closer. "Now, *you*, Crooked Leg, will distract the mother with a riddle while the rest of you capture the chick."

Crooked Leg tossed his head with irritation. "Tell her a riddle? I don't see the point. I haven't laughed at one in a hundred years!"

"If you don't tell a riddle," said Hookeye, "you might as well admit you're a valraven. She'll attack first and rip you to pieces!" He glanced at the others. "Any other stupid questions?"

Another valraven raised one feather and spoke in a cocky voice. "Why does it matter if she attacks us? We're immortal!"

The other valravens nodded and made little hisses of agreement.

"I'll tell you why, idiots!" said Hookeye. He cast a glance toward the trunk of the tree. "Cromwell! Are you there, old fellow?"

"I'm right here, Hookeye!"

Just above them, the dismembered head of a valraven poked out of a cleft in the trunk. It snapped its beak enthusiastically and winked at the others in spite of its sad condition.

"Where's the rest of you?" said Hookeye.

"Not exactly sure!" replied Cromwell. "Oh, wait, *there* I am!"

The other valravens followed Cromwell's glance and saw the headless body of the valraven waddling around the bottom of the tree. It struck the trunk, fell, then got up and walked into the tree again, then collapsed on the ground.

"Imagine being separated from your head for eternity like Cromwell here!" said Hookeye.

For a solemn moment, the ghouls considered this awful prospect.

"Oh, I've got a riddle!" said Crooked Leg suddenly. "What cures an empty stomach?"

"What?"

"*Nothing,*" groaned Crooked Leg.

"That's a riddle only a valraven would understand, you fool!" scolded Hookeye. "Think of something else."

The morning sunshine didn't last long. By noon, the sky hung in a dark gray limbo, as if it knew that there was wickedness afoot and was trying to warn the world.

Endora could feel the dismal mood. She would never have strayed from the nest, but she couldn't let Paladin starve. The weaker he became, the harder it would be for him to learn to fly. So she waited, watching the street, hoping a passerby might drop something she could feed him.

From between the leaves, Hookeye watched Endora, his cruel eye fixed upon her.

And so hours passed, the mother guarding her baby while the predator waited with his fellow assassins until the pale wintry sun lingered over the horizon, reluctant to let night bring on all the evils that lurked in its dark folds.

Finally, a woman passed, pushing a stroller; the little girl riding inside dropped her wedge of apple onto the sidewalk.

Hookeye immediately growled to his valravens, "Get ready now."

Poised to fly, Endora felt a tremor of panic. Why was it so quiet? Then she looked at Paladin, sleeping, and still so small and vulnerable. She rose slightly and peered around.

The five valravens stood perfectly still against the dark trunk of the oak tree.

With a swift movement, Endora left her nest and swooped down.

Hookeye's cold eye blinked at Crooked Leg, who fluttered awkwardly from the oak tree.

On the sidewalk, Endora seized the apple wedge and was about to fly up when a very scruffy raven appeared before her. Her heart beat fast. *Friend or foe?* she wondered. If it had been nighttime, she would have known by the glowing yellow eyes, but in the gloom of this wintry day the only way to tell was with a riddle.

"What moves as fast as a peregrine falcon yet always remains on the ground?" she asked.

Crooked Leg tried to speak, but his voice had disappeared. He remembered Hookeye's warning. He coughed. Then choked.

"The answer is *his shadow,*" Endora said. When he didn't laugh, her neck feathers sprang up in alert.

Crooked Leg tried to giggle, but an ugly gagging hiss came out.

Endora lunged, striking the valraven sharply between the eyes with her beak. Stunned, Crooked Leg collapsed backward onto the ground.

*That was too easy,* thought Endora. *It didn't seem like he was going to attack me. This was just a diversion.* She stretched her wings, desperate to get back to the nest.

"Paladin!" she cried.

Awakened by her cry, Paladin saw birds tearing at the biggest twigs of the nest, ripping them from their moorings. The nest wobbled violently.

Paladin kept still, remembering what he had been taught: make no movement, make no sound.

A shower of sticks clattered to the pavement below. With eager shrieks and throks, the valravens worked quickly, unraveling the carefully woven nest, clawing at the soft lining of its interior, throwing pieces over the rim in a frenzy to find their quarry.

A sudden earsplitting *COARK!* interrupted their task.

The mother raven swooped in, seizing one valraven by the throat.

"How dare you attack my home!" cried Endora, while the confused valraven gagged, clawing helplessly at the air.

Endora held him tight in her talons as she flew toward a cluster of chimneys on a nearby rooftop. In the next instant, she dropped him down a chimney. Poof! A cloud of smoke mixed with charred black feathers burst from inside.

The second attacker didn't see Endora coming because she bore down upon him from above, seizing his wings with her talons. He wailed and hissed in protest; she swung the valraven into a thick cluster of barbed wire on a fence. The more the creature struggled, the more he shredded to pieces, until he was nothing but feathers and bones dangling from the wire.

When Endora flew back to finish off the last ghoul, a terrible sight filled her eyes. The artfully built nest with its secret bottom had been devastated. Nothing remained but the stark gray branch of the oak. She circled the pavement, fearing that Paladin had fallen, but there was only debris scattered on the ground.

Then, above the nearest rooftop, she saw a valraven flying with a small object dangling from its feet.

"Oh, my poor darling!" she gasped.

As she soared toward the assassin, she saw that it was holding the secret compartment of the nest, a tangle of fluff, string, and twigs containing Paladin.

Swaying unsteadily beneath the valraven, Paladin realized the danger he was in. He peered out and saw a rooftop. It was only a short jump below. The chick leaped, flapping his sparsely feathered wings as furiously as he could. *I can do it*, he told himself. *I will fly!* But as hard as he tried, he felt the air pass swiftly through his feathers as he spiraled down. The wind whistled unkindly as he struck the tarry rooftop, lost his breath, and tumbled head over heels.

Bruised and dazed, Paladin heard a cry from far above. He opened his eyes and saw Endora circling him. He raised one wing, and gave it a flick to say, "I'm all right, Mama!"

Now Endora gave chase to the valraven, who had just noticed he had lost his valuable cargo. He dropped the nest, dodging Endora's first swoop.

At the second swoop, he snapped his beak at her wing, gashing her.

Wounded and surprised, Endora fluttered in the air for a moment, trying to summon her strength. *Come on, Endora,* she said to herself. *Only one more valraven. You can do it!* She flew higher to begin another attack. This time, when the valraven tried to snap at her again, she struck him hard with the point of her beak, and he uttered a hissing moan.

Wasting no time, Endora tore at the valraven's wing with her talons, and a clump of greasy black feathers fluttered down. She attempted one last lunge, tearing at his other wing, but the attacker struck her with his beak, and Endora felt the most awful pain. She thrust once more at the

valraven, and with a fearsome COARK! he plummeted to the
street below.


Paladin was dusting off his feathers when he heard his
mother land.

"Are you . . . all right, my darling?" she asked.

His eyes turned to her, vulnerable and terrified. "I still
can't fly."

"You will," she assured him.

"It'll take forever."

"Promise me you'll keep trying," she whispered.

This reply startled Paladin. It sounded as if she wouldn't
be there to see him do it. Then he noticed the blood on her
wing. "Mother? You're wounded," he said anxiously.

"I'm fine," she replied, but her next words were even more
faint. "Promise me something else, Paladin." She winced.
"Promise me you'll remember who you are."

"What do you mean?" he asked.

"It's in your blood to make sure the torc stays out of
evil hands—just as your grandfather did and your ancestor
Muninn. Promise me?"

Paladin was frightened by his mother's request. "Yes, but
*you'll* help me, won't you?"

"As long as I can," she replied. "But if anything happens to
me, my darling, you must seek your amicus."

Startled, the young raven glanced at her wound again, but she had preened her feathers to conceal it.

"Remember, you will find your amicus by using what you have learned from me. It's that simple."

His mother seemed to be preparing him for something scary and terrible. A world without her.

# ❋ Paladin's Amicus ❋

**O**n that very same afternoon, Gabriel was walking home from school with Abby. The sky was grim and dark; a chilly wind rushed them along the street with a peculiar kind of urgency. Abby shivered and buttoned the two layers of cardigans she was wearing.

"So," she said. "What do you think the next question should be?"

"You mean, for the desk?" replied Gabriel.

"Exactly."

A look of yearning appeared on Gabriel's face. "There's only one question," he said. "Where is my father? And I'm going to find out, no matter what it takes. I just know it's all connected to Corax."

Abby adjusted her glasses. "Interesting," she said. "Because I've been thinking about the torc mentioned in your dad's diary. Do you think your dad found it? And that's why—"

"He disappeared!" Gabriel nodded. "Wow, Abby, that makes perfect sense!"

By this time, they were walking up their block. Almost at

once, Gabriel felt that something was most definitely wrong. He stepped into the street, which was scattered with broken twigs and sticks. Quickly he glanced up at the oak tree: the raven's nest was gone.

"Gabriel? What is it?" asked Abby.


Endora was in pain, yet she took to the air holding Paladin, determined to get him to a safe spot. She chose one of the wide window ledges of the Finley house.

The moment she landed, a dark bird alighted on the wrought-iron railing a short distance away. Even in the dim light, she could see the empty gap of his missing eye. The other one stared ruthlessly at her.

"So kind of you to bring the young one to me," he said in a hoarse snarl.

Endora drew in her breath. "You can't have him."

"I take what I want," replied Hookeye. He moved toward her.

Endora's neck feathers sprang out in warning and she blocked his way.

"Don't worry," said Hookeye in a soothing tone. "Corax, Lord of Air and Darkness, will make good use of this young fellow's talents. He seeks the torc, and your precious little one will—"

"You'll never take him!" cried Endora.

Hookeye noticed the bloody wound on Endora's wing. A

smile appeared at the corners of his beak. In a flash, he lunged forward, but Endora was quicker, and seized the one-eyed valraven by his throat.

Up they fluttered, the valraven struggling and scratching with his talons while Endora summoned every last bit of strength to keep her beak clenched on his neck as she prepared one final dive.

At the end of the street, a large oil truck came roaring toward Gabriel and Abby. Its headlights jiggled as it picked up speed.

"Gabriel!" Abby said anxiously, pulling him back onto the sidewalk. "What is wrong with you!"

A sense of tremendous danger had gripped Gabriel; he couldn't speak. Instead, his eyes were drawn to a raven up in the air. She was in pain (he could feel it), and she was struggling against a shabby-looking raven with fierce yellow eyes, barely restraining it by the throat. In a desperate moment, she saw the truck and seemed to resign herself. She swooped down, leading the other bird into the truck's path. There was a terrible impact as a cloud of feathers burst from the front of the truck. As it rattled away, the street became mournfully silent.

A wave of grief engulfed Gabriel. When he missed his father, he felt this way—sad, abandoned, and confused. He wiped his eyes hurriedly before tears appeared, and turned to Abby. "She was fighting a valraven. But why did she give up her life?"

"I guess it was the only way to protect the little one," Abby replied. She pointed to a spot on the second-floor windowsill of his house. Alone, in the corner, a small, fuzzy baby bird lay trembling. Its small black eyes blinked at them.

It was on Trudy Baskin's windowsill, so they decided it would be wiser to retrieve the chick from outside rather than risk going into her room. Abby suggested making a pyramid of upside-down trash cans. Gabriel climbed up to the sill. He placed the little orphan gently into the side pocket of his coat, and clambered back down and held it out for Abby to see.

"Sweet little thing," said Abby. "Its mother wasn't going to let that disgusting valraven get near him."

The next thing that happened surprised both of them. The fledgling's beak opened, and in a frail, high voice, he spoke:

"What can you take from someone, but never keep?"

Abby and Gabriel stared, astonished.

"What can you take from someone, but never keep?" repeated the bird, looking anxiously from the boy to the girl.

"Take from someone, but never keep . . . ," said Abby.

"A temperature?" said Gabriel.

The fledgling nodded, and it laughed—a croaky, joyous raven laugh.

"I've answered a raven's riddle," said Gabriel, his eyes wide with excitement.

# ❀ The Orphan ❀

It was one thing to read about talking ravens in a diary, quite another to be spoken to. Abby and Gabriel pinched each other to be sure they had seen and heard the same thing. Abby's pinch was particularly sharp, and Gabriel gasped with pain.

"Ow!" he said. "Well, I'm definitely wide awake."

Paladin looked at them with a trembling stare. He was swooning with hunger, grief, and exhaustion, but he hadn't forgotten his mother's last words of advice. *You must seek your amicus.* He looked from the girl to the boy, searching for some link, a shared feeling of some sort. Almost immediately, he recognized it in the boy, the same bond he'd felt in the nest, watching Gabriel walk to school every day—they had the same urgent mission. Paladin spoke it aloud.

"Corax must not find the torc."

"What?" said Abby, looking at the fledgling.

Gabriel trembled. "Corax must not find the torc. He *knows*, Abby."

Relieved to see that Gabriel understood, the bird said one last thing: "I am Paladin." Then, overcome with relief, he closed his eyes and rested in Gabriel's palm.

"Paladin," repeated Abby. "Wow! This is no accident: your father's disappearance, finding this bird, the riddle, Corax. It's all connected. You have to take him inside, Gabriel."

Gabriel nodded. As he walked up the steps, he looked at Abby anxiously. "Are you going to tell anyone about this?"

"Are you kidding?" she replied. "I'm still in trouble for painting the toilet!"

She crossed the street to her house, then turned to him and uttered another *yippee!*

Gabriel entered the house and hurried down the stairs to the kitchen. He wasn't planning to tell Aunt Jaz that the bird had talked (at least, not right away), but the moment she saw the raven in his arms, she seemed to know. Her eyes crinkled with affection and excitement, as if she had been waiting forever for this moment.

Her first words, however, were restrained. "Oh, the poor little dear," she said, and turned to show Gabriel that Trudy and Pamela were in the kitchen, too.

Trudy said nothing until her daughter attempted to stroke the chick. "Pamela, don't you dare touch that thing," she snapped. "It's probably full of parasites. It belongs outside. Gabriel, put it out right now!"

He glared back. "I have to feed him; he's barely alive." He began searching the refrigerator for leftovers.

Trudy turned to Aunt Jaz. "Jasmine, talk sense into him! What if this creature spreads disease?"

Gabriel looked imploringly at Aunt Jaz.

"Gabriel's father took care of a wounded raven," Aunt Jaz told Trudy.

"I should have known." Trudy sighed, and her eyes flashed at Gabriel. "Like father, like son."

"Actually," retorted Gabriel, "you'd be surprised who else in my family was interested in ravens—"

"That's enough, Gabriel!" said his aunt sharply. She pointed to the laundry room beyond the kitchen. "You can keep the bird in there, out of harm's way."

Gabriel placed the raven in a basket lined with an old towel and set it in the laundry room. All through dinner, he had to fight the desire to check on the baby bird. Afterward, he offered the raven some scraps from his plate. The bird did not eat but buried his head in his chest and fell asleep.

Gabriel kept Paladin company for as long as he could that evening. Eventually his aunt came to ask him to go to bed.

"Aunt Jaz? He spoke to me," he whispered. "He said, 'Corax must not find the torc.'"

His aunt's boomerang eyebrows tilted with concern. "Remarkable. He must have sensed that you knew about the whole matter. A good sign that you are evenly matched. Raven and amicus."

Gabriel regarded her with surprise. "Why didn't you ever say it would happen to me?"

"I wasn't sure. And if it didn't happen, I knew you'd be very disappointed," she replied. She was solemn for a moment, and it occurred to Gabriel that Aunt Jaz must have been envious of her brothers.

She put a hand on his shoulder. "It's still time for bed, my dear."

Gabriel returned the baby bird to its basket. He followed his aunt upstairs and said goodnight at her bedroom door.

"One thing, Gabriel?" she whispered.

"Yes?"

"Trudy doesn't know the truth about Corax, and I would prefer to keep it that way."

"Okay," he said. "But she talks about my dad as if he was no good and Corax was some kind of hero."

She shook her head. "Your father is most definitely a hero."

"I'm going to prove it to her!" he promised.

Aunt Jaz's expression softened. "Gabriel, when your father found a raven, it changed him forever—just as it changed Corax." She searched his face. "Life may never be so simple for you, either."

"I'm ready," he said.

PART TWO

# ❋ The Bird Man ❋

Gabriel barely slept that night, worrying about Paladin's safety. Before school, he offered the bird more food and reminded Trudy not to open any windows in the laundry room.

"Why would I want to go near that thing?" she replied.

It was impossible for him to concentrate in class. He watched the clock's hour hand plod slowly round its face all day, and when the last bell rang, he sprinted all the way home.

"Gabriel, will you please slow down!" begged Abby, who was hurrying after him.

"I have to check on the baby raven," he said.

"I'm sure he's fine!" Abby puffed.

Gabriel scrambled down the stairs and into the kitchen with Abby following. The laundry room lay beyond a glass door. When Gabriel reached for the knob, he stopped dead in his tracks.

Through the glass, he could see an enormous raven with tattered, oily feathers, and gnarled, filthy claws on the washing machine. The bird had shredded Paladin's little basket. There was no sign of the baby raven. The door into the backyard hung open. With ripped threads dangling from its craggy beak, the bird sneered at Gabriel. Its eyes flashed a sickly shade of yellow.

Gabriel burst in, swinging his backpack at the bird. "Get out! Shoo!" he cried.

The valraven hissed at him and flew out into the yard. Gabriel slammed the door shut. Holding back tears, he peered around the laundry room.

"Oh, no!" cried Abby.

The two of them looked everywhere, horrified. It was so unfair. The poor little raven had barely survived a day.

At last, Gabriel solemnly began to gather up the bits of the basket.

A voice spoke behind them.

"Gabriel?"

It was Pamela.

"Gabriel? He's right here. . . ."

She entered the room cradling the baby raven in her hands.

Gabriel heaved a sigh of relief. "What happened?"

"I just got home from school," Pamela explained. "My mom left the back door open. She said the laundry room was very smelly. I told her never to do that again." Pamela shook her head and stroked the little raven. "He was trembling, so

I wrapped him up in my scarf and took him upstairs, where it was warmer."

"Where's your mom now?" asked Gabriel.

"Shopping. Why?"

Gabriel didn't say anything. He hurried upstairs and entered the study. Slowly he approached the painting of Corax. It seemed to stare at him with an expression of grim amusement, but Gabriel glared back defiantly.

"I won't be like *you*," he told the portrait. "I'm on my father's side."

When Gabriel returned to the kitchen, Abby and Pamela were trying to offer the baby raven some chunks of cheese, but the bird kept turning its beak away.

"He won't eat," said Abby. "It's been almost a day without food. He must be starving."

"I pass this shop on Union Street every afternoon," said Pamela. "Pleshette's Exotics, I think it's called. There are birds in the window. Somebody in there might know about feeding ravens."

They put Paladin in a shoe box with plenty of holes punched in the lid and headed out just as Trudy was walking in with two bags of groceries.

"And where are you going?" She frowned.

"The bird store," said Pamela. "I'll be back in an hour."

"What about your practicing?"

"Mother, I always remember to practice," Pamela replied.

On the way to Pleshette's, Abby turned to Gabriel. "You're not going to mention the *riddle* to the shopkeeper, are you?"

"Definitely not," said Gabriel.

"You didn't tell me about a riddle," said Pamela, surprised. "Did the chick say a riddle like the raven in your father's diary?" Her eyes lit up. "Gabriel, are you an *amicus*?"

"I don't know," he replied. "But when I found him, I got this strange feeling. . . ."

"Then you *are*," said Pamela, giving a wistful sigh. "I wish I could be an amicus."

Abby nodded. "Me too."

They had walked about five blocks when Abby noticed something. "Do you see we have company?" she asked the others.

"Who?" asked Pamela, glancing around. "I don't see anyone."

"You're not looking in the right direction," said Abby softly, and she tilted her head up.

Six ravens were sitting upon a branch near the intersection.

Wondering if they were valravens, Gabriel clutched the shoe box tightly. But looking more closely, he realized that these birds were much more handsome, their feathers smooth, their beaks elegant.

As the children walked, the six ravens followed their progress, alighting at every intersection, until they reached Union Street. Here, the children turned and came to Pleshette's Exotics, a dark storefront with a tin awning. The six ravens immediately became agitated, rocking sideways on their feet and splaying their neck feathers with squawks of protest.

"What's wrong with them?" asked Pamela.

"They don't seem to like this place," said Abby.

"C'mon," said Gabriel impatiently, "we need some advice."

Once they were inside the shop, the cries of the ravens faded. *Exotics* was definitely the right word for the pets on display. Gabriel saw a small gray hawk, a blue-necked cassowary, and a rather unhappy-looking raven in a cage. There were also cabinets of odd-colored jewels, and oddities encased in glass spheres—beetles, clocks, keys. Inside one cage was a parrot that appeared to be blind, for its eyes were almost white, and it kept muttering, "Go away!"

Pamela found a stringed instrument made of a tortoise's shell; she plucked a string and a bizarre noise filled the air, like a forest of crickets. A small bald man hurried from the back room and seized the instrument from her. He wore a vest, a green poker visor, and spectacles with tinted lenses perched on little extensions. Gabriel guessed they were for examining precious stones.

"I count three children with no adult!" he said, tapping a sign that read NO UNACCOMPANIED CHILDREN.

"Wow! Good counting!" replied Abby. "How are you at counting jelly beans?"

Mr. Pleshette glared at her. "Come back later with your mommy or daddy." He seized a broom, as if he might brush them out of the store.

"Please," said Gabriel. "We need some advice."

The man's expression became more hostile. "*Free* advice, I suppose?" He shook his head. "I don't have time!"

"You don't look that busy," countered Pamela, who had noticed a crossword puzzle on the counter.

Abby gave it a quick glance. "Oops, you missed one. The word is *liar*."

Pleshette snatched the puzzle out of her hand. "I wasn't finished!"

"Then you aren't busy," concluded Gabriel. "I found this baby bird," he said, showing him the shoe box.

The man frowned. "I don't buy birds."

"Yes, but you *have* birds," observed Abby.

"Please, we just want to know how to feed it," said Pamela.

"It's a raven," added Gabriel.

Pleshette suddenly became alert. "Did you say *raven*? Let me see." He removed the lid and peered at Paladin. "Very strange," he murmured.

"Strange?" repeated Abby.

"Ravens don't give up their young easily. How did you come across it?"

"The mother was being attacked by another raven," said Gabriel.

"Unlikely." Mr. Pleshette sniffed doubtfully. "Ravens don't attack each other unless . . ."

"Unless what?"

A secretive look appeared on Pleshette's face. "Tell me, has this raven done anything *unusual*?"

"Like what?" replied Gabriel warily.

"Talk? Mimic? Repeat? . . . Tell a *riddle*, perhaps."

Abby, Gabriel, and Pamela shared a glance.

Pleshette pressed his hands together with a triumphant smile. "Children, you came to the right place. I'll take this one for five dollars."

"You said you didn't buy birds," said Abby.

"I don't recall saying that."

With a skeptical stare, Abby said, "You'd better write down *liar* before you forget that, too."

"Look," said Gabriel, "I just want to be sure that I'm taking the right care of him."

"Ravens are omnivorous. That means they'll eat all kinds of food—eggs, raisins, peanuts, sesame seeds, chicken, ground beef—but no dairy."

"Aha!" exclaimed Abby. "No wonder he wouldn't eat cheese or drink milk!"

"Never offer them milk," admonished the man. "When he starts to stand, give him a perch so he doesn't damage his tail feathers. He'll teach himself to fly. Simple as that. Remarkable birds. Intelligent beyond compare. And with some of them, it's possible to do extraordinary—"

Suddenly, the man blinked frantically, as if he regretted revealing this last detail.

"Extraordinary what?" asked Abby.

"*Nothing,*" snapped Pleshette. "Look, stupid children, I'll pay you thirty dollars for the bird. That's ten dollars each. Go get yourselves ice cream or candy or firecrackers."

"I'm not selling him," insisted Gabriel.

Pleshette rolled his eyes. "Make it ninety dollars. That's thirty for each of you. Go to the horse races, play the slots, buy cigars, I don't care."

"Cigars?" protested Pamela. "We're kids!"

"Kids?" The man rolled his eyes again. "Runaways, probably. Up to no good, I'll bet. I should call the police!" He picked up the phone.

"We're not runaways; we live here," said Abby.

"Prove it. Where d'you live?" said Pleshette, glaring at Gabriel.

"Six-oh-eight Fifth Street," said Gabriel. "Call my aunt, she'll tell you."

Pleshette shrank at the mention of another adult. He lowered the phone and sighed. "Okay, you drive a hard bargain.

I'll make it three hundred for the little bird. In cash, no questions, don't tell anyone!"

"Thanks for the advice," said Gabriel, replacing the lid and leading his friends out of the shop.

As soon as the children were back on the sidewalk with Paladin, the six ravens took to the air and flew off.

Abby turned to Gabriel. "Do you think they were trying to warn us about that guy?"

Pamela looked a little ashamed. "It's my fault. I thought he could tell us something useful."

"Are you kidding?" Abby replied. "He told us a lot!"

"Yeah, Pamela," said Gabriel. "I was the one who made the worst mistake."

"You did? How?" replied the girls.

"I gave him my address."

# ❈ The Prisoner ❈

That evening Gabriel offered the baby raven sweet-and-sour chicken; Paladin gobbled it down. In the morning, he pecked heartily at scrambled eggs; in the afternoon, he ate raisins, peanuts, and sesame seeds; in fact, the only thing he didn't eat was one of Trudy's homemade muffins. After each feeding, the chick curled up in his box, but not without looking at Gabriel first. When their eyes met, Gabriel felt an intense bond of trust.

"He hasn't talked again," he admitted to Abby. "But I feel as if he's in my head."

"In your head?" repeated Abby. "Oh! The way your father talked to Baldasarre. Try talking to him—without speaking, I mean."

After the next feeding, Gabriel sat quietly beside the box and focused his thoughts on the bird. *How are you?*

A feeling suddenly popped into his head—a very tender, vulnerable feeling. Gabriel was sure it was an answer. The word that described this feeling was obvious: *sad.*

*Do you have any family left?* wondered Gabriel.

*All alone*, came the reply.

*You're safe here. I'll take care of you.*

Gabriel put his hand on the rim of the box. The raven chick regarded him with small black eyes, then rested his head gently against Gabriel's hand.

The next Saturday, Trudy broke a tooth while biting into one of her own muffins. She had to make an emergency trip to the dentist. The minute she was out of the house, Gabriel invited Abby over, and they hurried up to Pamela's room to see if she could get the writing desk to reveal more answers.

Without hesitation, Pamela began playing a jaunty tune, and in less than a minute they heard footsteps trotting up the stairs.

The desk, draped in a paisley shawl, nudged the door open. When it saw Gabriel and Abby it trembled (although they weren't sure how it could see), then lurched into a jig with a jump, a kick, and four hops.

"You have to admit it's pretty good," Abby whispered.

At the end of the song, the desk began to stamp on the floorboards for more music. It was acting like an impatient three-year-old, so Abby shook her finger at it.

"Deskie," she said sternly, "you can have more music if you let us ask a question!"

Stamping its front legs in protest, the desk slumped down in front of Pamela, who lowered her violin to show that she wasn't going to play. Frustrated, the desk raised one taloned foot and pulled off the paisley shawl, tossing it into a corner of the room. The children waited for this sulk to pass. Reluctantly, the desk dragged its feet toward Gabriel and offered its lock to him.

Inserting the key, Gabriel concentrated on the small engraved word on the lid: *Ask*.

"Did my father find the torc?"

This time, the lid seemed to pop open of its own accord.

A postcard was sitting in the middle compartment.

It was blank on the message side, but the other side showed a photograph of a man seated at a familiar-looking writing desk.

"It's my dad!" Gabriel said. "That's his study."

"What does the picture mean?" asked Pamela.

As she spoke, parts of the photograph began to move. First the curtain fluttered. Then a raven flew in from the window; it dropped a roll of parchment into Mr. Finley's hand and whispered something in his ear. Mr. Finley lowered his head, frowning, as if he had received tragic news. He nodded to the raven, who flew out of the window again. Mr. Finley unrolled the parchment to examine it.

"Adam," said a voice.

A visitor had entered the room in the picture. He wore a dark velvet topcoat and trousers. Two large black wings extended from his shoulders, and one taloned claw clutched a cane.

"Corax?" whispered Abby.

"So my little brother is all grown up," said the visitor in a cold, crisp voice. "I understand you have a child—a little boy. Nine years old."

"That's correct." Adam Finley replied cautiously.

Gabriel thought that his father was very brave to stare back at those frightening coal-black eyes, the gaunt cheeks, and the sharp, beakish nose.

"Oh, I get it," whispered Abby. "If you were nine, then this happened three years ago!"

"The boy's name?" Corax continued.

"Gabriel."

"I'm so pleased to have a nephew," said Corax. "He will serve me well."

"Serve him well?" whispered Pamela anxiously. "What does that mean?"

Gabriel didn't reply. He was terrified.

"And I believe you are to be congratulated for something else," continued Corax. "Finding the extraordinary torc of Huginn."

Adam Finley nodded solemnly. "Yes, Corax. At great personal cost, I found the torc."

"So you were right," Gabriel whispered to Abby. "My dad *did* find it."

The half man, half raven unfurled his coal-black wings, which pulsed threateningly as he held out an open claw.

"I'll take it, then."

Adam shook his head. "It's not here, Corax, but I can assure you it is safe."

"Safe?" Corax's great black wings shook violently. "Understand me, Brother. I don't plan to leave empty-handed. Give me the torc."

Chilled by Corax's cold voice, Abby clutched Gabriel's arm so tightly that he almost dropped the postcard.

"That is impossible," Adam Finley replied. Replacing the ribbon on the rolled parchment, he put it in the writing desk, closed the lid, and locked it with a familiar-looking key. "You see, my raven, Baldasarre, hid the torc where even I cannot find it."

Corax's cold eyes settled on the desk. "Why should he hide it from you?"

"Because of its tragic history," said Adam.

"I only know its legend," replied Corax. "But you are a scholar, so tell me what you've learned."

Adam pressed his fingers to his temples for a moment. "I'm not clear on all the facts, except for this. After Muninn won the torc from Huginn—"

"Stole it, you mean!" interrupted Corax.

"I believe Huginn agreed to a duel of riddles but lost," replied Adam.

Corax waved one claw peevishly. "The details don't matter!"

"Oh, you'll find they *do* matter—a lot," said Adam. "Once Muninn won the torc, he tried to use its power for good. He wished for something else—a staff that would repel the attack of a valraven. Then he wished for a hiding place where the torc could never be found. That should have been the end of it, but the torc continued to exert its dark, mischievous force. It *wanted* to be found, and after a thousand years, I was the unlucky one to stumble upon it. So when it brought tragedy into my life, I begged my amicus to hide it."

"And what did Baldasarre do with it, Brother?" said Corax impatiently. "I have great plans for the torc. Armies to lead. Wars to win. Your warm, sunlit world is my next domain, and I need the torc to rule it."

Pamela gasped. "His next domain? Does he mean *here*?"

"Shhh, let's listen," said Gabriel.

"If you don't tell me," Corax continued, "my valravens will get to Baldasarre and tear him to pieces to find it."

"That's also impossible," Adam replied coolly. "Dear Baldasarre has passed away. The torc is out of your reach."

Corax collapsed his wings in frustration. He looked sharply at his brother. "Out of *my* reach, you say? Then another can find it? Who?"

"Don't tell him," whispered Pamela.

Adam Finley shook his head, and the children breathed a sigh of relief.

Corax beat his wings impatiently and paced the room. "Baldasarre must have left clues." His cold, dark eyes probed his surroundings and settled on the key in Adam Finley's hand. "And since every raven loves a riddle, it stands to reason that

Baldasarre left his clues in a riddle." His eyes settled on the desk. "A riddle in *here!*"

He wrenched the key from Adam's hand and turned it in the lock. The desk's carved raven legs tottered with fear as Corax wrested the lid open, but every compartment was empty. Furious, he dragged his claws across the surface.

"Explain!" he cried.

"You might have guessed the desk is bewitched," said Adam.

"I'll have it crushed and burned!" said Corax.

Adam shook his head. "What a shame to burn a desk containing the only clue to the torc's whereabouts."

Corax's expression shifted into a crafty smile. "Who can retrieve its contents?"

"Someone as pure as you once were, but wiser than you'll ever be."

Corax narrowed his eyes at Adam. "Don't speak to me in riddles!"

"Isn't it obvious?" Adam replied. "Baldasarre wanted the torc to fall into the right hands. One of noble and generous character, unspoiled by evil, who could find the torc with the help of a raven."

Corax nodded slowly. "*A twelve-year-old.* Your son is next in line. How clever. And I must wait three years for him to come of age? Very shrewd, Adam, but I shall simply take him with me to Aviopolis and keep him until he turns twelve."

Adam shook his head. "Just as a caged bird can't fly, a

caged mind forgets how to think. Corax, do you honestly believe that a child raised in your dark, miserable prison of a world will find the torc that eluded you all these years? I guarantee it will be lost forever. Interfere with him in any way and your hopes will be dashed."

This wiped the smile off the demon's face. Corax arched his wings in frustration. "You think you have fooled me," he muttered. "But let me remind you that your son will require an amicus. I shall hunt down every raven. Imprison those who defy me. When the boy turns twelve, I will make sure his raven serves *me*!"

Abby's eyes lit up. "So *that's* why Paladin was being attacked when we found him. Corax intended to use him against you."

"And that's why the key came on your twelfth birthday!" added Pamela.

"And why my father always told me so many riddles," said Gabriel. "So I could solve Baldasarre's riddle."

Meanwhile, in the magic postcard, Adam Finley made a last appeal to his brother. "Please, Corax," he said. "Reconsider the path you've chosen. Come back home. It's not too late."

The half man, half raven brooded for a time while his dark, velvety wings flexed ominously. "I don't understand you, Brother," he replied. "Why would you pass up the chance to possess a necklace that grants any wish?"

"Because it never brings happiness," Adam replied. "The dwarfs created it to sow mischief, despair, and revenge."

"Revenge!" The demon's cold heart thrived on this emotion. "Here is my revenge—you shall be imprisoned with me until the torc is mine!"

Corax leaped forward, his enormous wing feathers spread out so wide that they filled the postcard, and he soared through the opening in the window.

Gabriel let out a cry for his father, but there was nothing he could do. Adam Finley had vanished from the picture. Running his finger desperately around the edges, the boy wished he could reverse what he had just seen, merely for a last glimpse of his father, but the picture showed an empty room.

"So your dad is in Aviopolis," murmured Abby.

"Wherever that is," added Pamela.

# ❋ Learning to Fly ❋

Some places simply cannot be found on any map or computer. Gabriel spent the next week looking for a clue to Corax's domain. Perhaps no human had been there—or, more to the point, no human had ever returned from it.

Meanwhile, Paladin was in a big hurry to learn to fly. If Trudy slipped out to go shopping, Gabriel would let him practice in the living room, but the raven kept crashing into the furniture. It worried Gabriel so much that he made a careless remark.

"Can't sparrows fly in just a week or two?"

"I am not a sparrow!" Paladin sputtered indignantly. "Sparrows are idiots! I'm a *raven*, the smartest bird alive!"

"I'm sorry. I didn't mean to insult you," Gabriel said.

"Maybe you didn't *mean* to, but you did," replied the raven. "Let me remind you that human children take a year just to *walk*!"

"True."

In the following week, Paladin made great progress. He

learned to take off, land, and hover. The boy and the raven became so accustomed to sharing their thoughts that they could argue without speaking a word out loud. Most of their quarrels had to do with paravolating, because neither knew exactly how to do it.

*Could we try flapping our wings at the same time?* suggested Paladin.

*But I don't have wings,* replied Gabriel.

*Don't argue, just flap your arms instead!* Paladin answered.

Flapping his arms for several minutes, Gabriel slumped into a chair, sweaty and frustrated. *I feel silly.*

*You looked ridiculous!* laughed Paladin.

*You're not helping very much.*

No matter how they tried, they couldn't merge as Adam Finley had with Baldasarre.

Paladin's wings developed a handsome blue sheen, and his neck feathers formed a very dignified ruffle around his sleek black neck. He could be quite charming, too. He bowed to Aunt Jaz in the evenings, which Gabriel knew was a high compliment. In return, Aunt Jaz told Trudy Baskin that the bird could be fed in the kitchen.

"But his germs!"

"Trudy, I think we can agree that the bird is quite clean."

Pamela offered peanuts to the raven, who would now accept them from her with a courtly bow.

"Isn't he just amazing!" she cooed.

"I doubt he's any more intelligent than a trained parrot," snapped Trudy.

Paladin repeated Trudy's words, with the same snippy tone: *"I doubt he's any more intelligent than a trained parrot!"*

Before breakfast, Gabriel would pose a riddle to Paladin.

"When do strawberries get upset?"

"Hmm." Paladin noticed a jar on the table. "I know," he said. *"When they get in a jam!"*

Then Gabriel exploded in laughter, and the bird uttered *throk throk throk*s of glee.

Pamela watched their conversations with quiet yearning. One evening, she came to Gabriel with a favor. "May I please tell Paladin a riddle?"

"Sure," said Gabriel. "Go ahead."

"Okay," she said, looking nervously at Paladin. "It goes like this: Who shows up at breakfast, never appears for lunch or dinner, but comes twice for dessert?"

Paladin cocked his head at Pamela thoughtfully, then said, "The letter 's.'"

"Yes, that's it!" said Pamela.

Paladin laughed giddily. *Throk throk throk!*

"That was pretty good," Gabriel told Pamela.

Pamela sighed. "I wish I had a raven."

"I don't *own* Paladin," Gabriel reminded her. "Aunt Jaz told me that I could take care of him but one day he would probably decide to go his own way."

The girl's smile faded. "You're still so lucky!" She stamped angrily upstairs.

Gabriel tried to talk to Pamela later. He paused by her door, listening to the sad song she was playing on the violin. The music stopped for a moment, but when he tapped on the door, it resumed.

The next day on the way home from school, Gabriel complained to Abby about Pamela's sulk.

"I feel exactly the same way," Abby admitted. "You're telepathic. How cool is that? You have a fantastic power nobody else has!"

"Oh, yes, a *fantastic* power," mocked a voice. Somes Grindle had just caught up with them. "You're both so very special just because you know what goes up but doesn't come down or what's black and white and red all over! When's your next club meeting?" he said scornfully. "Don't forget your badges and T-shirts!"

Glaring at the two, Somes barged past, knocking Gabriel into the fence so that he dropped his backpack.

"Pest!" muttered Gabriel.

Abby stared after Somes. "Poor Somes. I think he feels left out."

"Yeah, poor Somes," Gabriel said wryly, picking up his backpack. He left Abby at her gate and crossed the street.

But when he got to his house, he saw two men standing

at the gate. The first had a familiar face: he wore a green poker visor and spectacles with extra lenses perched on the corners. Beside him stood a tall gentleman wearing a long tweed coat with a crimson silk scarf around his neck. But the most striking thing about him was the bird sitting on his shoulder—a magnificent raven as white as bone.

## ❀ Aviopolis ❀

"Ah, there he is!" said Mr. Pleshette to his companion. "Young man, I just came by to see how you were doing with your raven."

"Okay—why?" said Gabriel cautiously.

Pleshette withdrew his wallet. "I have decided to make you an even better offer for—"

"He's still not for sale."

"Not for three thousand? A fine box of Cuban cigars, a case of excellent Madeira wine, or a pair of hand-stitched Italian shoes?"

When Gabriel shook his head, Mr. Pleshette frowned. "I see. Disappointing, very disappointing indeed. Then allow me to introduce you to Mr. Crawfin here."

"How do you do, young fellow?"

The gentleman beside Pleshette had not spoken; it was the bird.

"Oh!" said Gabriel to the bird. "Fine, thank you!"

"Let me introduce my amicus," said the white raven. "Mr. Septimus Geiger."

Gabriel took another look at the tall man. He wasn't much older than Pleshette, but his hair was white and his skin was rugged, like that of someone who had traveled great distances in all kinds of weather.

"A pleasure, my lad, a great pleasure," said Septimus Geiger, shaking Gabriel's hand. Casually, he reached into his pocket and tossed a mouse into the air.

The white raven caught it in a swift movement and devoured it. Then the bird tilted his head curiously at Gabriel. "So, my young friend, what's the difference between a churchgoer and a donkey?"

"A churchgoer and a donkey?" said Gabriel. "Hmm." He thought for a moment. "Well, a churchgoer sits and prays, but . . . I'm sorry. I don't know the answer to that one."

"One sits and prays, the other spits and brays!" Crawfin chuckled, his laugh as rusty as a garden gate. *Cachh! Cachh! Cachh!*

Septimus regarded the bird sternly. "As riddles go, I don't think it's especially funny. At least, it's not worth all that *cackling!*"

Crawfin turned to Gabriel. "I think it's a pip!" He nibbled at Septimus's ear. "I deserve an extra mouse for that riddle."

"I think you've had enough," scolded Septimus.

The bird stared at his amicus. "Do I tell *you* when you've eaten too much?"

Sighing, Septimus dug into his pocket, produced another

small white mouse, and held it up by the tail. Crawfin gulped it down in an instant.

All this time, Mr. Pleshette had been glancing impatiently at his watch. "As we have no further business to discuss, I'll be on my way," he said, looking miserably at Gabriel.

"Bye," said Gabriel.

When Pleshette reached the end of the block, Gabriel expected the shopkeeper to turn and offer him something else ridiculous, like a bearskin coat and snowshoes, but the man rounded the corner and disappeared.

"Poor Pleshette," said Crawfin. "He doesn't understand that a raven and his amicus have an unbreakable bond. Septimus and I go together like salt and pepper."

"Eggs and bacon," added Septimus.

"Fish and chips," said Crawfin.

"I have a fine eye for valuable things—" said Septimus.

"And I have the talent for stealing them," added Crawfin. "I'm the one with the courage and—"

"No, *I'm* the one with the courage," protested Septimus.

"You have all the courage of a *hedgehog*!" snapped Crawfin.

As they argued, Gabriel began to wonder what they wanted from him.

"Dear boy," said Septimus, sensing the boy's confusion, "we bring news of your father."

Nothing else could have convinced Gabriel to invite such strangers into his house. Eagerly, he led them down to the kitchen. There was no sign of Trudy, which was a relief.

"So, about my father . . . ," Gabriel said. "Where is he? What's happened to him? Is he okay?"

Septimus raised his hand. "He is in fine health, I assure you. Until just recently, I was imprisoned with him in Aviopolis."

"Really?" said Gabriel. "Do you know where Aviopolis is?"

"Of course I know where it is," whispered Septimus, pointing downward with dramatic emphasis. "Corax's dim, cavernous realm lies miles right beneath us! A maze of polished stone, marble, anthracite, and alabaster. A city of birds, ruled by Corax and his hordes of valravens. In its center lies a fortress containing thousands of prisoners. Your father and I were captives together with only bread, water, and friendship to sustain us. He wants nothing more than to come home, dear boy. I promised I would aid his escape, which is why I am here!"

Gabriel couldn't believe his good luck. "And you say it's miles beneath us? Where exactly—"

"I understand you have a raven friend?" interrupted Crawfin.

"Yeah, but—"

"Well, we must be introduced immediately!" said Septimus.

"But I really want to know more about my dad," Gabriel replied.

"Patience, lad. One hand washes the other, does it not?" said Septimus.

This was an odd reply, but Gabriel saw that he had no choice but to fetch Paladin. When he explained about the visitors the young raven raised his neck feathers warningly. *If they came with Mr. Pleshette, are you sure they can be trusted?* he asked.

*Septimus is a friend of my father's,* Gabriel explained.

*You mean, he* said *he's a friend of your father's,* the raven corrected him.

When they returned, Paladin regarded Crawfin with a wary glance and immediately challenged him with a riddle. "What can burn you without fire, and lie without speaking?"

"A carpet," said Crawfin. *"Caw, caw, caw!"*

Paladin laughed, but then pinched Gabriel's shoulder with his foot, signaling that he wasn't quite ready to trust them.

Septimus sensed their doubt. "Relax, my friends," he said. "We are just like you! A raven and his amicus!"

"Tell me, can you actually fly together?" asked Gabriel. "Para—"

*"Paravolate,"* interrupted Septimus. "Let me demonstrate!"

Rising from his chair, the man flexed his fingers. "Now, it's rather like jumping while standing still. You have to *think* about jumping, without actually moving your muscles."

Locking his glance with Crawfin's, he made a small upward gesture with his finger and promptly vanished.

Gabriel looked around the room.

"Oh, I'm right here, dear boy." Septimus's voice spoke

merrily from the mouth of the white raven. "Or, if it's prefer-
able to Crawfin, he may travel in my form."

Suddenly, Septimus reappeared, and the white raven vanished from sight.

"Why would a bird want to be human?" asked Gabriel.

Septimus tried to reply, coughed, then removed the remains of a mouse tail from his mouth. "Crawfin," he snapped,
"it appears you didn't finish your snack!"

The white raven rematerialized on the chair and gulped
the mouse tail from the man's fingers. "I can answer that," said
Crawfin. "There are perils to being a raven. If, for example,
we are among great horned owls or falcons, it is far prefer-
able to be human. To be eaten by an owl is a very nasty way
to go."

"And there is one other benefit," added Septimus. "Together, our differences are diminished and our similarities are
enhanced. Crawfin and I are smarter when we merge . . ."

"And more determined," added Crawfin.

"Can we talk about my father again?" said Gabriel. "How
do you get to Aviopo—"

"All in good time, my boy," interrupted Septimus. "We
have explained how to paravolate. Now we have a question.
The location of the torc, if you please?"

Gabriel felt Paladin pinch his shoulder in caution. "How
is it you know about the torc?" he replied.

"Oh, every sparrow, finch, and chickadee knows about
the torc!" said Crawfin.

"Well, I don't know exactly where it is. All I know is that there's this riddle, hidden away, that explains where to find it."

"Ah! So where is this riddle?"

"Why didn't my father tell you, if you were such good friends?" asked Gabriel.

Septimus's expression became shrewd. "Smart boy!" He slapped his knee and laughed. "You're being careful, and rightly so! Your father would be proud of you!"

The man didn't look entirely pleased, however. Gabriel decided Septimus was a bit like sunlight moving on water: Quick. Elusive. Deceptive.

It was then that Pamela walked into the kitchen, back from school. Gabriel introduced his guests, who turned their attention to her with the same intensity they had given him.

She gasped when she saw Crawfin. "What a beautiful bird!"

"Thank you, my dear," said the bird. "You're very pretty yourself."

"Would you like to hold him?" said Septimus.

"Oh, I'd love to," gushed Pamela.

Crawfin hopped obligingly onto her wrist. She stroked his white feathers with a look of utter rapture.

"So, about Aviopolis . . . ," said Gabriel.

"About that *riddle*," Septimus countered. "I hope your father put it in a very safe place."

"Safe enough," replied Gabriel.

Septimus smiled craftily. "Then *you* know where the riddle is?"

Gabriel bit his lip, furious at having admitted this.

Crawfin nuzzled Pamela gently with his beak. "I'll bet this house has some clever hiding places, eh, my dear?"

"Oh, yes. The best hiding place is in a desk," Pamela replied. "But it's magic, nobody can open it unless—"

"*Pamela!*" Gabriel interrupted sharply. "Don't you need to practice?"

The boy's anxious expression was all she needed to realize she had made a mistake. "Excuse me," Pamela said, handing Crawfin back to Septimus. "I have to practice my violin." Slipping Gabriel an apologetic glance, she hurried upstairs.

Now Septimus turned to Gabriel and spoke in a smooth, seductive tone. "Don't you see how simple this is? You want your father back . . ."

"And we need the riddle that explains the torc's location," said Crawfin.

They were so determined, so insistent, so *devious*, thought Gabriel, but he kept his lips sealed tight. They were *too* clever.

The sound of Pamela's violin playing echoed from the staircase.

"Ah, how sweetly she plays," said Septimus. "She must be like a sister to you."

When Gabriel remained silent, Septimus and Crawfin shared a glance. It became obvious to them that he would reveal nothing more.

"Well, we must be off," said Crawfin, hopping onto Septimus's shoulder. "If you should change your mind, just tell any little bird you see."

"Any little bird?" Gabriel said curiously.

"Sparrows, finches, chickadees—they'll pass it on," added Septimus with a wink.

Gabriel escorted the pair up the stairs and out the door. "Goodbye," he said, relieved to see them go.

Septimus raised one hand with an elegant flourish and promptly vanished, leaving the white raven hovering in midair.

"Until next time!" said the white raven, then soared upward into the evening sky.

*Do they really know your father?* Paladin asked Gabriel.

*I only know they really want the torc,* replied Gabriel.


Gabriel waited until after dinner to discuss the visitors with Aunt Jaz. When he had explained what Septimus told him, she looked concerned.

"I don't know who this man is, Gabriel. You're right to be cautious," she said.

"But what if Septimus is telling the truth?" said Gabriel. "And my dad's really in prison, and the torc can free him? I have to do whatever I can to help."

Aunt Jaz's eyebrows tilted together in Paladin's direction.

"Perhaps you should begin by practicing what this Septimus person taught you."

It took a few moments for Gabriel to understand what she meant, but then a wondrous thought crossed his mind, and he looked at Paladin.

"You mean—*paravolate?*"

# ❊ The First Flight ❊

It was late evening when Gabriel stepped out into the backyard with Paladin on his shoulder. A cool breeze sent the last of autumn's yellow leaves spinning down onto the flagstones. The sky, a fathomless nighttime blue, seemed utterly out of reach.

*What if it doesn't work?* wondered Paladin.

"What if it *does*?" said Gabriel.

Paladin jumped onto a wooden patio table, then rocked nervously on his feet. He had only flown in a confined room. To be out at night in a sky full of dangers, well, this was another thing entirely.

Sensing the bird's anxiety, Gabriel stroked his sleek black head. "You don't have to fly tonight if you're scared."

Paladin stamped one foot. "That's the *last* thing I am." Then he cast Gabriel a concerned glance. "Actually, it's you I'm worried about."

"But I *want* to fly!" said Gabriel.

"Yes, but in order for us to do it *together*, you must think and move like a bird. That may be the problem. You don't understand what flying is all about."

"Okay, Mr. Know-It-All, go ahead, explain it to me," said Gabriel with amusement. He realized that Paladin hadn't forgotten his remark about sparrows learning to fly in just a week.

Paladin began with the parts of the wing. "First, there are the metacarpals, which are like your fingers; then the radius and ulna. The real work is done by the humerus, which is the bone from your elbow to your shoulder. Go ahead, stretch it!"

Gabriel flexed his shoulders, then spread his arms into a graceful upward reach. He did this several times until the raven gave him an approving nod.

"Nice," said Paladin. "Now, Septimus said you had to imagine jumping while standing still. But when you jump, concentrate on your wings instead of your feet!"

Gabriel nodded and silently recited the parts of the wing. *Humerus, radius, ulna, metacarpals.* It was a bit like a spell. *Humerus, radius . . .*

Taking a deep breath, he jumped!

In an instant, the world blurred, then sharpened. Gabriel's eyes were suddenly on the sides of his head instead of facing front. He realized his shoulders had dropped backward and his torso had shrunk; the sensation of lips vanished; his legs narrowed while his toes parted until they seemed impossibly wide. He looked down and saw a shiny breast of fine black feathers and two taloned feet. He paused to examine the handsome pair of black wings on his shoulders and felt himself topple backward with a thump.

*Gabriel!* snapped Paladin. *Will you please pay attention! Imagine if I stopped moving your legs while you were trying to walk! You'd fall on your face!*

*Sorry!* he replied.

After some maneuvering to get upright, they prepared to take off again.

*Just remember, I'll do the work!* said the bird.

As Paladin spread his wings, Gabriel felt the air swirl in eddies around him. It was thick, thick as water, thicker, even. He remembered wearing rubber flippers in a swimming pool and pushing himself forward with a strong flick of his foot. It was like that now, except that Paladin's wings gripped the air with even more strength.

One thrust and they left the ground.

Two thrusts and they were above the fence.

Three, four, five, and the house seemed to fall away beneath them.

The higher they got, the giddier Gabriel felt. When a breeze blew by, strong and steady as a freight train, they caught it and spiraled upward. Suddenly, Paladin stopped flapping and Gabriel panicked that they would drop, but amazingly, they coasted smoothly over the city, which was all the more beautiful for being so small and so far below.

It was blissful.

*I like this!* said Paladin.

*I love this!* answered Gabriel.

They passed through some low clouds and the glittering streetlights below became cloaked in an amber haze.

*Paladin, are you seeing everything I'm seeing?* Gabriel wondered.

*Of course. Do you think I'm doing this with my eyes closed?*

*Well, I suppose it's possible that one of us could sleep while the other did the flying,* Gabriel replied. *If we were traveling really far, I mean.*

They swooped back down over the neighborhood and saw people walking along the sidewalks. Gabriel wanted to shout out "Hey! I'm flying!" until he remembered that he was in the body of a bird.

But then Gabriel recognized one person—a tall boy walking at a slow, reluctant pace.

*Look,* he said. *That's Somes! Let's follow him.*

So the raven spiraled lower and shadowed the big boy's slow progress up the hill.

Somes carried a grocery bag. He stared at the ground, kicking at a twig as he made his way in long, languid steps. Presently, he arrived at a gray clapboard house with a shingle that read GRINDLE.

Gabriel and Paladin alighted on a nearby tree to watch.

Somes paused at the bottom of the stoop, as if the last thing he wanted to do was enter. He sat down and folded his arms. Suddenly, the front door opened and a tall, unshaven man wearing a baseball cap stood in silhouette.

Somes jumped up, clutching the bag.

"Finally back, huh?" the man said. "Took you long enough."

"Sorry," replied Somes.

"Let me see what you got," said the man, reaching for the bag. *"Peaches?* Didn't I say pears?"

"You said peaches," said Somes. "I wrote it down somewhere." He began turning out his pockets.

"No, I said pears."

"Peaches, see?" Somes replied nervously, holding up a slip of paper.

The man grimaced. "Think you're smarter than me?" He cuffed Somes's ear with the flat of his hand.

The boy flinched in pain. "Why did you do that?" he cried. "I got you exactly what you asked for!"

"Don't talk back to me! Idiot!"

With that, the man delivered a sharp blow to the boy's face, then walked back into the house with the bag.

The boy stood motionless, one hand covering his eye, weeping softly. After a moment, he turned, as if he sensed he was not alone. On a low tree branch, he noticed a raven. The two stared at one another for a moment; then Somes walked into the house.

Now boy and raven flew toward the East River. The water was dark and magnificent, rippling with reflections from the

windows of office buildings, and they could see traffic rolling silently like small beads of light along the streets. Soon,
however, Gabriel began to feel an ache in his wing muscles,
and he heard Paladin thinking.

*I'm tired. Let's go back.*

*Yes,* agreed Gabriel, and they headed toward home.

Paladin alighted in the backyard and Gabriel jumped free.

"That was amazing!" he whispered.

"Not bad," said Paladin, puffing out his neck feathers, obviously very proud of himself.

Quietly, Gabriel tiptoed upstairs with Paladin. The moment he got into his bedroom, Pamela appeared at the door.

"I just wanted to say I'm sorry . . . ," she began.

"It's okay," said Gabriel. He was too excited to be upset,
and immediately described soaring through the air and the
gorgeous flight over the bay. He also told her about seeing
Somes struck by his father.

When he finished, Pamela looked slightly peeved. "What's
the matter?" he asked.

"I just wish it had been me, that's all," she said. "My life is
so boring. Nothing ever happens to me."

"Wait, what about the dancing desk?" said Gabriel.

"Oh, sure," she said. "It was fun the first time, but it's
nothing like what happened to you tonight. To fly, and have
a friend like Paladin read your thoughts?"

"Why don't you try it with him?"

Pamela sat down with Paladin on her arm. The raven and

the girl stared at each other for a long moment, but it was obvious that it wasn't working. Magic between two minds is a mysterious thing. It happens quite simply, or not at all. Like friendship. Or love.

"It's no good." Pamela sighed. "You're just lucky, Gabriel."

With that, she headed back to her room.

# ❈ The Abduction ❈

On their way to school the next morning, Abby prodded Gabriel for details about his flight, but she became very quiet when he described the incident with Somes and the peaches.

"Poor Somes," she remarked. "Imagine how awful it would be, living with a father who hits you for fun!"

"Yeah—and he took it out on me a few times," Gabriel said.

"It kind of sounds like you spied on him," Abby replied.

Gabriel reacted with surprise. He recalled his father's diary description of Corax spying on his friend Thomas and realized how easy spying was for him to do now. He frowned, wondering if there were other changes coming over him—worse things.

Somes arrived at school with an ugly purplish bruise around his eye. As he weaved his way to his desk, he ignored Gabriel's sympathetic glance.

"Are you okay?" Gabriel asked.

"I'm fine," snapped Somes. "Don't I look okay?"

Gabriel decided to let him be; but a few moments later, Somes tapped him on the back. "Aren't you going to ask how I got it?" he said, pointing to the bruise.

"Sure," said Gabriel reluctantly. "How?"

"Simple," said Somes. "I was, um . . . reading. Yeah, reading while I was walking. Had the book right up in front of me, and *bam!* I walked smack into a pole. Hit me right in the eye."

Gabriel lowered his voice so that no one else could hear. "C'mon, Somes. Nobody's going to believe that. You hate reading anything."

"Seriously," Somes insisted. "That's what happened!"

Gabriel spoke in a whisper. "Look, I don't care what your excuse is. I mean, I *do* care. I'm sorry about what happened last night. Just make up something that people will believe."

Somes blinked at Gabriel, wondering how he knew. He hadn't seen anybody around but that raven on the branch.

On the way home, as Gabriel passed a group of sparrows twittering from the bush in his neighbor's front yard, the birds suddenly quieted down. It was just the way a group of kids talking about you might fall silent as you pass them. One of the sparrows fluttered off the bush and dropped a slip of paper before him. Gabriel caught it in his hand.

Written on it was a familiar name, with an address. On the reverse side was a note:

*My dear lad, I have your musical friend Miss Baskin with me and wish to arrange her safe return as soon as possible. It might be a good idea, on your way to my apartment, to bring the item from that remarkable desk that will help us in our urgent quest.*

*Sincerely yours,*

*Septimus Geiger*

Gabriel recalled the cunning expression on Septimus's face as he left Gabriel's house. Septimus must have realized how he could use Pamela to get what he wanted.

Aunt Jaz greeted Gabriel at the bottom of the stairs with Trudy.

"Gabriel," she said, "have you seen Pamela?"

He felt his stomach roll. "No—why?"

Trudy's forehead broke into worry lines. "I'm very concerned—very concerned! I called the school. They say she left at the usual time. She should have been home an hour ago. She's never this late!" Her shoulders quivered and her small eyes became red and moist.

"Maybe I can help . . . ," Gabriel offered.

Blinking back tears, Trudy replied scornfully, "You? What can you possibly do? The less you have to do with her, the better!"

"Now, now, Trudy," said Aunt Jaz.

Gabriel retreated to the laundry room to tell Paladin what had happened. The raven already knew what Gabriel was thinking. *Yes, of course, we have to rescue Pamela!* he said.

*I'd better get the parchment from the desk,* said Gabriel.

*Isn't that just what Septimus wants you to do?* warned Paladin.

Gabriel shrugged. *If I can help free my father and get Pamela back home, I have no choice.*

Paladin tipped his head to the boy to show that he agreed.

When Trudy was busy talking on the phone in the kitchen, Gabriel took Paladin upstairs and slipped quietly into the study. He turned on the light and heard movement behind the door. The writing desk, draped in a yellow silk robe with a purple feather boa, tore into the hall.

"Here we go again," groaned Gabriel.

He followed the desk out, but it was waiting at the doorway. It stuck out one taloned foot, tripping him so that he tumbled down the stairs.

Furious, Gabriel rubbed the bruise on his forehead, staggered back up, and thrust his arm through the balusters, grabbing one of the desk's carved feet.

"Look, Desk!" he said. "Pamela's in trouble. It's an emergency!"

The mention of Pamela seemed to change the desk's attitude. It flapped its little wings eagerly, as a dog might wag its tail at the prospect of a walk.

Inserting the key, Gabriel whispered his question. "Now. How do I find the torc?"

Raising the lid, he saw a piece of parchment tied with red ribbon in the middle compartment. He unrolled it to find a set of verses written in scratchy lettering. It was a riddle, all right. But at that moment, a voice spoke from the staircase.

"Gabriel, what are you looking at?"

It was Aunt Jaz. When Gabriel explained about the note from Septimus and his plan to rescue Pamela, her boomerang eyebrows knitted with worry. "My dear, are you sure this is something you should be doing?"

"Well, I got Pamela into this mess," he said. "Who else can help her but me?"

Aunt Jaz nodded. "You know, that's exactly what your father would have said."

It felt good to hear this. Perhaps, Gabriel thought, he could bring Pamela back and help free his father. That would be amazing.

Aunt Jaz threw the window open. "I think it best if Trudy doesn't see you leave. She doesn't have a—"

"Flexible mind?" suggested Gabriel.

"Exactly!" replied Aunt Jaz.


In minutes, Paladin and Gabriel were high above Manhattan. This evening the city resembled a mysterious amber jewel—streetlights glowed through a faint mist, all the traffic noise was muffled, and the air felt charged and ready for something fantastic to happen. The boy and his raven flew over the dark rim of Central Park, looking for the first building on the corner: One West Seventieth Street.

A rolling mist circled the apartment building, lapping at its edges like waves around a lighthouse. On the rooftop was a terrace. Paladin alighted on its wall. A large fireplace glowed brightly through open french doors.

Gabriel separated from Paladin. He shook his legs to straighten them; then Paladin perched on his shoulder and the two entered a room with a roaring fire and a vast stone mantel that seemed more suitable to the residence of a duke or king. The white raven had a very cozy spot on a brass perch beside the fireplace.

"Welcome, welcome, welcome!" said Crawfin, his eyes glittering.

Septimus leaned forward from a great leather armchair, his face red and devilish in the firelight. "Welcome indeed!" he said. "What a pleasure! Come in, come in!"

As Gabriel's eyes adjusted, he noticed the walls were lined with bookcases and framed maps. An enormous globe of the earth occupied the center of the room. It was immensely detailed—there were oceanic trenches, rugged mountains, and islands poking like barnacles from the seafloor.

"Do you like it?" said Crawfin. "It comes in very handy in our line of work."

"What's that?" Gabriel replied.

Septimus poured himself a glass of golden liquid from a crystal decanter. "We travel the world in search of rare jewels, exotic medicines, and unusual creatures. Crawfin *obtains* them . . ."

". . . and Septimus," continued Crawfin, "always gets a good price!"

Gabriel guessed that Septimus probably did business with Mr. Pleshette, whose shop was full of curious items from all over the world. Something about Septimus's expression seemed to imply that these objects weren't always found in honest ways.

"I've been wondering—why did Corax imprison you, anyway?" asked Gabriel.

Septimus and Crawfin exchanged a cautious glance.

"Let me assure you of one thing," said Septimus severely. "I didn't steal anything!"

"And even if he did, no one can prove it," Crawfin added.

"All I did was sell him an item that didn't work properly." Septimus shrugged. "You don't throw someone in prison for selling a broken vacuum cleaner, do you?"

"You sold Corax a broken vacuum cleaner?"

"No, a *necklace*."

"A very expensive necklace that you *promised* would grant wishes." Crawfin smirked.

"I *hoped* it would grant wishes. It was silver, just like the real one," Septimus said indignantly.

"It didn't grant a single wish, but it did give Corax an ugly rash and a smell like rotten eggs. After he recovered, he threw Septimus in prison with your father," chortled Crawfin, provoking a nasty look from Septimus.

"So why did he set you free?" Gabriel asked.

"Aha!" said Crawfin. "Septimus promised to—"

Septimus closed his hand on the bird's beak to silence him. "Never mind that! I mean to help your father escape, dear lad. Now, did you bring the riddle that reveals the torc's location?"

"That depends," replied Gabriel. "Where is Pamela?"

"Crawfin, send her in!" Septimus replied, releasing the white raven's beak.

Crawfin uttered an indignant throk, flew across the room, and landed on the handle of a door. It opened to reveal Septimus's library, and Pamela, looking weary and disheartened.

"Are you okay?" asked Gabriel.

"Gabriel! Paladin! I'm so glad to see both of you!" she replied, running to them. "I've been so stupid. I trusted them when they promised to make me a raven's amicus—"

"*That's* what they promised?" interrupted Gabriel angrily.

Septimus put a hand to his chest. "I certainly tried!" He looked into the library. "Hobblewing! Where are you?"

A raven with bent tail feathers and a limp wobbled unsteadily across the floor. Ravens were proud birds, but there was something meek and unfortunate about this one. It offered a riddle in a timid voice.

"Whenever I come near, you wave, and yet we are not friends. Who am I?"

"Hmm," said Paladin. "Wave at you but we are not friends. I know! You are a *fly*!"

The two ravens broke into a rusty laugh, then shared a

quiet conversation. Eventually, Paladin returned to Gabriel, looking upset.

"This unlucky raven was captured by Pleshette before he hatched! Never even saw his mother! Imagine the fellow's life, Gabriel. Born alone in a cage, never learned to fly, no friends but that horrible shopkeeper. Trapped and alone with no companion! What could be worse for an orphan?"

"Terrible," Gabriel agreed.

Pamela looked at Hobblewing. "Is there anything we can do for him?"

Gabriel glared at Septimus, who fussed with his shirt collar. "Pleshette assured me this raven was one of his best. . . ."

"This bird needs his freedom," said Gabriel. "Let Hobblewing go, Septimus. And Pamela must also—"

Crawfin interrupted. "You were going to bring us something in return. The riddle that will lead us to the torc."

"Exactly," continued Septimus. "My boy, all I'm trying to do is get your father out of prison."

Gabriel wondered again how he could possibly trust these two.

*I don't trust them, either,* agreed Paladin.

*Yes, but I have to find my father,* Gabriel reminded him. *That's the most important thing. If there's even a chance that they can help us free him, Paladin, I think we have to take it. Don't you? Wouldn't you do the same thing if you could get your mother back?*

*Without a doubt!* Paladin replied.

So Gabriel demanded that Septimus send Pamela home

in a taxicab, but to be sure the promise was kept, he asked Paladin to accompany her.

*Consider it done,* the raven replied. *I'll return as quickly as I can.*

Crawfin grudgingly agreed to give Hobblewing flying lessons. Although Pamela was glad to have Paladin escort her, she asked Gabriel why he wasn't coming with them.

"So I can keep my part of the bargain," he explained.

"What's that?"

"To solve a riddle, of course."

# ❀ The Raven's Riddle ❀

Gabriel was just as excited to examine the parchment as Septimus and Crawfin. The verses were written in scratchy script by the raven Baldasarre. He read aloud:

"To those who seek this wondrous prize,
My humble verse please heed;
The mischief that this necklace brings
Hails from an ancient deed:

One thousand dwarfs raised arms against
A mighty chieftain's reign,
But this bold king imprisoned them
Beneath his great domain.

And so they forged a kingly gift,
With malice and invention,
A torc that would all wishes grant
To gain their swift redemption.

To thee I say, resist its lure,
Devised in evil plot.
Around the staff this torc must stay,
Its wickedness forgot."

When they had finished this part of the verse, Septimus's forehead, which had been wrinkled to start with, cleared with obvious amusement. "What a charming little rhyme!"

Gabriel frowned. "It sounds to me like a serious warning," he said. "Like signs on a fence that say 'Danger, Keep Out!'"

"Oh, yes," laughed Septimus. "I've always ignored those signs. Why, if Crawfin and I paid attention to Keep Out signs, we would be—"

"Out of business," interrupted Crawfin.

Septimus rubbed his hands. "This raven Baldasarre enjoys preaching a lot of gloom and doom, but I wish he would get to the point!"

"Let's move on," said Crawfin impatiently.

Gabriel passed his finger down to the next part of the verse.

"To find the torc, the seeker must
Prove worthy in its thrall,
Brave in spirit, warm of heart,
And selfless, most of all."

"That's me," said Septimus. "No truer words were said."

The white raven looked doubtfully at Septimus. "If that's you, I'm an ostrich."

"I was brave in my youth."

Crawfin rolled his eyes.

Gabriel read on:

*"A daring task must be performed*
*To gain that for which you yearn:*
*Give back the druid stone to those*
*Who pine for its return."*

"Druid stone? It sounds valuable!" Septimus's eyes brightened.

"And I wonder who pines for its return?" Gabriel said.

"It must be quite precious," Septimus declared. "What a shame to go to such trouble to find it, just to give it away to somebody else."

"Maybe Baldasarre means that this stone must be traded for the torc," Gabriel replied. "A selfish person would keep the druid stone and never get as far as finding the torc."

Crawfin smirked. "The boy makes sense." Septimus, however, rolled his eyes and gestured for Gabriel to continue.

*"On pillars made of granite stone,*
*Lady Justice rests her feet.*

*Be sure to charm her resident*
*Or, in despair, retreat."*

"*On pillars made of granite stone, Lady Justice rests her feet.* Well, that sounds like the big courthouse building downtown," guessed Gabriel. "It has pillars. The top of the building has a statue of a woman holding a sword and a flaming torch. I'll bet that her 'resident,' whoever it is, lives behind that statue and has this druid stone."

"What sort of creature would live up there?" said Septimus. "Rather a high place, I reckon. Windy. Cold. Very unpleasant this time of year." He and Crawfin shared a pointed glance.

"I don't know, but we'll just have to find out," said Gabriel.

"Now, isn't he a fine chap?" Septimus remarked to Crawfin. "Volunteering on such a dangerous mission!"

"I didn't exactly volun—" Gabriel said, but he was interrupted by a desperate noise—three weak throks. An exhausted raven appeared in the doorway, one wing drooping, his chest heaving.

# ❖ The Aerie ❖

"**P**aladin!" Gabriel cried. "What happened?"

"Attacked," gasped the bird.

"Oh, no! Is Pamela okay?"

"Home and perfectly safe," said the raven. "Your aunt fed me a few slices of bacon, then sent me back to you; but on my way I heard the croak of another raven above me, so I landed on a branch. Two other ravens landed on either side of me, so I greeted them with a riddle:

*"From hour to hour I wander,*
*As night and day go by,*
*Yet always anchored to my home.*
*Can you guess the reason why?*

"When I told them the answer was an hour hand on a clock, they didn't laugh."

"Valravens," murmured Gabriel.

"Exactly," said Paladin. "I took off as quickly as I could, but I could hear them behind me. 'Get him, get him!' they cried. I flew low over the rooftops, dipping between trees and washing lines, anything to dodge them, but they stayed right on my tail. Eventually, I found my way to the river. It was misty down there, so I hoped I could just disappear, but their eyes glowed yellow like flashlights through the darkness. One of them grabbed my wing, and I thought I was done for. Just then, a huge bird appeared out of the mist and the three began shrieking in terror. I'm almost sure it ate them, because one by one they cried out and then fell silent."

"Something that eats valravens?" repeated Crawfin. "What could it have been?"

"Well, I didn't wait to find out," replied Paladin. "If it ate valravens, it might eat me. I got lost in the mist for a while, then finally spotted the lights of the bridge. Halfway across the river, I happened to look up and saw it above me— terrible wings beating the air as silently as a ghost. I couldn't even hear a flutter from its feathers. And those talons! So big they could have plucked me out of the air and squeezed the life out of me!"

"An owl," said Crawfin.

"How did you escape?" asked Gabriel.

"I flew in and out of the bridge wires. At the end of the bridge I found a drainpipe just big enough to fit me," Paladin replied.

"Very wise, young Paladin," said Crawfin.

"I waited and waited," Paladin continued. "I could see the owl's vicious eyes peering from the mouth of the pipe. I've never been so terrified. Finally, it began to rain and he must have taken shelter somewhere. I know that owls can't fly in the rain, so I took a chance and climbed out. When I was aloft, I heard him calling after me. The nerve! As if he expected me to come back and offer myself up as his dinner!"

Crawfin cocked his head curiously. "Interesting. I should think an owl that big would have snapped you up in a few seconds."

"Yes, I know!" Paladin replied. "Mother always said that no one survives an owl attack. That's my second. I don't fancy a third one!"

"I hope the owner of the druid stone isn't an owl," murmured Septimus.

"The druid stone? What's that?" asked Paladin.

Gabriel explained the verses while Paladin listened.

"Well," Septimus said. "Best get on your way and find that stone!"

In moments, Gabriel and Paladin had paravolated and were soaring into the sky as one, heading south toward the big buildings where the courthouses were.

*The only thing I don't understand,* remarked Paladin after a few quiet minutes, *is why, if Septimus is such a good friend of your father's, he's not helping us? He didn't even offer to come along.*

*Yeah, I know,* replied Gabriel. *They were perfectly happy to send us off alone.*

Before they had time to wonder what dangers Septimus had foreseen, they spotted an enormous courthouse down below. It had a row of statues on the facade at the top. In the center stood a proud figure of a woman holding a sword in one hand and a flaming torch in the other. Her carved feet stood on a pediment resting across a row of granite pillars. In the niche behind the statue's head and shoulders, Gabriel spied a nest composed of very large twigs and sticks.

As soon as they swooped near, a piercing shriek turned their blood cold. An eagle with a helmet of brilliant white feathers and a massive hooked beak peered over the statue's head. Straddling the nest, it screamed another earsplitting warning.

*An eagle!* gasped Paladin. *The only thing worse than an owl. In fact, now I prefer owls. Is it too late to find an owl instead?*

*Paladin, we need the druid stone,* Gabriel reminded him.

*But I don't want to be an eagle's dinner,* said Paladin.

*I have an idea,* said Gabriel. *Land over there.*

Paladin alighted as far from the eagle as he could, in the pediment corner. They were sixty feet above the ground, and an icy breeze pressed them against the granite facade. It was exactly like a cliff, which made sense to Gabriel; only an eagle, he thought, would make a nest in such an unpleasant place.

"Okay, what's your idea?" asked Paladin.

The eagle was looking at them with a predatory glint in its eyes.

"Remember Crawfin telling us that ravens are sometimes safer in human form?" said Gabriel. "You should merge with me!"

Paladin jumped and immediately felt his body stretch to a boy's proportions. His toes felt ridiculously short, his arms weak and scrawny, but he liked being able to see directly in front for a change. Best of all, his trembling stopped.

With chilled fingers, Gabriel clambered across the lap of Lady Justice until he arrived just below the eagle's nest. Something crunched sharply beneath his feet. He looked down and saw many bones of small birds that had been eaten and discarded. His knees began to shake.

*How does one greet an eagle?* he wondered.

*Be very polite!* answered Paladin.

"Hi! I'm Gabriel Finley," said Gabriel.

The voice that replied was sharp, powerful, and contemptuous.

"I'm Tiberius." The eagle looked him up and down. "I suppose the geese sent you?"

"Pardon me? What geese?" said Gabriel.

"The Romany Geese. Those cowards. They've been begging for the return of the druid stone for years," muttered Tiberius.

*Interesting,* thought Gabriel. *Is the druid stone supposed to be returned to the Romany Geese? The verse never mentioned them.*

*Please concentrate, Gabriel,* interrupted Paladin.

"Yes, the Romany Geese," repeated Gabriel. "Any special reason why you don't want them to have it?"

"No special reason at all," murmured Tiberius. "Geese have very little to say. Oh, they make a lot of noise, but it's all for the attention. One could starve for lack of intelligent conversation with a goose. I would have given them the druid stone for a little chat or a joke or two." The eagle coughed bitterly into his wing.

"Really? You would have traded the stone for a joke?" asked Gabriel.

Tiberius gave a long-suffering nod. "I didn't choose this life. It's lonely at the top. Nobody jokes, nobody laughs, nobody goofs around. I suppose that's why I eat them."

The great bird tucked away a stray wing feather with his hooked beak.

"What if I offered you a riddle for the stone?" Gabriel suggested.

The eagle looked at him with interest. "It would have to be a good one, and if I guess it, no stone. Understood?"

"Of course," said Gabriel. "May I see the druid stone first?"

The eagle regarded him with one disdainful eye. "Don't you trust me?"

"It's only fair that you show me you have it."

"Fair," repeated the eagle. "Creatures often use that word with me. This isn't fair. That isn't fair. Let me tell you, nothing in life is fair." He sighed. "Well, I'm eager to hear your riddle, so I'll make an exception."

Tiberius dipped his head into the nest. When he reappeared, a small amber stone glittered between the points of his beak. It was honey-colored and quite clear, with a curious sparkle in the center, almost as if a flame was burning deep inside. Gabriel was astonished by its beauty.

The eagle placed the stone on the granite, just between his deadly claws.

"Well, hurry up. Let's hear it," said the eagle. "And if I guess it, you lose!"

At this point, Paladin asked Gabriel a silent question. *And if we lose . . . then what?*

*I don't want to know,* Gabriel replied while attempting to smile at the eagle.

"Okay, it goes like this," he said:

*"I shine like a dagger*
*Or a diamond tooth in a dragon's maw.*
*I grow larger as the cold night comes,*
*And shorter in the thaw.*
*What am I?"*

A grave intensity settled in the eagle's eyes, his black pupils flicking back and forth as he pondered.

"A beak is like a dagger," he declared. "But a beak doesn't look like a diamond. Perhaps a claw? Hmm. Larger as the cold night comes and shorter in the thaw. What kind of dagger grows or shrinks? That doesn't make sense." He fell silent for another few seconds, then flexed his talons. "I've got it."

Gabriel's heart sank. Tiberius looked so sure of himself.

"The answer is *nothing*."

"Wrong," said Gabriel, relieved. He reached up and took the druid stone.

Surprised at Gabriel's nerve, Tiberius rose from his nest, flexing his enormous wings. "You don't understand," he murmured gravely. "If I say the answer is nothing, then that is what it is. *Nothing!* Put the stone back!"

"That's not fair," said Gabriel, keeping the stone behind his back.

"Didn't I tell you already that nothing is fair!" snapped the eagle.

"Look, I'll tell you the right answer," Gabriel persisted, as he edged away. "An icicle is shaped like a dagger or a dragon's tooth, it can be clear as a diamond, and it grows longer when it's cold but shorter when it gets warm, because it melts, see? Icicle. That's the answer!"

The eagle blinked unforgivingly at Gabriel. "I am never wrong."

He leaped nearer the boy.

*Paladin, quick, it's time to switch places!* cried Gabriel anxiously.

Before Paladin could reply, the eagle swiped one claw at Gabriel.

Three bloody slashes appeared across his frozen wrist. Gabriel couldn't feel the wound, but the blood flew against his shirt in bright red streaks.

Hopping toward the boy, Tiberius uttered a menacing

shriek. Gabriel sprang backward, but there was nothing beneath his feet. Now air was rushing past him. He was falling swiftly. Below, he saw the granite steps waiting like a deathbed. And above? Tiberius swooped, no kindness in his eyes, just the murderous stare of a raptor preparing to rip out the heart of his victim.

*Jump!* cried a voice.

But how do you jump when you're falling?

*Jump, Gabriel!* repeated Paladin.

The eagle's savage scream was an inch away.

Suddenly, a bright amber light flashed from the palm of his hand.

Gabriel blacked out.

# ❋ The Romany Geese ❋

*Gabriel? Wake up!*

Opening his eyes, Gabriel found himself high above a barren salt marsh extending for miles along a shore. His first assumption was that the eagle was carrying him, but then he realized that he was actually flapping his own wings. Apparently he and Paladin had succeeded in exchanging bodies in midair—a pretty extraordinary feat in itself—as well as escaping the vicious bird.

Now he became aware of a brightly glowing object in his right claw that seemed to be pulling him downward.

*Paladin? Where are we?* he asked.

*I'm not sure,* replied Paladin. *But I think we've arrived.*

They spiraled toward a cove where gentle waves lapped the sand into soft ridges. On the ground, Gabriel separated from Paladin and stretched his arms and legs. A curlew cried a faint welcome. Gabriel examined the spot where Tiberius had slashed him, and the wound vanished before his eyes. The druid stone in his hand dimmed, retaining just a tiny trace of fire in its center.

*What about the eagle, Paladin? Why didn't he catch us?* Gabriel asked as they walked along the shoreline.

*I've been wondering that myself. I think it might be because of the druid stone. Do you remember me saying* jump?

Yes, said Gabriel, *but that's all I remember.*

*Then you missed the best part! I flew down between the pillars and the eagle followed, and each time he caught up with me I dodged my way around another pillar. It was the strangest thing, Gabriel. I knew my way even though I had never been there before. The stone led me!*

*But how did you get rid of Tiberius?*

*Aha!* said Paladin gleefully. *An eagle may be bigger and stronger, but he can't change direction like a raven. So finally, I did a high dive toward a pillar and turned at the last moment. Ha! You should have seen him fly into the granite. What a colossal thump! Old Tiberius flopped to the ground like a sack of potatoes.*

*Paladin, that was incredibly brave,* said Gabriel.

The raven puffed out his neck feathers proudly. *Well, yes, I suppose it was. Anyway, I was wondering how to find these Romany Geese and the stone began to glow again, and suddenly, I knew which way to fly. No wonder they want it back.*

Across the stark beach they noticed figures dotting the landscape. Thousands of geese, but not like any Gabriel had seen before, watched the boy and his raven approach. Their heads were black; their long, graceful necks were striped; their bodies had a white circle upon the chest; and their wing feathers were speckled. Mute and elegant, the Romany Geese turned to observe their visitors.

At that instant, they noticed one Romany Goose step forward and approach them. She had a graceful walk quite unlike a normal goose's waddle.

"You must be Gabriel and Paladin," she said. "I am Ulyssa."

The goose's voice was warm and very soothing. She blinked at them with large brown eyes.

"You know our—"

"Names? Yes, we've been expecting you!" She sounded like a motherly librarian, so accustomed to answering questions that she never needed to hear the whole sentence.

"But I was almost eaten by—" began Paladin.

"Tiberius? Oh, he would never be a match for Baldasarre's grandson!"

"Then you also knew *I* would—" began Gabriel.

"Solve Baldasarre's riddle? Of course we knew you'd find the druid stone! You're Adam Finley's son."

Gabriel enjoyed the compliment but felt frustrated that the goose kept guessing his questions, so he replied with the shortest question he could think of. "How?"

"A boy raised on riddles and a smart raven: you're a perfect pair. Naturally, it's different from being *knowledgeable*, as we geese are." Ulyssa betrayed a very smug little dimple in the corner of her beak.

"Why is it diff—"

"Because our wisdom comes from roaming. The stone has always led us. We know where the best saffron blooms grow, where the wolves nurse their young, where elephants go to grieve. I could tell you where to find the most beautiful orchids on five continents."

"Do you know where to find the torc?" asked Paladin.

The goose's amused dimple reappeared. "Oh, yes," she said.

"And my father?" said Gabriel anxiously.

Ulyssa sighed. "I wish I could tell you, but you must follow the course you have begun. You have both proved yourselves uncommonly brave, which is Baldasarre's first test," she said. "May I have the druid stone?"

"Here it is," said Gabriel.

The goose took the stone in her beak and promptly swallowed it. She smiled pleasantly. "A reward comes with the return of the druid stone. You must be very cold and hungry. Perhaps this would be the item you most desire?"

A silver tureen appeared beside the goose. Steam curled from beneath the lid, promising something warm to eat. Gabriel's stomach growled.

*Remember why we're here!* Paladin reminded him.

"No thank you," Gabriel said to the goose. "We're trying to rescue my father, so the torc is what we're looking for."

"Ah! Then you require this." The goose turned her head to the left, and Gabriel saw a stick lying on the sand. It was roughly the length of a broomstick, twisted by age like a piece of driftwood. It didn't look very special at all.

"But isn't the torc a *necklace*?" he asked.

"So it is," said Ulyssa. "But long ago, the raven Muninn

used the torc's magic to enchant a staff of ash wood. The staff is the only thing that can destroy a valraven. When the torc is wrapped around the staff, it will come to you when summoned."

Gabriel remembered his father discussing a staff with Corax on the moving postcard, but he felt disappointed. Such powers might be useful, but he still wished Ulyssa had offered him the torc. He was also very hungry.

With a longing glance at the tureen, Gabriel turned to Ulyssa. "Well, thanks very much," he said, picking up the stick.

The moment he did so, hundreds and thousands of honks erupted across the beach. The geese who had been watching were giving their approval, gyrating their necks and clapping the sand with their webbed feet.

"Very good," said the goose, and smiled again. "Gabriel, you have passed the second part of the task. You are steadfast, and this quality will serve you well indeed! Take the staff in hand and remember its valuable gifts!"

"So where exactly is the—"

Ulyssa interrupted again. "I promised Baldasarre that I would abide by his wishes. I cannot lead you to the torc."

The goose turned to join her flock, which had already begun taking to the air. The graceful birds needed to flap their wings only once to get aloft.

Gabriel looked doubtfully at the stick. Then he noticed that the silver tureen was still on the ground.

"Oh, excuse me, you left your—"

"Have something to eat before you go." With a wink, Ulyssa raised her great wings and set off.

The tureen happened to contain the very thing Gabriel most wished for: a bowl of steaming oatmeal studded with fresh blueberries, raspberries, and walnuts and drizzled with butter, maple syrup, and cream—perfect for a cold morning on the beach.

Full-bellied and quite pleased with themselves, the boy and his raven had no sooner eaten than the tureen vanished. Far above the gray sea, they noticed the Romany Geese flying in a perfect V formation, honking a farewell.

Gabriel looked at the staff and saw a slip of paper attached to it with a knot of string. He pulled it loose and was about to examine it when Paladin nudged him with his beak.

"We're not alone," he said.

In the distance, a white bird was approaching. Suddenly, a gentleman with snowy hair and a long coat materialized on the beach. When the bird landed on his shoulder, the man drew a mouse from his coat pocket and tossed it into his companion's mouth, then waved at Gabriel.

"I am so proud of you both!" cried Septimus. "Such bravery! To best an eagle is one thing. To win the trust of Romany Geese quite another!"

"You saw it all?" said Gabriel. "You were following us?"

Septimus put his hand to his heart. "My boy, I promised Adam Finley I would watch over his son like my very own."

"But I almost died!" said Gabriel.

Septimus dismissed this remark with a wave of his hand. "Trust me, we were there to make sure you didn't. Isn't that so, Crawfin?"

Crawfin cocked his head wryly at Septimus, but he said nothing.

"What does that paper in your hand say? Let's have a look."

## ❋ Horned Assassins ❋

**G**abriel unfolded the paper. It was covered with more of Baldasarre's scratchy lettering, like a bird's tracks in the sand. He read it aloud:

> *"If my power you seek to claim,*
> *Beware my awful curse.*
> *I'll trade the good that lies in you*
> *For something vastly worse.*

> *"My horned assassins guard me where*
> *The peacocks safely roam,*
> *Where lions roar near bleating lambs*
> *And mighty tigers moan."*

"Clearly this explains the torc's whereabouts," said Septimus. "But where on earth do lions roar near bleating lambs?"

"Well, that can only be a zoo," said Gabriel.

"And these horned assassins?" worried Septimus. "Who can they be?"

"The little zoo in Brooklyn doesn't have lions or tigers, but the Bronx Zoo does," Gabriel replied. "I bet we'll find horned animals there, too."

The dawn sky was a soft peach color, and the zoo felt strangely busy for such an hour. Dark forms paced back and forth along the fenced enclosures, emitting whoops, brays, barks, and wails. The cries of large cats merged into one grand chorus. Apes taunted and chuckled, as if they all knew that a riddle had summoned these visitors.

They visited the rhino paddock, elks, ibex, goats, and water buffalo, but Gabriel sensed each time that they were on the wrong track. He turned the staff in his hand, wondering if there was a clue carved in its surface. It was very smooth, and strangely warm to the touch, but it offered no answers. He consulted the piece of paper that had been attached to it.

"Look," he said to the others. "The verse says horned *assassins*. Well, water buffalo and goats aren't really assassins."

"Gabriel," said Paladin, "the bird that chased me over the river had horns."

"It was an owl, right?" said Gabriel

"Yes. A great horned owl, I think."

Gabriel laughed. "That's it! *An owl!* And what's the best place to hide something from valravens? A place full of their worst enemies. *Owls!*"

\*   \*   \*

The Birds of Prey building was black and windowless. Paladin dug his talons nervously into Gabriel's shoulder when they arrived at the entrance. "I can't go in there," he said.

"I understand," said Gabriel gently. "But you just out-witted an eagle."

"Only because I had the druid stone. This is much worse!"

An idea popped into Gabriel's head. "Look," he said, "we'll do exactly what we did with Tiberius. If you merge with me, the owls won't even know you're here."

"Splendid!" said Crawfin. "I'll do the same with Septimus."

Gabriel and Septimus advanced through the eagle and hawk section and came to a room marked NOCTURNAL PREDA-TORS. Inside, it was pitch black, the air thick with dust and feathers. Gabriel noticed large eyes glittering in the darkness and felt a violent quiver of panic in his chest.

*Sorry, it's just me, trembling,* Paladin told him.

But it wasn't just Paladin; the staff vibrated so intensely it resembled the throb of a very low piano string. Something extremely important was in this room, something that ex-cited the old gnarled piece of wood.

Hostile hoots and suspicious whispers filled Gabriel's ears. As he became accustomed to the darkness, he saw three very large owls sitting upon a tree limb. Their heads had pointed feathery tufts resembling horns, and they regarded him with keen scrutiny and sharp beaks. They were horned assassins, to be sure.

Septimus gasped. "There it is!" He pointed to a bright object wrapped around the limb. It was a three-quarter necklace of dull silver, each end tipped with the head of a raven. Its cold blue glow was eerie and disturbing.

Gabriel swallowed, feeling only dread at the sight of it. He remembered the verse's description. *Forged . . . with malice and invention.* He didn't trust its merciless gleam. But he reminded himself that he only needed it to help his father, and cheered by this thought, he felt his courage restored. He turned to the owls; they regarded him with shrewd, inscrutable stares, flexing their daggerlike talons to remind him that this quest wasn't over yet.

Gabriel's knees began to shake. Without thinking, he clutched the staff more firmly, and to his surprise, the wood replied with a strong, reassuring warmth that spread from his fingers up the length of his arm.

The torc's effect on Septimus was different; his eyes took on a hungry, covetous stare. Its dark magic seemed to beckon to him. Eager to touch it, he clambered over the low wall that separated visitors from the owl habitat.

The reaction of the owls was swift. They clustered together on the tree limb, covering the necklace with their claws.

Septimus frowned. "Move over, big fellow!" he said harshly, batting an owl with one hand.

The owl's gaze settled on Septimus with cold scrutiny. Then it leaned down to him, as if to whisper tenderly.

"Ow!" cried Septimus, putting a hand to his ear. Blood dribbled between his fingers. "How *dare* you bite me?"

The owl shrugged; in a velvety-smooth voice it replied, "How dare *you* take what is not yours?"

"Not mine?" sputtered Septimus. "I happen to be a very close friend of Adam Finley's!"

"Then where is the staff?" the second owl said.

*So* that's *why the Romany Geese gave you the staff,* said Paladin excitedly.

Septimus appeared to realize this, too, for a shrewd smile appeared on his face. He turned to Gabriel.

"My good lad," he said. "Come join us! Don't be shy!"

Gabriel turned to the owls. "May I enter?" he said.

"Step forward, Son of Finley," replied the first owl.

"*You* are welcome," added the second, with a haughty glance at Septimus.

As Gabriel climbed over the wall, their scrutiny was so intense that he felt as if they were peering into his heart.

The third owl spoke: "Young fellow, we admired your father. It saddens us that he has been taken." The owl eyed Septimus doubtfully. "Finley was unusual among men— honest, forthright, and kind."

"And he knew a good riddle," added the second owl. "Do *you* know any riddles?"

"Lots," said Gabriel.

"Of course, we owls prefer *puns*," added the third owl. "Do you know what a pun is?"

"Sure," said Gabriel. "A joke that uses two meanings of a word."

"Proceed!" said the first.

All the owls leaned forward, eager to hear.

*Go ahead! Tell a pun!* said Paladin.

"Okay," said Gabriel. "Why is there always something to eat in the desert?"

"Why?" asked the first owl, followed by a chorus of other owls, all repeating "Why?" This tempted Gabriel to smile, since owls are known for saying *who*, not *why*.

"Because of the sandwiches there," said Gabriel.

"Sandwiches?"

"The *sand which* is there . . . ," he explained.

There was a silence. Then one owl coughed, followed by another, followed by a third. The entire chamber seemed overcome with coughing. Gabriel began to wonder if his pun had made the owls ill.

*No, that's owl laughter,* explained Paladin.

Indeed, the three owls perched before him were now doubled over, wheezing and coughing like old men. In the back of the room, little owls were bobbing up and down in hysterics; one owl completely lost his balance and swung upside down on his perch.

"Sandwiches?" Septimus muttered. "What's so funny about sandwiches?"

When the three owls had recovered, the oldest blinked approvingly at Gabriel.

"Very good, Son of Finley. The torc is yours."

In that instant, there was a loud *CRACK!*

The tree limb snapped exactly where the torc had been wrapped around it, and clattered to the ground. The owls took to the air in a disorganized flurry and settled onto more secure perches.

Septimus uttered a cry. "But where is—"

He didn't finish his sentence because a blindingly brilliant light enveloped the room—so cold, bracing, and unpleasant that the owls blinked, shielding themselves with their wings and uttering woeful hoots and moans. As Gabriel clamped a hand over his eyes, he felt a jolt from the staff, as if it had been struck by a charge of electricity.

Slowly, the light began to fade and Gabriel felt the staff become considerably heavier. He took his hand from his eyes and saw that the torc was now wrapped around the upper end of the staff; the eyes of its two raven heads still glowed white-hot, like iron fresh out of a forge. They quickly faded to dull metal, then, in mere seconds, became tarnished and barely distinguishable from the wood. Gabriel guessed the staff had a neutralizing effect on the torc, damping its extraordinary power.

Septimus uttered a disappointed sigh. "Such a shame."

"You have been warned of the torc's devilish power?" asked the second owl.

"Yes," said Gabriel. "But I don't quite understand why they go together—"

"Both staff and torc will assist you in finding your father," explained the third. "That is your next quest."

"But I thought the torc harms anyone who uses it," said Gabriel.

"Quite true, which is why Baldasarre set tasks that could be completed only by someone *brave in spirit* . . ."

"*Warm of heart,*" added the second owl.

"And *selfless, most of all,*" added the third. "Its black magic will do *you* the least harm; while in the hands of another, it will be disobedient and ruthless! Keep it upon the staff at all times!"

"I understand," said Gabriel.

"One more thing, young Finley," said the first owl. "Tell the ravens we owls are not as bloodthirsty as they believe. We take care of our kin, as others do. We hunt for a purpose, not for pleasure."

*What about the one that hunted me last night?* murmured Paladin.

Gabriel said, "Excuse me, but my amicus, Paladin, was almost eaten by a great horned owl just a few hours ago!"

"That is not so. We share the same enemies," said the third owl. "That owl was Caruso. He tried to help your friend by escorting him, but the young raven misunderstood his good intentions."

Paladin felt too indignant to contain himself. He jumped free of Gabriel.

"A likely story!" he snapped, his neck feathers rising in fury.

At once, the owls leaned forward, poised to attack, but the first owl turned his head completely around, addressing an owl in the very darkest part of the exhibit.

"Caruso? Please answer for yourself!"

A plump, scruffy horned owl hopped out of the shadows to face Paladin. The young raven immediately began bobbing and weaving, as if preparing for a fight.

"Grandson of Baldasarre! A chick off the old block!" quipped Caruso.

"You mean a *chip*," corrected Paladin.

"I was punning," the owl explained. "Young Finley's father once saved my life, so I was obliged to do a tit-for-tat, one-tern-deserves-another,  robin-the-rich-to-help-the-poor  sort of thing." Caruso paused to burp. "Young Paladin, do you remember the three valravens chasing you that night?"

"Yes," admitted Paladin.

"Well, I've never been fond of fast food, but they were three very happy meals!"

Several owls began coughing in amusement.

Paladin immediately forgot his anger. In gratitude, he extended one foot, dipping his head in a raven bow. "Thank you," he said.

"Don't mention it," whispered Caruso. "And I sincerely mean that! Don't want sparrows knowing that my hoot is worse than my bite, do I? If word gets out that I spared the life of a raven, I'll be the laughingstock of the flock."

"I promise," said the young raven.

All this time, Septimus had been rocking impatiently. He put a hand upon Gabriel's shoulder. "Come, lad," he said. "The zoo staffers will be making their rounds soon. We'd best be on our way."

"Thank you," said Gabriel to the owls.

"Son of Finley may always count on our aid!" they replied, and tipped their heads in unison.

# ❀ The Torc and the Staff ❀

A boy and a man, each with a raven on his shoulder, hurried along the zoo's paths. Eventually they came to one of the turnstile gates. After they passed through and found themselves on a tree-lined boulevard, Septimus turned to Gabriel, patting him on the back.

"You handled yourself brilliantly, lad. Now, let's have a look at this torc, eh?".

Before Gabriel could protest, the man snatched the staff and ripped the torc from it.

That very second, the torc began to glow unpleasantly— an eerie blue glow that made Septimus look craven and hungry.

"Septimus," Gabriel cried. "The owls warned me to keep—"

"Gasbags!" he interrupted. "Never heard such blather in all my years." He turned the necklace in his hand. It glowed stronger, brighter. His fingers tightened around it.

"Not just the owls," persisted Gabriel. "The geese also—"

"Geese are full of do's and don'ts. Pay them no mind!"

*He's not listening,* said Paladin to Gabriel. *I'll bet he's already under some kind of awful spell from that thing.*

Indeed, Gabriel wondered if he was hearing the torc itself talk, for the man's face was changing from one wretched expression to another, almost as if he were a puppet.

Gabriel tried to reason with him again. "Septimus, *please* listen! The verses warned that for every wish the torc grants, it takes something in return, something precious!"

*"Enough!"* roared Septimus in a high, unfamiliar voice.

In the same instant, the torc flashed, and Gabriel found himself on the ground, breathless, with a heavy pain in his chest.

Paladin nudged his cheek gently with his beak. *Are you all right, Gabriel?*

"Something hit me!" he gasped.

Septimus rubbed his eyes, as if coming out of a trance. "It wasn't me," he said indignantly. "All I did was wish that you would be quiet."

Crawfin alighted near Gabriel. "Remarkable," observed the bird. "It granted Septimus's wish!"

Gabriel scrambled to his feet. "Hey," he said. "Put it back on the staff before you make another—"

"I've got a better idea," interrupted Septimus. "You keep the staff, I'll keep the torc!" Throwing the staff into the thick underbrush, he slipped the torc around his neck, where it glowed blue against his skin.

"Wait!" cried Gabriel.

Septimus made a quick flourish with his hand and vanished. The white raven uttered a triumphant *caw!* and flew up over the treetops.

"Let's go after them!" said Paladin.

Gabriel jumped, but once they were in the sky, they saw no sign of the white raven. They had no idea whether he had gone home or had perhaps headed to the place called Aviopolis, or someplace else altogether. It seemed wiser to retrieve the staff from the bushes.

Gabriel pressed his way through sharp brambles, his hands pricked and bleeding, until he found the gnarled piece of wood.

Defeated and sad, Gabriel turned for home, wondering how he could have lost the torc so easily after solving so many riddles and risking so many dangers. It was a catastrophe.

*Will we ever see them again?* Paladin wondered.

Gabriel had no answer for his friend. The owls had told him that being brave, warm of heart, and selfless would protect him from the torc's black magic, but it hadn't helped him against Septimus. He felt so foolish for trusting him. Most of all, he was disappointed at being no closer to finding his father. It seemed that with every step forward, he slipped backward again.

Bleakly, Gabriel gazed up at the horizon where Crawfin

had disappeared. A breeze shook the nearby trees, and the whisper of leaves filled his ears. Were they mocking him or was it just a careless wind?

Gabriel tried to shake off the ache in his heart by picking up his stride. Paladin swayed on his shoulder but held on tight, sharing his despair.

# ❋ The Mausoleum ❋

It was still morning when the disheartened pair arrived home. Trudy had taken Pamela to school, so Aunt Jaz made breakfast for Gabriel while he told her the whole adventure. After describing how Septimus and Crawfin flew away with the torc, he rested his head in his hands in frustration.

"I failed, Aunt Jaz."

"Nonsense!" she said. "You and Paladin not only rescued Pamela, you found the druid stone, returned it to its owners, then got the staff *and* the torc."

"But we lost it."

"We still have the staff," Paladin reminded him.

"Yes," said Gabriel. "But the whole point was to help my father. I should never have believed Septimus."

"You had no choice," replied his aunt.

"I'll never make that mistake again."

"Gabriel!" his aunt replied with astonishment. "I hope that if you *ever* have to choose between trust and selfishness, you'll make the same mistake. We all get second chances. Septimus will be back. Mark my words."

Gabriel was unsure if Aunt Jaz knew something she wasn't telling him, or if she was just being hopeful.

Gabriel got to school in the middle of math class. Abby could tell that he had important news, but she had to wait until they could talk in a secluded corner of the library during study hall.

When he explained, she was most disappointed to have missed the adventure. "Oh, I wish you had let me come," she whispered. "Who knew owls love puns? I wonder if that goes for other birds. I bet woodpeckers prefer knock-knock jokes. Maybe larks like limericks and puffins prefer palindromes!"

"Yeah, Abby, but it's gone."

"Well, the owls said it was disobedient and ruthless. Maybe it will try to escape from Septimus and come back to you."

"One thing the owls said was really confusing," said Gabriel.

"What?"

"They said that they have the same enemy as us."

"Hmm. Valravens, maybe?" said Abby. "Or Corax. Oh! Remember when we saw him talking to your father in that weird postcard? He said, *'Your warm, sunlit world is my next domain, and I need the torc to rule it.'* The owls *must* have been talking about him."

"Scary," said Gabriel. "Corax has to be stopped, which

means we have to get my dad out of that prison in Aviopolis as soon as we can. . . ."

Abby's eyes shined when Gabriel said *we*.

"The question," Gabriel continued, "is how to get there?"

Rubbing her glasses furiously with the hem of her skirt, Abby gasped. "I've got it!" she said. "Ask the writing desk!"

On Saturday, with Trudy out shopping, Gabriel, Abby, and Pamela lured the writing desk into Pamela's bedroom with another jig. Pamela played three measures on her violin and the desk crept timidly up the staircase wearing a beret and a woolen vest. Immediately it jumped into a vigorous step dance. After the third slip jig, it collapsed in exhaustion and offered its keyhole without a fuss.

"How can I get to the place where my father is prisoner?" asked Gabriel.

Another postcard appeared in the middle compartment. On it was a photograph of a small marble building standing among gravestones.

"What's that?"

Abby's smile faded. "It looks like a mausoleum."

"What's a mausoleum?" asked Pamela.

"A monument with coffins of all the members of a family inside. Cemeteries have lots of them."

An awful thought struck Gabriel. "Is the desk telling us my father's dead?"

The three were silent. Gabriel sat down, staring grimly at the postcard.

After a moment, Pamela spoke. "No way. I don't believe it for a minute. That can't be what it means."

"Why not?"

Abby's eyes lit up. "Because you asked *how* to get to the place where he was being kept prisoner. That's an entirely different question."

"A mausoleum," said Gabriel, "that leads to Aviopolis?"

PART THREE

# ❀ Somes Grindle ❀

Gabriel Finley wasn't scared of him anymore, and this bothered Somes Grindle.

When he poked Gabriel from behind, Gabriel didn't tremble. When he asked for homework answers, Gabriel ignored him. Something had changed, something secret and important.

Somes felt envious of Gabriel these days and wished he knew Gabriel's secret because he wished for more courage himself. He was sick of being picked on by his father.

Mr. Grindle worked for the Quinn Bakery, whose motto was *Love in a Loaf*, with a picture of a big red heart on a loaf of bread. It was on the T-shirt he wore each night at the bakery. Somes didn't understand how his father could have a furious temper wearing such a motto. His father's best friend, Arturo, worked in the bakery with him; Arturo was as friendly and calm as anyone could be. *Love in a Loaf* made sense on Arturo's shirt.

Arturo once told Somes that his father was a much happier man when he was married, but that was a long time ago.

Somes couldn't remember his mother. She had married again and had little children of her own somewhere in Florida.

When Somes stepped out of school, he saw the bakery van and decided to take a long walk instead of going home.

He rambled south for ten blocks, then east along the freeway embankment, then up the ramp to the cemetery, his hideaway.

He studied the names on the tombstones along the empty paths and wondered about the people who had lived a hundred years ago. He liked the statues of angels, the monuments, and the mausoleums. They seemed such happy little places with their stained-glass windows and tidy interiors. One mausoleum had letters carved on the outside that read ELKIN, and inside were the names of a family: DAVID, JUDY, JANE, and JEFFREY. He imagined that if things got really bad, he could always hide out with the Elkins for company. He wasn't scared of tombs. He didn't believe in ghosts. When you live with someone who shouts and gets angry about nothing at all, a mausoleum seems the most peaceful place in the world.

By the time Somes arrived home that evening, he was tired and hungry. The house was dark and quiet. In the kitchen he saw a brown bag with the *Love in a Loaf* motto and started to open it.

"Where have you been?" His father was waiting in the darkness.

"Just walking," Somes replied.

"What about your homework?"

"I'll do it now. First I need something to eat."

"Get cracking," said his father. "If you wanted to eat, you should have come home in time for dinner."

Somes looked at him—there was stubble on his cheeks and a sneer on his face.

"Dad, I'm starving," he said.

His father raised his voice. "You should have come home on time!"

Somes looked at the bag again. That motto—*Love in a Loaf*—made him feel indignant. The man worked in a bakery; he brought bread home every day—the warmest, most delicious loaves. It seemed cruel not to let him eat.

In the next moment Somes did something he had never done before.

He grabbed the bag and ran out of the house. He heard his father shout behind him, but he kept running. Clutching the loaf against his chest, he ran until all he could hear was his heart beating, his breath whistling high and shrill. At the cemetery fence, he threw the bread over and clambered after it, then sprinted straight to the mausoleum marked ELKIN. When he had closed the door behind him, he sat on the marble floor, ripped off hunks of bread, and gobbled them down.

It must have been around midnight when Somes woke up. A great scarlet moon hung in the sky; he was peering through the red stained glass of the mausoleum door. He had been woken by a conversation.

"Is it safe to talk?" said a raspy voice.

"Of course it's safe. The only humans here are dead humans!" replied another.

"We must be on the lookout for Septimus Geiger, the sparrows say, for he has the torc!" said a stern voice.

"If any of you see him, pluck out his eyes."

"If you can't pluck out his eyes, bite off his fingers."

"Yes, but if he has the torc," replied the stern one, "he could cast any of us into oblivion."

A sharp voice interrupted: "Corax will reward any one of us that captures the necklace!"

Somes scrambled up and pressed his forehead to the glass, trying to make out who was talking, but there wasn't a person to be seen. All he could see was a tree with a group of tattered black birds perched on one bare branch.

"One thing is clear—when Corax claims the torc, he'll rise from Aviopolis to rule the skies."

"Yes," sighed another. "It won't be long now."

The birds flew off and the conversation stopped.

*Birds talking?* Somes wondered. *I must be dreaming.*

He turned the handle of the door, which made a rough, grating noise. It was colder outside, and his teeth began to chatter.

With the full moon shining above, he noticed three mausoleums standing in a dignified row—each had two pillars in front and bronze gates. The family names were carved into the marble. WHEELER, THORPE, and FINLEY.

*Finley?* Somes wondered if Gabriel's family owned the mausoleum. He approached it and noticed something peculiar: a procession of ravens had been engraved beneath the Finley name.

Somes peered through the circular hole in the bronze mausoleum gate: the little building was empty. There were no names on the walls, no signs of anyone buried there. Where there should have been a floor, there was a set of steps that descended into darkness.

## ❊ The Disobedient Torc ❊

Gabriel kept the staff in a corner of his bedroom. It looked like any broom handle—a very old, weathered, and slightly warped one. Sometimes he would wrap his hand around it, just to remind himself that his last adventure hadn't been a dream. If he kept his grip firm for a minute or two, a wonderfully reassuring warmth would emanate from the wood, and his doubts would disappear. This was how he managed to get through the next few weeks as he planned what to do. He had asked Aunt Jaz about mausoleums, but she told him that most were the size of a small room and led nowhere.

Winter swept very suddenly over the city; puddles began to freeze and there was a harsh bite to the air. Gabriel noticed flocks of birds heading south for warmer weather; in spite of this, some chattering little birds lingered at the windows of the Finley house.

*Eavesdroppers,* explained Paladin.

*What are you talking about?* asked Gabriel.

*Those birds have been told to spy on you,* explained the young raven. *I listen to their silly conversations all day long. Most of the time, they're trading gossip about where the best birdseed spots are, but once in a while, they mention you.*

*Me?*

*Yes, they call you "Son of Finley," like the owls. "Where is Son of Finley?" "What is Son of Finley doing?"* mimicked Paladin. *Somebody important must want to know.*

This explained why Gabriel saw finches and robins on his classroom windowsill. There were spies everywhere.

*Watch what you say,* Paladin warned him.

In the second week of December, an early snow blanketed the city, transforming it into a softer, whiter, quieter version of itself.

Aunt Jaz sent Gabriel out to shovel the sidewalk; the boy brought his raven with him. He had taken only three steps before he stopped and stared at the elegant perfection of the snowfall. It was the kind of world a demented pastry chef might have created: dollops of snow on every car, every lamppost, gate, staircase, chimney, and rooftop—as pretty as a dessert.

The little birds appeared to have been driven away by the storm. With the daily clamor of sparrows, starlings, swallows, and robins gone, there was just silence. A beautiful silence. Paladin shivered on Gabriel's shoulder, astonished by the sight of his first snowfall.

*How wondrous,* he said.

*Yes,* agreed Gabriel.

Ravens are playful birds; they enjoy snow exactly as

children do. Gabriel took Paladin to Prospect Park. They wandered past the hill where most children were sledding and found a clear slope hidden in the woods. Gabriel set Paladin on a plastic sledding saucer and encouraged him to go for a ride. The raven went careering down the hill, bobbing his head excitedly.

*Again!* cried the bird when Gabriel found him toppled in a drift.

They took a bigger slope and rode together, Paladin nestled in Gabriel's lap, crashing past bushes and rolling in the deep drift at the bottom.

After one of these tumbles, Gabriel lay in the snow, blinking up at the stark gray sky, when he noticed an awful sight: a man with a tormented face, streaked with filth, staggered toward him.

"Help me! For heaven's sake, help me!" the man moaned.

Gabriel recognized the voice, but not the blistered, bloody face or the terrified eyes. His snow-white hair was scorched to the scalp, his elegant tweed coat ripped, muddy, and threadbare.

"Septimus?"

"Yes, lad, so it is," sobbed the man. "Or the little that's left of him!"

Paladin landed on Gabriel's shoulder. "Where's Crawfin?"

Septimus sobbed. "My oldest friend, my dearest friend, poor Crawfin. Gone forever, and it's all the fault of that cursed necklace!"

"Because of the torc? Why? What happened?" asked Gabriel.

Uttering a groan, the man wrung his hands. "The torc! That awful torc! It all began when Crawfin and I decided to celebrate our good fortune at the finest restaurant in town."

"*Your* good fortune?" Paladin snapped. "You mean, after you stole the torc from Gabriel!"

The exhausted man winced. "I wanted the best! Steamed lobster, caviar, shrimp cocktail, and champagne. Didn't have to ask, I just wished and everything was brought to me. Dishes I had only dreamed of. Waiters attended to my every whim!"

A smile appeared on the man's face, but then the horror reappeared. "The food wouldn't stop. I told them I was finished, but waiters brought more until plates were stacked on top of each other! Then the chef came running from the kitchen, offering pastries, truffles, mousse! No sooner did I finish one thing than he pressed something new to my lips. The look on his face, scared, miserable, *spellbound*, as if doing it all against his will!"

Septimus paused to scratch feverishly at his neck before continuing.

"I staggered into the street with Crawfin on my shoulder, but it didn't stop."

"What didn't stop?" asked Gabriel.

"People offering me things."

"What kinds of things?"

"Whatever they possessed!" Septimus cried. "An old man offered me his hat, a woman offered me the little dog she held in her arms, a mother offered me her children! Imagine! Her *children*! And it wasn't as if she wanted to give them to me—she was *compelled*."

"Why didn't you wish it to stop?"

"I did, but the torc ignored *that* wish." Septimus raised his hand to his collar. "Instead, it began to grow hot around my neck."

"Hot like a sunny day?" said Paladin.

"No—hot like a poker. I tried to remove it, but it was stuck to my skin, burning me like a branding iron!"

"So what did you do?"

"I passed a men's clothing shop and carelessly wished I could replace my shabby coat. At once, the pain stopped, and I thought, *Aha! It just wants me to wish again. How simple!* I went in and the shopkeeper was happy to help me, although . . . he also had that strange expression."

"Spellbound?" said Paladin.

"Yes." Septimus nodded. "I chose a handsome new tweed coat. The shopkeeper told me I could have it for free. But while measuring the sleeves, he saw they were too long. 'I'll have the tailor fix them,' he said. Then I heard him on the phone ordering the tailor back to work—the man was at home with a sick child—but the shopkeeper screamed. He, too, was *compelled*!

"I decided to stop wishing. I left the shop. Outside, I tried to pull the torc off again, but it . . . vanished. When I felt for it with my hand, I realized it had burrowed *under* my skin, like a giant splinter."

"Under your skin?"

"I told Crawfin it had disappeared. He accused me of hiding it. I showed him my neck, but he didn't believe me. He said I had betrayed him."

Gabriel remembered a line of the verse about the necklace: *I'll trade the good that lies in you for something vastly worse.*

"My best friend attacked me!" sputtered Septimus. "Snapped at me, tore at my clothes to find the torc while I was shouting that I'd never do such a thing. He told me I was a villain and a thief!"

Septimus's rugged face turned pale.

"So I wished him gone for good." Raising a trembling hand to his mouth, he whispered, "Right before me, my dear old friend, my constant companion, my amicus, *burst* into flames. Poor Crawfin. Making the most piteous and wretched sounds. I tried to stop the wish. I wished him back, but it was too late." Big tears rolling down his cheeks, Septimus drew a filthy gray handkerchief from his ripped coat pocket and dabbed at his face.

"My old friend," he blubbered. "Lost because of a foolish wish. And you know, it's impossible not to wish in your head. One can't help wishing."

A dark shadow crossed his face. "Then the valravens came. Those deadly, cursed birds. Although they serve the master of Aviopolis, I thought I had the power to send them away. . . ." He pointed to his charred neck with puzzlement.

"But they ignored my command. Or perhaps the torc ignored my wish." Here, Septimus looked at Gabriel with a shudder. "They began asking me their riddles. If you don't answer a valraven's riddle, it will go for your eyes, and when you are blind, your flesh!"

Septimus described how the birds flocked around him asking riddles he couldn't answer, and how he ran to escape them, climbing beneath cars, crouching under trash cans, fighting off their attacks with bloody hands. He stared up at the gray sky. "Thank heavens for the snow; it scared them off. I never cared for snow before, but now I appreciate it for bringing you, my boy. Your father, Adam Finley, knows everything about the torc. Only he can help me. I can't go back to him without the staff and the torc."

Septimus held out his hand.

"Give the staff to me."

"Sorry, Septimus," said Gabriel, shaking his head. "I can't."

"Of course you can!" the ravaged scarecrow pleaded. "I helped you find it in the first place. Where would you be without me?"

"If you'd listened to me, this would never have happened," Gabriel reminded him.

As Gabriel trudged up the slope, the man followed, scratching at the dark scar around his neck and taunting him. "Only I know where your father is! Aviopolis. A cavernous

city of birds far under this earth. There's a maze of passage-
ways to get there. I know the way!" He grabbed Gabriel
roughly. "Give me the staff!"

Gabriel shook his head.

"Then I'll *wish* for it!"

Septimus raised his head and mumbled his wish. Suddenly, a blue glow appeared under the scorched flesh of his
neck.

"Oh, no," murmured Gabriel.

Paladin uttered a cry as something flew across the
clearing.

A large pole hurtled toward Septimus. Its blunt end struck
him hard in the chest. Septimus quickly realized it wasn't the
ash wood staff. Then a nearby thicket began to sway and
snap as one by one, branches broke off and whizzed toward
him. Dodging each missile, Septimus could see that the torc
had granted his wish in its own mischievous way. With sticks
flying toward him from every direction, he gave up and cow-
ered in one spot as he was buried in a pile of kindling.

Then, as abruptly as it had started, the blue glow vanished from his neck and the forest became silent. Septimus
clambered out of the pile and implored Gabriel, "Don't you
see? You must actually *give* it to me."

When Gabriel refused, the man bared his teeth and
seized him by his shirt collar.

"Give it to me or I'll wish *you* gone for good, like Crawfin!"

"Septimus, this isn't you, it's the torc!" cried Gabriel.

"Give me the staff!" screamed the man, his fingers tightening around the boy's neck.

Gabriel struggled to pry off Septimus's grip, but he couldn't breathe; he was going to faint.

*Jump!* cried Paladin.

Releasing his hands, Gabriel spread his arms like wings.

In the next instant, Septimus found himself choking nothing but thin air. He looked up and recognized Paladin circling overhead.

"Please help me! I—I—I didn't mean to hurt you," he stammered. "If you change your mind, tell the sparrows, and they'll tell me!" With that, Septimus scratched his neck furiously, turned, and staggered into the woods.

# ❈ Farsighted ❈

"**Y**ou did the right thing," Paladin told Gabriel as he walked home.

"Did I?" said Gabriel, rubbing his throat. "Shouldn't I help my father any way I can?"

Paladin reminded Gabriel that the staff was too important to give to a man who never kept any of his promises.

Abby was shoveling her sidewalk when Gabriel came by. When he asked her advice, she agreed with Paladin. "You can't trust him," she said, "but there is a way that you could help your father *and* Septimus."

"How's that?"

"Go to this mausoleum the desk showed us and have Septimus lead you down to Aviopolis," said Abby.

"Yes, but where is the mausoleum?"

The one person who could have told them was having a hard week.

"Somes," Ms. Cumacho snapped, "will you please focus!"

She had been very impatient with him because he wouldn't concentrate on his work. When everybody was supposed to be reading, he stared out the window.

He lowered his face to his textbook so that his eyes were just a few inches from the page. *Focus.* He was trying, but it was so hard.

That was when a lightbulb went off in Abby's head. After school that afternoon, she and Gabriel stopped Somes as he came down the steps.

"Somes, can I ask you a question?" said Abby. "Have you ever had your eyes checked?"

"My eyes?" he replied. "Why?"

"Well, you do this thing that I used to do before I got glasses."

Abby demonstrated by holding a book just inches from her eyes.

"So?"

"Maybe that's why reading is so hard. You should see an eye doctor."

"I can't." Somes couldn't imagine his father being willing to take him.

"Well, guess what? My mother's an eye doctor. I could ask her to look at you right now."

He regarded her skeptically. "Why would she do that for me?"

Abby talked Somes into walking with them to her mother's office, six blocks away. Ms. Chastain was a small woman who wore glasses herself. Gabriel noticed that she had Abby's inquisitive stare. She dabbed drops in Somes's eyes and told him to sit with Abby and Gabriel in the waiting room. Later, she gave him an eye test and made adjustments on a machine in front of his face.

"Your near vision is very poor, Somes," she said. "I'm going to give you a prescription for reading glasses. You must wear them whenever you read."

"I hate reading," he replied.

"I understand, because it's all blurry." She smiled. "It's about to get much easier." She wrote a prescription and sent the three kids to an eyeglass shop around the corner.

Somes halted at the door. "I can't pay for glasses."

Abby explained that her mother had arranged payment. "All you have to do is pick them out. It's a breeze."

A few days later, when the glasses were ready, Abby and Gabriel went back to the shop with Somes. He examined one of his schoolbooks. Words that had been fuzzy and difficult to read were now sharp and clear. "Wow," he murmured. He gave Abby a cautious glance. "Thank you."

Abby smiled. "You're welcome, Somes."

Then he looked at Gabriel. "Did you know that there's a mausoleum in the graveyard with your name on it? It has ravens all along the top. There are stairs leading down somewhere."

"Ravens? Stairs leading down?" Gabriel turned to Abby, wide-eyed. "I bet it's the entrance to Aviopolis! The first time I met Septimus he told me it was 'miles right beneath us!'"

"It makes perfect sense!" agreed Abby. "Somes? Will you show us?"

Hurrying through the windswept cemetery, the three friends were barely able to contain their excitement. When they found the mausoleum, they approached slowly, quietly, the way you might approach a cliff edge.

Somes tried to turn the bronze gate's handle, but it was either very rusty or locked. He couldn't open it, so he pointed through the gate at a staircase that descended into darkness.

"It looks like it goes on forever," said Abby.

"Let me get this straight," said Somes. "You think a guy is keeping your dad down there?"

"Well, he's sort of a half-raven, half-human guy called Corax," replied Gabriel.

"Corax," repeated Somes. He told them about the conversation he had overheard in the cemetery.

"Probably valravens," Gabriel said.

Somes looked at him doubtfully. "C'mon. Birds that talk like people?"

"You'd be surprised," said Abby. "Valravens serve Corax. They're flesh eaters. You're very lucky they didn't attack you."

"That's crazy."

"I know it's hard to believe, but it's true," said Abby.

Although he was full of astonishment as Abby explained the Finley family's history and Gabriel's unusual friendship with Paladin, what most impressed Somes was something else. "Your dad must be pretty cool for you to go to all this trouble," he said. "Do you really think you can rescue him?"

"Well," said Gabriel, "I have to try."

Staring down the darkening steps, Somes nervously asked, "Hey . . . Do you think . . . Can I come with you guys?"

"Sure, but it's dangerous," Gabriel warned him. "We don't know what's down there."

Somes looked at Abby. She had a small, excited smile.

"Count me in," he said.

# ❖ Where Is Septimus? ❖

Pamela guessed that Gabriel had a plan, because he ate Trudy's latest soup without comment. Trudy assured them it was a minestrone, but there were objects bobbing in the mixture that resembled shoelaces and rubber bands, and the smell was like moldy boots left in an attic.

Even Trudy noticed Gabriel's hearty appetite. "*Somebody* seems to have changed his mind about my cooking!" she remarked.

"What? Oh, right," said Gabriel.

Pamela followed Gabriel outside after dinner. He stood alone in the backyard, holding the staff.

"Where's Paladin?" she asked.

"Oh, I asked him to take a message to Septimus by way of the sparrows," he explained.

"I see," she replied enviously. Recently, she'd attempted to befriend the writing desk by trying to talk to it in her head. It did not reply.

"Hey, guess what? I found out how to get to Aviopolis." Gabriel told Pamela all about the mausoleum and the staircase he hoped would lead him to the bird city. "So we're planning to rescue my—"

"I'm coming," interrupted Pamela.

He nodded. "I figured you'd want to, but listen—it could be dangerous."

"What could be dangerous?" asked a voice.

Trudy was standing in the doorway. "Pamela? Where are you going with *him*? Tell me right now!"

Gabriel noticed that Aunt Jaz lingered behind Trudy, listening.

"Mother, I'm going to Aviopolis."

"*Where?*" asked Trudy.

"It's nowhere, seriously," said Gabriel.

"I doubt that," snapped Trudy. "And you, young lady, are not going out all night like last time, worrying me to death. Now, where is this place?"

To Gabriel's horror, Pamela repeated everything he had just told her.

"It's . . . it's an amazing city full of birds," she said. "It's miles beneath the earth, and very hard to get to. We think you enter through the cemetery and walk down a deep staircase!"

Trudy's reaction was a surprise, however. Her anger melted and she gave her daughter a small, indulgent smile. "Oh, I see," she said. "Sometimes I forget that you're still a child with an imagination. Look at the time. You still have practicing to do, dear!"

"Yes, Mother." Pamela shot Gabriel a sly glance, then followed Trudy back inside.

Aunt Jaz, however, didn't look as amused. "Gabriel," she said, "if you were any other boy, I would tell you to forget about this. Stay at home, enjoy your childhood." Then her voice softened. "But you are like no other boy. To talk to ravens, fly with them, and unlock the secret of a necklace that has been a mystery for a thousand years—well, I don't quite know what to say, except that you are your father's son, and if anyone can help him, it is you. But please be very careful."

Gabriel promised her that he would.

Once Aunt Jaz had walked back inside, Paladin arrived, breathless and agitated.

"Bad news," he said. "Nobody's seen Septimus in a week. The valravens may have gotten him."

Gabriel and Paladin flew to Septimus's rooftop terrace apartment. What they found was a shock. Every window had been shattered; the french doors swung carelessly in the breeze; plush armchairs had been pecked to pieces, their stuffing spilled across the floor. Many of the valuable pots and vases Crawfin and Septimus had gathered (or stolen) from all over the world had been picked up and dropped on the hearth to reveal their contents. The grand fireplace that once crackled with a blazing fire was now a dark hole.

A tatty-looking raven with a jagged beak and a blistered, featherless neck looked up when Gabriel and Paladin entered.

"Answer me this! Whenever I introduce myself, people turn and walk away. What is my name?"

"Hmm," said Paladin. "Is it *Goodbye?*"

"Well done, Paladin," whispered Gabriel.

The valraven, however, was furious that the young raven had solved the riddle so quickly. It flew at them, sharp talons extended, but Gabriel removed his coat and used it to bat the valraven away. It hurtled across the room, toward the enormous mantel, and dropped into a large stone urn perched on top.

Gabriel immediately clamped a lid on the urn. The bird squawked and struggled inside.

From the other room, a second valraven appeared. "No necklace here," it muttered, then noticed Gabriel and Paladin. Raising its wings threateningly, it said, "Where is Septimus Geiger?"

"I was looking for him myself," Gabriel replied.

"Looking?" The valraven smiled viciously. "You'll have no need of your eyes when I'm finished."

It fluttered across the room and perched in the ashes of the fireplace, searching for its companion. "Grinderbeak? Where are you?"

At that moment, the urn began rocking violently above him.

"Grinderbeak! Show yourself!" snapped the valraven.

The urn tottered, then tipped off the mantel and shattered upon the valraven below, silencing them both.

Gabriel surveyed the pillaged room. "Now, where could Septimus be?"

"Do we really need him?" asked Paladin. "The mausoleum leads down to Aviopolis, I'm sure of it."

"Yes, Paladin, but we have to find my dad in a maze of passages, and Septimus knows exactly where he is."

Suddenly, a voice came from behind them.

"What gets wet when it dries?"

Gabriel turned with Paladin, but they couldn't see who had spoken.

"What gets wet when it dries?" repeated the voice.

"Wet when it dries? Doesn't make sense. How can something get—" began Gabriel.

"A towel!" replied Paladin with a laugh.

A chuckle of raven laughter came from the old globe in the center of the room. A crack appeared in the lower hemisphere, right between Paraguay and Argentina, and the scruffy raven from Mr. Pleshette's shop flew out.

"Hobblewing!" cried Paladin.

"Greetings, old friends!" said Hobblewing. "Look, I've learned to fly!"

"Excellent," said Paladin. "Say, have you seen Septimus anywhere?"

"Why, of course," said the bird. "I'm his lookout." He

raised his head and uttered three sharp throks in the direction of the fireplace.

Cinders began to fall from the chimney into the grate. Suddenly, two boots dropped down, followed by trousers and a long coat. A figure as gray as ash dusted himself off to reveal snow-white hair and a weatherbeaten face.

"Young Finley?" He sniffed. "I didn't expect a visit from you."

"Septimus," said Gabriel, "my friends and I think we found an entrance to Aviopolis in a graveyard."

The man looked disappointed that his secret had been discovered. "*You* found it? I had forgotten how inquisitive children can be."

"Yeah," continued Gabriel, realizing his advantage. "So if you help me find my father—"

"*Help you?*" Septimus said bitterly. "Go find him yourself."

As Gabriel wondered how to get him on board, he noticed the ugly scar around his neck.

"Septimus," he replied, "I'm sure my father would help you remove the torc if you showed me the way there."

Suddenly, Septimus's face turned eerily blue. "Remove it?" he snapped in an unnaturally shrill voice. "*Never!*"

Surprised that these words sprang from his mouth, Septimus winced and corrected himself in a desperate whisper. "No, no, it's all for the good. Must get rid of it, quickly, quickly!"

## ❖ The Journey Begins ❖

**S**eptimus wanted to set out for Aviopolis as soon as possible. This pleased Gabriel, so they agreed to meet the next evening at the cemetery.

Gabriel and Paladin flew home discussing the plan.

*Are you sure we can trust him?*

*Not really,* replied Gabriel. *There's no way I'll let him have the staff.*

In the morning, Gabriel explained the plan to Pamela; on the walk to school, he told Abigail; and he slipped a note to Somes during math.

At dinner, Gabriel and Pamela ate great helpings of Trudy's eggplant ragout, a purple and black broth that smelled like skunk cabbage, knowing they would need plenty of energy for the evening's adventure.

Gabriel stepped out of the house first, with Paladin on his shoulder and staff in hand. Pamela appeared a moment later, holding her violin case.

"Do you really want to bring something that valuable?" said Gabriel.

"Mother thinks I'm practicing," Pamela explained. "Besides, if it works on writing desks, it might work on other things."

Gabriel nodded. "I never would have thought of that."

Abby raced across the street wearing rubber boots (one yellow, one purple), four cardigans, and a heavily stocked backpack slung over her shoulder.

"Where's Somes?" she asked.

"Meeting us at the cemetery," Gabriel explained.

They set off along wet Brooklyn streets, past dark storefronts, dimly lit restaurants, and bright bodegas with neon lights glowing in the gathering fog, toward the cemetery that rose on a hill overlooking New York Bay. Aside from the mournful echo of a ship's horn, the city was quiet. Gabriel imagined most people were nestled warmly in their armchairs or curled up in bed, unconcerned about a world far beneath the earth ruled by a villainous half man, half raven.

He was excited at the prospect of rescuing his father, but terribly anxious, too. If they got lost, who would know where to find them? Who would look so far under the ground, or even imagine a city populated by birds, dominated by the Lord of Air and Darkness?

The moon was just a fuzzy smear behind the clouds as they entered the cemetery gate. After searching, they found the Finley mausoleum and waited for Somes. The wind began to blow unkindly, chilling their ears and biting at their cheeks. When a security guard drove by, flashing his searchlight, the children scattered to keep out of sight.

\* \* \*

As Somes prepared to leave the house, Mr. Grindle arrived with a pizza box. He squinted at the boy's glasses. "Where'd you get those?"

"A nice lady gave them to me," Somes replied, adjusting them. "She checked my eyes and said I needed them for reading."

"A nice lady, huh?" His father sniffed. "Well, glasses can't make a dumb kid smart."

Somes frowned. "I can see better. I can read better."

Unimpressed, his father put down the pizza box. "Sit. I brought dinner."

Somes hesitated. He was very hungry, but he had to go.

"Are you late for a train?" snapped Mr. Grindle. "Sit."

His stomach was growling, so Somes took a seat. He wolfed down a slice and was halfway through a second when his father spoke.

"Now," said Mr. Grindle. "Suppose you tell me where you were going?"

"Cemetery," said Somes.

"Cemetery? Why?"

Somes shrugged. "It's safe there."

Suddenly, Mr. Grindle's hand flew out and slapped Somes on the cheek, sending his glasses flying across the floor. Somes picked them up tenderly. "You almost broke them!" he cried.

"I told you, glasses can't make a dumb kid smart."

"I'm not dumb," Somes replied, putting the glasses on.

His father raised his arm to slap him again; but this time, Somes was ready. He raised his hand, catching his father's wrist, and he twisted it. The man let out a cry and fell off his seat.

"I'm not dumb!" Somes said angrily.

With a fresh slice of warm pizza cradled in his hand, Somes ran out of the house—and he didn't stop running until his father's shouts had faded in the soft rumble of evening traffic.

When Somes arrived at the cemetery, a low-hanging mist encircled the gravestones. He listened for voices, but all sounds were muffled here. He wondered if the dead kept things nice and quiet. Had his friends forgotten about him? Even though he had eaten, Somes felt a lonely ache in his chest. He tossed away the last crust of pizza and leaned against the Finley mausoleum.

Moments later, Gabriel arrived with Paladin on his shoulder, Abby and Pamela by his side. He saw Somes, then noticed three dark birds alight above him on the roof of the mausoleum.

"Somes! Step over here, carefully," said Gabriel.

Paladin addressed the birds. "Tie me up and I'll walk all day. Loosen me and I'll sit still. What am I?"

The birds didn't answer.

"I am a pair of sneakers!" said Paladin. When the birds didn't laugh, he nodded at Gabriel. *Definitely valravens.*

The ghouls stared from Paladin to Gabriel, pining for a time when they had their own human companions. This feeling passed quickly. Their eyes burned a sicklier yellow and their bitterness reappeared.

"Son of Finley!" said the first valraven. "The Lord of Air and Darkness wants the torc."

"I don't have it," replied Gabriel.

"Deliver it—or die!" added the second.

Gabriel felt a sudden tremor come from the staff in his hand. The ancient wood grew warm; its heat jumped to his fingertips and traveled up his arm into his shoulders. Quivering, the staff began to turn, its tip pointing at the birds.

Out came a loud *pop!*

The first valraven disappeared, leaving only a cloud of black feathers fluttering down.

"Cool," said Gabriel, staring at the staff. "This is what the Romany Geese said it would do." He turned the staff toward the remaining phantoms.

*Pop! Pop!* Two more clouds of feathers.

"How does it do that?" Somes looked at Gabriel with amazement.

"I have no idea," said Gabriel.

"Look out!" exclaimed Paladin.

There was a cry from the mist. A man in a long coat came

running, waving his arms wildly. Two valravens pursued him, their yellow eyes piercing the fog.

"Septimus!" said Pamela.

Gabriel raised the staff and pointed it at one of the valravens. There was another abrupt *pop!* and the valraven vanished, leaving a few bones and feathers scattered on the ground. Gabriel pointed the staff at the next valraven and it disappeared just as swiftly.

"Ha ha! You wretches! That'll teach you!" Septimus shook his fist triumphantly. Facing Gabriel, his gaze turned cunning. "Well done, lad. Now, let's have a look at that marvelous thing, eh?"

Gabriel pulled the staff to his chest. "I don't think so."

"Dear boy . . ." Septimus's expression shifted quickly to disappointment. "You still don't trust me?"

"I trusted you *once*," Gabriel reminded him.

The man's shoulders dropped; he searched the group for a sympathetic face, but there wasn't one.

Meanwhile, Somes had also been admiring the staff. "Can I hold it, Gabriel?" he asked.

"Sorry, Somes," said Gabriel. "But I think I'd better keep it for now."

The big boy frowned, embarrassed to be treated just like Septimus in front of the others. Septimus noticed this immediately and offered his hand.

"We haven't met. I'm Septimus Geiger."

Somes shook his hand and gave his name. Septimus smiled, filing away the information. Suddenly, his hand was grabbed by Abby and given a vigorous shake.

"We haven't met either," she said. "I'm Abby Chastain. I know all about you! And you've already met Pamela."

At the mention of Pamela, Septimus's smile faded. "Charmed," he muttered.

"So," said Abby, turning to the mausoleum. "How do we get in?"

The gate was made of tarnished bronze. The circular hole in the very center was the right size for a raven. It was wrought in braided metal, with two raven heads meeting at the bottom, just like the torc. Paladin perched upon it and looked to see if there was a lock on the inside but didn't find anything. They all took turns trying to turn the handle, but it wouldn't budge.

"Why put a gate here that doesn't open?" Gabriel wondered.

"It's clearly not an entrance for humans," said Septimus.

"How did you get through when you escaped?" asked Abby.

"I merged with Crawfin and entered through the hole. Valravens can come and go—that's what it's for. If you look carefully at the gate, there are symbols." He pointed to a symbol of a tower. "Here, you see the citadel of Aviopolis."

"What's a citadel?" asked Pamela.

"An inescapable fortress," said Septimus. "It was there that Adam Finley and I were imprisoned by Corax."

Abby looked at Septimus. "If it's *inescapable*, how did you escape?"

Septimus rubbed his hands nervously. "It's complicated."

"Even better. Try me," persisted Abby.

Septimus frowned. "Well, I made a pledge."

"What kind of pledge?"

The man sighed. "A pledge that I would find the torc . . . and bring it to Corax."

"What?" cried Gabriel with disgust. "*That* was your pledge? To help him? How could you do that, Septimus?" Disheartened, the boy shook his head. "You called yourself a friend of my father's."

Septimus squirmed. "Look, no matter what I *said*, all along my plan was to rescue my good friend Adam Finley! Cross my heart!"

"Except that when you had the torc, you didn't rescue him," charged Gabriel. "You went to the finest restaurant in town, remember?"

"You can't imagine its awful power!" said Septimus, clawing at the torc that festered under his skin. "Surely one can make mistakes and be forgiven?" He gazed imploringly at the children, but they turned back to the gate.

"If it doesn't have a keyhole, there must be a trick to it," said Abby.

All this time, Somes had been staring at the gate handle. "There are words," he said, adjusting his glasses to look closer.

"Here!" Abby removed a flashlight from her backpack, focusing the beam to reveal four lines etched in the metal:

*All who wish to enter here*
*Must first a binding oath declare.*
*To Corax swear thy loyalty,*
*Then watch the gate swing wide for thee.*

"*Swear thy loyalty?* I'm not going to do that," said Gabriel.

"There's no other way in, dear boy!" sputtered Septimus. He dropped his voice to a whisper. "Look, you don't have to mean it. If you just say it, the gate will probably open."

"Yes, but a *binding oath* means a promise," said Abby.

"I can't believe the fuss you're making," said Septimus. "Why, I've made promises my whole life that I didn't—"

"We know that," interrupted Gabriel.

"Look at it this way," the man replied. "Sticks and stones may break my bones, but words can never hurt me. Here, I'll go first."

Winking at the children, Septimus grabbed the handle and spoke into the hole. "I, Septimus Geiger, traveler and seeker of fine curiosities, hereby pledge loyalty to Corax, Lord of Air and Darkness!"

Those last words echoed unnaturally, as if his pledge

extended far beyond the door, down into the depths of Aviopolis.

Moments later, a sound came back, deep and ominous like a thunderclap, the handle turned, and the gate slowly creaked open.

Septimus laughed, and with a jolly grin, stepped inside.

The gate immediately began closing. Just in time, Somes grabbed a stone and wedged it into the opening. "Gabriel," he whispered, "use the staff!"

Gabriel jammed the staff into the gap and pried the gate open a bit more. The staff quivered violently and he felt its familiar warmth spread into his fingers and arms. It appeared to be fighting the very magic that commanded the gate.

"Everybody in!" said Gabriel, and the children hurried into the little building. Then Gabriel drew out the staff and the gate slammed shut with a bang, pulverizing the stone into dust.

Ahead lay a staircase that wound down in a seemingly endless spiral. The right side had no railing, just darkness. The children took their first steps clinging to a stone wall on the left side while trying to imagine, deep below, a city of birds—a city called Aviopolis.

# ❋ Somes and Septimus ❋

The little group walked together for a while, but everyone had a different pace, and they gradually separated into two clusters. Abby produced two flashlights from her backpack. Septimus and Somes led with one light; Abby followed with Gabriel, Paladin, and Pamela.

Somes brooded as he walked with Septimus. He wished Gabriel trusted him, but he felt like the odd man out—last to know about ravens, riddles, and Gabriel's extraordinary power. The man next to him smelled of ashes and mice and kept rubbing the unpleasant scar around his neck. Why was he stuck with this loser?

Septimus was silent for an entirely different reason. A voice had started talking to him in his head.

*Ah, my old friend,* it said. *You've come back when I thought you had forgotten all about me.*

*Crawfin? Is that you?* replied Septimus doubtfully. A throbbing pain in his head seemed to accompany each word.

*No, it is your Lord and Master—Corax!*

The man's face collapsed into horror. *My Lord, of course. Greetings!*

*Don't you remember your promise to me?* "Set me free," *you begged.* "Get me out of that cell and I'll bring back the necklace."

The voice was mocking and abrasive—like a bone grinding into broken glass.

*How is it that I can hear you in my head?* wondered Septimus. *I thought I could only talk to my amicus this way.*

*Oh, Septimus, my foolish friend. He who pledges loyalty to Corax opens the gate of his own soul. Did you not realize?*

*Yes, but—*

*In return for your pledge, I may speak to you whenever I wish*, said Corax. *I can see inside your thoughts. All your forgotten promises. All your tricks. All your lies. For example, I know now that you never intended to help me. You're a selfish man, Septimus. And you must pay for it.*

Septimus raised his hands to his head, horrified at what might happen next.

*Please, don't hurt me!* he begged, for the pain was getting worse.

*Redeem yourself by serving me. You have the torc but not the staff. I want them both.*

*The boy never lets go of the staff*, Septimus replied. *I've tried, believe me!*

*There is another boy, a stronger boy. Use him to get it. Whatever happens, the staff must not reach Adam Finley. If it does, my valravens will hunt you down and take your eyes first!*

Septimus uttered a small whimper, then put his hands up to his eyes. Somes looked at him warily. Sensing the boy's scrutiny, Septimus attempted a jolly smile.

"Your company is a pleasure, dear boy," said Septimus. "You and I, sadly, are in the same rut. No one trusts us."

"Why do you say that?" said Somes.

"I saw you being humiliated," Septimus replied.

"Humiliated?"

Septimus nodded. "Gabriel wouldn't lend you his staff, would he? You know why? Because it makes him feel important. Better than the rest of us. It's a bad sign when a fellow thinks himself superior to his friends. A very bad sign."

"I don't care." Somes shrugged. "He can have it."

"But is it *right*?" murmured Septimus.

"I told you," muttered Somes. "I don't care."

"Perhaps, but after you did him such a great favor?"

"What are you talking about?"

"Why, you helped everybody get through the gate," said Septimus. "How enterprising! How skillful! You're a lad of great potential; it's a shame, that's all."

"What's a shame?"

"Not to be trusted by anyone. But never fear. *I'll* stand by you, my good lad. You have a friend in me." Septimus gave him a chummy pat on the back. "That's a promise!"

# ❋ Musical Light ❋

The travelers had been walking for an hour when their flash-lights dimmed, then fell completely dark. Fearful of taking a wrong step into the abyss off the right side of the staircase, they came to a halt.

Septimus uttered an exasperated sigh. "Well, it seemed a good idea to come this way," he said to Gabriel. "Still, I see no choice now but to give up and turn back."

"What are you talking about?" said Gabriel. "No way!"

"Right, no way!" agreed Abby, Pamela, and Somes.

Outnumbered, Septimus winced uncomfortably. "Well, the last thing I would say is 'give up'!"

"You just did," said Pamela.

"And I doubt it's the last thing you're ever going to say," added Abby.

Septimus blew his nose. "Nonsense! I never . . . It was more of a philosophical position."

*He doesn't make any sense at all!* Paladin remarked to Gabriel.

"Let's have a snack and think what to do," said Abby. Dipping into her backpack, she passed around pieces of her sister Viv's taffy. Even in the damp darkness, the salty candy raised their spirits.

"Somes?" Abby whispered.

"Yes?"

"It was incredibly clever of you to think of keeping the gate open with a rock."

"Oh. Thanks."

"It was genius," added Gabriel.

"Great, Somes," Pamela chimed in.

Septimus sniffed. "Not that I'm asking for praise, but if I hadn't opened the gate by pledging to Corax, none of you would be here."

"Thank you, Septimus," the children replied with considerably less enthusiasm.

"Oh, please. It was nothing!" Septimus said with a little laugh.

*If it was nothing, why did he mention it?* Paladin remarked to Gabriel.

"Does anyone else hear that?" said Abby.

There was a noise in the air shaft beside the staircase— the very distinct sound of wings fluttering. It came and went, as though something (or many things) were flying past in the darkness.

"Birds," said Pamela.

"Yes," said Septimus. "This staircase is a passageway between the world above and the city of Aviopolis. Only birds live here now."

"Who lived here before?" asked Pamela.

"An army of dwarfs, imprisoned for trying to overthrow their king."

"I remember this story," said Gabriel. "It was in Baldasarre's parchment. The dwarfs were jailed in dungeons underground. They made the silver necklace as a gift to the king so he'd release them."

"Precisely," said Septimus. "They were brilliant silversmiths, and dwarf silver was highly prized. But the king didn't trust the gift."

"Why not?" said Abigail.

"His raven, Muninn, thought it was a trick," Septimus explained. "They were banished underground for years. When the king went down to free them, he found the most marvelous city and the dwarfs long gone."

"Why did they go?" asked Pamela.

"Isn't it obvious? An underground palace without sky or sun is still a prison," said Abby. "They probably dug their way to freedom."

"Nevertheless, it's one of the wonders of the subterranean world," said Septimus. "A shame we won't see it."

"We're going to see it," Abby replied.

"Yes," said Gabriel. "We're definitely going."

Septimus uttered a sigh. Then there was another fluttering sound nearby.

"More birds? How do they know where they are going?" wondered Gabriel.

"Who cares?" muttered Septimus. "We risk our peril walking in the dark for miles before we reach the bottom. This is hopeless. Now, let's turn around. Who agrees with me? Somes?"

Then another bird flew by; as it chirped, Gabriel noticed a faint flash of light on the wall. "Did anyone see that?"

"I saw nothing," replied Septimus. "As I was saying—"

"Wait, it was a flash!" interrupted Pamela.

Several more flashes lit up the walls as birds flew past them, down the shaft—flashes so faint that they would never have been seen in the glare of their flashlights.

"What's doing that?" Abby wondered.

"Something in the air?" suggested Somes. "Like the birds' chirps are making light!"

"It must be the high notes, because our voices have no effect," said Pamela.

Paladin uttered a high chirp. The wall flashed faintly.

"Hardly enough light to see a staircase," complained Septimus.

"I have an idea," Pamela said, unlocking her violin case.

She played a high note on the violin and a strong orange light lit up the walls.

"Do it again!" said Gabriel.

Pamela played another long note, then a trill. This time,

several colors shimmered across the staircase. Now the children could see the thousands of steps heading down below, and many birds of all shapes and sizes flying up and down the shaft.

"Way to go, Pamela!" said Abby.

"Marvelous," muttered Septimus bitterly.

As Pamela played a scale on the violin, a quivering series of colors danced upon the staircase wall, and the children walked on.

"Be careful you don't fall and break your neck, dear!" said Septimus.

"Marching bands walk and play at the same time," Abby reminded him.

"I was never fond of marching music," he replied.

Ignoring Septimus, they continued forward. Pamela played as Gabriel steadied her with one hand, holding the staff and violin case in the other.

Presently, the music was drowned out by an unearthly shriek that turned the walls a deep blood-red. A bird with glowing yellow eyes spiraled down the shaft and swooped, claws extended, toward the violin.

"Pamela, look out!" warned Abby.

The music stopped suddenly and all was dark. There were sounds of a struggle.

"Help!" Pamela cried.

"Where are you?" answered Gabriel, for he had lost his grip on her.

"It's got my violin!"

Gabriel fumbled for his staff, dropping the violin case, which clattered down the staircase. He pointed the staff above him.

There was a sudden *pop!* and then a faint smell of rot.

"Pamela?" called Gabriel.

"Pamela!" said Abby. "Where are you?"

"Here!" replied a very anxious and weak voice.

Gabriel fell to his knees and felt along the side of the steps that edged the abyss. He found her fingertips gripping the very edge. Pamela was gasping as she held on.

"Give me your other hand!" he cried.

"I can't. I'm still holding the bow!"

Gabriel reached down and tightened his grip around her forearm. Slowly, he hoisted her up. "There," he said. "We've got you!"

Trembling, Pamela rested on the steps. Then she came to an alarming realization. "I've lost my violin. . . ."

"No worries!" announced Paladin, alighting on Gabriel's shoulder, the neck of the violin in his talons. "Now we'd better get going. More valravens are sure to be on their way."

As Pamela started playing, light returned to the staircase, and the others smiled, relieved to be able to see each other again.

"That was brilliant, Paladin!" cheered Abby.

Septimus uttered an exasperated sigh. "While you congratulate yourselves," he snapped, "some of us wish to carry on!"

He placed his hand on Somes's shoulder.

"Come, dear boy. Nobody appreciates us."

# ❊ The Gatekeeper ❊

After several minutes of walking, the pain throbbing in Septimus's head intensified.

*Well, Septimus?* said Corax. *Can this boy Somes be relied upon?*

*I believe he and I have much in common,* Septimus replied.

*Good. Then I have no need for either of the girls.*

*Surely you're not asking me to—*

*Oh, you cowardly fool, you're no more capable of killing anyone than you are of keeping your promises. Since our little group is so fond of riddles, my gatekeeper shall complete that task. Listen carefully to my directions. . . .*

It was a surprise to everybody when Septimus pointed out a doorway that was barely noticeable in the wall of the staircase.

"As I recall, we must make a turn here," he told the children.

"But you said we had to walk all the way to the bottom," said Gabriel. "I remember."

"Did I? I don't believe so." Septimus laughed, but his smile wilted under Abby's intense scrutiny. "What is it, young lady?"

"You change your mind faster than a chameleon changes its colors."

Septimus attempted another laugh. "Look, it doesn't matter what I said before. You asked me to help you find the way. This is it!"

"Is your nose getting longer?" Abby replied.

Septimus directed them through the doorway with one of his graceful gestures.

They entered a long hall of stone. Several torches flickered, casting little pools of light along the floor. On the walls were carvings of human armies in battle against great flocks of black birds with glowing eyes. The faces of the soldiers and birds were fearsome and sharply drawn.

"I have a bad feeling about this," said Pamela, putting her violin away. "What about you, Somes?"

Somes shrugged toward Gabriel. "He's the leader."

"I can assure everyone that this is the correct path," Septimus said.

*What's wrong, Gabriel?* Paladin asked, sensing Gabriel's doubts.

*I'm not sure,* Gabriel replied. *But back on the staircase, I had a hunch that my father went that way, too. I felt something close and familiar about it.* He looked around doubtfully. *Not here. He never came this way. I'm positive.*

Paladin gripped Gabriel's shoulder. *I have an idea. I'll continue down the staircase and see where it leads.*

Gabriel stroked Paladin for a moment. *Thank you.*

*We're going to find your father, Gabriel. Don't worry.*

*You'll look out for valravens, right?* Gabriel said.

*Of course,* Paladin replied. *I've dealt with eagles, I can manage any old valraven.*

As the raven left Gabriel's shoulder and disappeared into the darkness, Septimus shook his head. "On his way back home, eh? Scared, I suppose."

"No more scared than you," said Gabriel. "Now let's go."

The hall zigzagged a few times. At every corner, the children expected to arrive somewhere, but each turn revealed another long corridor.

Eventually, however, they found a large room paved with flagstones. There was an arched doorway with a portcullis—a heavy gate that could be raised and lowered with a chain. A bird could easily slip through the gate, but it would be impossible for a person.

Guarding the portcullis was a very large valraven. It sat upon an iron perch, its eyes glowing at the group with faint amusement. The curve of its beak was impudent and harsh, and it spoke through a clog of saliva that dribbled from the corners of its mouth.

"None may enter Aviopolis, domain of the Lord of Air and Darkness," said the valraven, "until they answer a riddle!"

Abby's face lit up. "Cool!"

Somes turned to her with disbelief. "A riddle?" he groaned. "Are you serious?"

"Answer or perish," the valraven said.

Septimus gave Somes another jovial squeeze on the shoulder. "I know how you feel, lad. It doesn't seem fair, does it?" He pitched a glance at Abby and Gabriel. "Especially when *some people* have an unfair advantage."

Septimus approached the valraven. "Look here . . ." He paused, shot the others a fake smile, then resumed in an urgent whisper. "I happen to be as *loyal* to his Lordship as you. So, between you and me, surely you could grant a favor."

"Certainly. You may go first, Septimus Geiger!"

This wasn't what Septimus had in mind at all. He rubbed his scorched neck, then proceeded to scratch all over his scalp in a fit of anxiety.

The valraven spoke the first riddle in a dry, unamused tone:

> *"I travel to earth with the greatest of ease,*
> *Borne on the breath of a northerly breeze.*
> *Shapes have I many, words I speak none;*
> *Quickly I die in the bright warming sun."*

As Septimus muttered the riddle to himself, Gabriel tried to solve it. *I travel to earth with the greatest of ease . . . on a northerly breeze. It must be something that falls through the sky—either rain or snow,* he thought. *Quickly I die in the bright warming sun. Definitely snowflakes.*

Hoping the answer would just spring into his mouth, Septimus offered a string of answers. "Airplanes? Acorns?

Clouds? Raisins? Popcorn? Soot! Screwdrivers? Bottle caps!" he cried frantically.

The valraven shook his head.

Gabriel thought it was odd that the ghoul permitted Septimus so many wrong guesses.

"Weeds? Berries? Buttons? Umbrellas? Tea leaves? . . . Snow!" cried the man, finally.

"Correct," snapped the valraven. Raising one claw, he pulled a chain hanging beside the perch and the portcullis rose, letting Septimus pass. At once, the portcullis dropped, striking the stone floor with a deafening crash.

"Next!"

From the other side of the portcullis, Septimus gave Somes an enthusiastic nod. "Never fear, lad!"

Trembling from his knees to his fingertips, Somes looked at the others' concerned faces and felt terribly alone. They couldn't possibly understand how difficult this was for him.

"You can do it, Somes!" said Abby.

Her smile surprised him. Then Gabriel stepped forward and held the staff out.

"Take it," he whispered. "It'll stop you from being scared. Just let your mind play with the riddle. It's only a game!"

Astonished, Somes took the staff in his hand. The valraven narrowed his eyes, then recited:

*"I'm a gift to you the day you're born.*
*I'll last you till you're dead.*

*But rarely will you use me—*
*Many others will instead.*
*What am I?"*

Somes immediately became aware of a comforting
warmth in the staff. It tingled his fingertips, then worked its
warmth along his arm and up into his shoulders. A soothing
feeling he remembered from drinking hot chocolate, or eating toast with cinnamon and sugar. He felt better than he'd
ever felt before.

Relaxing, Somes let his mind wander. What gifts had he
received from his father? He couldn't think of very many.
Then the answer came to him—so simple, so obvious, almost
ridiculously obvious:

"It's my name."

The bird hissed and reached for the chain. The portcullis
rose and Somes joined Septimus on the other side.

"Well done," Septimus whispered. "You showed them all.
They probably didn't think you could do it. Now it's going
to get interesting!" Septimus's eyes strayed down to the staff,
but Somes clutched it tightly.

Abby stepped forward to face the valraven.

*"I've four legs and a sturdy back,*
*Yet eat no food or drink,*
*But serve my lord and lady,*
*Without the brains to think.*

*The mighty lion runs from me*
*When my legs rise up in fury,*
*Yet quietly I serve beneath*
*A judge and all his jury."*

Pamela turned to Gabriel, worried. "Why is Abby's question so *hard*? Septimus had such an easy one, and so did Somes."

Abby rubbed her spectacles, quivering with the excitement of a racehorse ready to burst from the starting gate.

"Okay," she said. "You say it has four legs and a sturdy back and the lion runs from it? Hmm. I don't think it's an animal. What else has four legs? A table? But a table has no back!"

A drip of saliva stretched from the valraven's beak all the way to the ground. His meal stood before him, fussing with her eyeglasses.

Abby's brain, however, was whizzing along. "So," she said. "What lies beneath a judge and jury? A floor? No. Must be something else. A chair! And a circus performer uses a chair to tame a lion! That's it! My answer is a *chair*!"

The vexed bird hissed with dismay and tugged the chain to the portcullis. As the gate rose, Abby sailed past it, sticking out her tongue. She uttered a contented sigh as she joined Septimus and Somes. "Well, that was a juicy riddle! I wish I got two!"

"Two?" repeated Septimus, dubiously.

Somes gave Abby an admiring glance.

Now it was Gabriel's turn.

*"He who grandfathered you*
*Was father to me.*
*He who gave thee life*
*Was brother to me.*
*You, me, and he,*
*Each one a raven's amicus.*
*Who am I?"*

This was hardly a riddle, thought Gabriel. *My grandfather is this mystery person's father. My father is the mystery person's brother. Each of us is a raven's amicus.* The answer was very obvious. *Why have I been given such an easy question when Abby's was so hard?* he wondered.

"Corax," he answered.

The valraven didn't seem surprised. He pulled the chain raising the portcullis, and Gabriel looked back at Pamela. She was shaking like a leaf.

"Do what Somes did," he said to her. "Let your mind play with the riddle."

"Somes had the staff," she reminded him, her lower lip trembling.

The portcullis slammed shut behind Gabriel. Pamela

stepped up toward the valraven, who beckoned with a voracious leer.

*"I may sit on a scale,*
*But I cannot be weighed.*
*One step down I am flat.*
*One step up I go . . . fa!"*

"Fa?" repeated Pamela, her voice faint.

Gabriel's heart sank. This was the most difficult riddle he had ever heard. He looked at Abby. She shook her head. "*Fa?* What does that even mean?" she said.

"I may sit on a scale, but I cannot be weighed?" repeated Pamela, bewildered.

The valraven shifted on his perch, running his black tongue hungrily along the edge of his beak, certain that at least one of the girls Corax wanted eliminated would be gone.

Gabriel pressed his head against the portcullis.

Pamela's eyes searched the chamber, as if the carvings on the walls might offer an answer. Her fingers were shaking so much that the violin case began to slide from her grasp.

Gaping with triumph, the valraven dribbled a streak of saliva down his breast. "No answer?"

"I—I—I . . ."

The bird raised his wings, preparing to strike.

The violin case struck the floor. As Pamela steadied it, a thought crossed her mind.

"*Wait!*" She shook her head. "Wait. It's . . . it's a *musical* riddle."

"Time's up!" snapped the valraven.

"Notes can't be weighed," Pamela reasoned. "But they sit on a musical scale. *One step down I am flat, one step up I go fa.* Well, a *flat* musical note is a lower note, and if *fa* is the next note on the scale, do, re, mi, fa . . ." She smiled. "The note is *mi!*"

"Correct, but too late!" cried the ghoul.

Pamela shook her head. "It's not too late! Septimus took forever. He gave you a zillion answers before he got the right one."

"*Too late!*"

The bird hovered above his perch, then lunged.

Suddenly, there was a *pop!* and a big shower of black feathers floated down to the flagstone floor.

Pamela found herself standing alone.

"What happened?" said Abby.

They turned and saw that Somes had pointed the staff through the portcullis and destroyed the raven. Nobody looked more astonished than Gabriel.

"Why didn't I think of that in the first place?" he muttered to Abby.

Abby shrugged. "I liked answering mine."

"Pull the chain!" shouted Somes.

Pamela grabbed her violin case, pulled the chain, and slipped under the rising portcullis. She immediately threw her arms around Somes and gave him a tight hug.

"That was awesome!" she cried.

Somes blinked and hugged her back.

Septimus glared at him. "What possessed you to do that?"

"It was the right thing to do," Somes replied.

# ❋ Paladin's Pursuer ❋

Let us go back a few minutes earlier, to when Paladin parted from Gabriel.

The raven flew down through the center of the staircase. It was frightening, because he didn't know where the bottom was. Eagles, hawks, and falcons fly straight down to catch their prey, but ravens rarely do. Paladin began to worry. An increasing smell of rotting meat intensified his panic.

Then he became aware of wings beating the air just above him.

Perhaps you've had that eerie feeling when you walk at night, the sense that someone is matching your footsteps, step for step. Paladin was sure he was not alone. Then he remembered something Twit, the gossiping finch, had told him about Corax:

"He's the size of a man—no, *twice* the size! With black wings as big as sails! He soars in complete silence, plucking smaller birds from the air with the appetite of a devil."

This memory had Paladin trembling. Even though he knew Twit had been exaggerating, he could think of nothing but a monstrous creature bearing down from above, swallowing him in midair without so much as a burp. Gasping, Paladin decided to catch his breath on the staircase. Perhaps if he could just listen, his worries would evaporate. So he tilted his wings to land, bumped clumsily against the wall, dragged his talons to break his momentum, and somersaulted down three steps. It was a very painful, embarrassing touchdown.

*Whoosh!* Something flew past. It was impossible to see, and almost as impossible to hear, but the rush of air assured Paladin it was enormous. Just a few feet away, he heard the rasping sound of talons scraping on stone and guessed that the bird had landed.

For a chilling moment both predator and prey stood silent in the darkness.

Paladin's fear quickly became a stouthearted kind of courage. *If I were that big, I would eat my victim immediately,* he told himself. *It's not fair to let a bird worry himself to death. How dare he be so silent!* Paladin felt so indignant that he cried out, "You there!"

"Greetings," came a deep and gravelly reply.

"I have a riddle for you," said Paladin, determined to find out what kind of a bird he was dealing with.

"Proceed," said the stranger.

"How stupid is a sparrow?"

"I cannot answer that," replied the voice in the darkness.

"Why not?"

"No owl cares to be insulted," came the reply. "Or did you think I was a peanut?"

"A peanut?" said Paladin. "What do you mean?"

"Peanuts can be salted or insulted." The owl burst into a vigorous coughing fit.

"Oh, that's a terrible pun!" complained Paladin.

"Speaking of terrible, I just saw you land on those steps. Best imitation of a bowling ball I've ever seen!"

"I'm still learning," Paladin replied indignantly. "You sound just like Caruso, the owl who saved me once before."

"'Tis I, nose, and throat," quipped the owl as he fluttered up to join Paladin.

"What are you doing down here?"

"I've come to help you on your mission. I heard about it from the sparrows. Remember, ravens and owls have the same enemies."

"Oh, Caruso," cried Paladin with relief. "I'm lost, hopelessly lost!"

"'Tis better to be loved and lost than never to have loved at all," replied the owl, giggling.

Paladin offered a polite chuckle, then proceeded to explain about Septimus and the torc, and Gabriel's plan to rescue his father. When he finished, the owl told him that he had traveled too far.

"How do you know?"

"We owls see better in darkness. You missed an entrance to Aviopolis a short way back. Follow me!" said Caruso.

# ❧ The Bridge to the Citadel❧

"**Y**ou guys were great," Gabriel told Abby and Pamela. "Those were really hard riddles."

"Yes, they were," admitted Abby. "Septimus, on the other hand—"

"I can assure you," interrupted Septimus, "mine was exceptionally difficult."

Nobody replied, not even Somes, who had guessed the answer before Septimus did.

"I promise you," Septimus continued, "I didn't choose to come here!"

"But you did," replied Gabriel. "You need my father to help you."

"Let's not dwell in the past, my good lad. The point is, we got by that awful creature!"

The group had arrived at a ledge. Before them lay a grand and terrifyingly deep underground cavern, its walls dotted with small chambers. This, at last, was the city of Aviopolis. The bottom of the cavern (if there was a bottom) was too far to see. In its center stood an immense tower of stone with thousands of candlelit windows that flickered in the darkness.

"Look at all those windows! They're so pretty," said Pamela.

"Each is a cell," said Septimus. "The citadel is a prison for all who refuse to serve Corax. Many are ravens, hanging in cages, forgotten and doomed."

In spite of this grim description, Gabriel felt a glimmer of hope. He sensed his father's presence again. Perhaps, in one of those windows, Mr. Finley was looking out right now. It wouldn't be long, Gabriel told himself, before they might be together for the first time in three years.

Getting to the tower was a problem. Gabriel saw no way to reach it across the dark abyss. Septimus, however, led them to a point in the cavern rim where a stone bridge became visible. It was ancient, with great cracked steps of rock leading upward to a narrow span that arched high over the abyss, then descended to the citadel.

The closer they came to the bridge, the more anxious everybody felt, for the stone railings had broken away, leaving only a jagged path that narrowed to the width of a cafeteria tray in some places. With nothing to grasp, it would be like walking a balance beam; and to make matters worse, small chunks of the bridge seemed to be dropping from the edges every few moments.

"I wouldn't like to walk across *that* thing," said Pamela.

"Me neither," said Abby. "So, where *do* we cross, Septimus?"

"I'm afraid this is the only way," said Septimus.

"Unless you have wings," added Somes, who pointed out something the others hadn't seen: far below their ledge, hundreds of birds were circling the citadel, riding on the air currents in a counterclockwise direction like schools of fish swimming.

It took a few moments for their eyes to take in the scene. They saw linnets, herons, storks, albatross, and many birds they had never seen before. The birds were singing, a sound that might have been beautiful in a valley at dusk, but in this echoing chasm was a nightmarish mix of squawk and gabble.

Now that it was obvious that the bridge was nothing more than a crumbling ruin with a perilous path, Gabriel raised his hand. "Anybody afraid of heights?"

Abby, Pamela, and Somes raised their hands.

"Great," said Gabriel. "Septimus, how about you?"

Septimus's face had turned green. In fact, he couldn't even look at the bridge—a brief glance had caused his cheeks to swell.

"Haven't you crossed before?" asked Gabriel.

Septimus took a deep, shuddering breath, and stammered, "N-n-never took the bridge. Terrible fear of big open spaces. Nausea. Vertigo. Awful."

"How did you cross the chasm the first time?" wondered Gabriel.

"I paravolated with Crawfin."

Pamela regarded him doubtfully. "If you flew, why weren't you scared? It's still a big, open space."

"As I've told Gabriel, when you and your amicus merge, your similarities are enhanced and your differences erased," Septimus explained. "Crawfin had no fear of wide-open spaces, so his confidence erased my fear. On the other hand, his greed for the torc was multiplied by my own—which is why we fought."

At that moment he was interrupted by the echo of a rock tumbling from the bridge; it struck a larger boulder, which triggered bigger pieces to fall. A small rockslide rumbled into the darkness as the children watched with bleak faces. It appeared that even if they got across, there was only a slim chance the bridge would be there for the return journey.

"Well, I'll give it a try," said Pamela. "It's the only way to get to Gabriel's father."

Somes gave a thumbs-up. "I'm in," he said.

"Me too," said Abby, impressed by the others. She gave Gabriel's hand a squeeze.

Gabriel smiled warmly at his friends. He silently wished he could complete the journey alone with Paladin. Where *was* Paladin? It seemed his amicus had been gone for hours.

An odd figure greeted them at the entrance to the bridge—a squat-looking bird, like a very large turkey with a long neck and a bulbous beak. It had a clipboard under one wing, and waved its free wing enthusiastically. "Greetings, visitors! Humans! What a pleasant surprise," she said in a bubbling voice.

"Oh," whispered Abby with astonishment. "It's a dodo!"

"Aren't they extinct?" said Pamela.

"I thought so," said Abby. "I remember reading that sailors killed the last ones for food, hundreds of years ago."

"Then why would it be glad to see people?" murmured Somes.

"Maybe they're just stupidly friendly," suggested Abby.

"*Dodo*, what a perfect name," said Somes.

The dodo stepped forward. "Welcome, oh welcome indeed, to the Chasm of Doubt. Crossing it is the only way to enter the citadel of Aviopolis!"

"Chasm of Doubt? Why is it called that?" asked Gabriel.

The dodo blinked. "I'm not sure."

She balanced on one muscular foot, withdrew the clipboard from her wing with the other, and pulled a pencil free from the clip with her beak. "So, what are your names?"

"I'm Gabriel. This is Abby, Pamela, and Somes."

"And Septimus Geiger, at your service, ma'am," said Septimus in a sickly voice.

As the dodo took down their names, Gabriel stared at her. She wrote with a pencil in her beak as easily as anyone writes by hand, her eyes blinking pleasantly at the children like a kind elderly grandmother's. Her beak was the most extraordinary thing—much too big for her face, sculpted with absurd curves. Her wings were dark brown, with fluffy gray tips; her feet were yellow and very thick and muscular, with talons that must have been good for crushing clams and other mollusks. Gabriel noticed a lot of razor-clam shells spread about the entrance. He guessed that the dodo snacked on them when she had nothing else to do.

"Pardon me," asked Abby. "Why do you need our names?"

"Oh, I don't know," laughed the dodo, patting herself on the chest. "If I didn't take your names, I doubt I would need to be standing here!"

Gabriel noticed that there were no other names on the dodo's list.

"Are we your first visitors?"

The dodo looked puzzled. "I doubt it."

"Well—how long have you been here?" asked Pamela.

The dodo blinked. "I'm not sure if I know."

"You don't know?" repeated Pamela. "Or you don't know if you know?"

"I'm doubtful," admitted the dodo. She gave them another daffy smile.

"Can we go ahead, then?" asked Gabriel.

"Of course," said the dodo. "I doubt that the bridge is very strong, so you should cross one at a time. It's a long walk and we don't want accidents, do we? Now, who will go first?"

The children regarded the bridge with fresh concern.

Septimus, who was nearest to the bridge, dusted off his hands. "Well, my lad, I have brought you as far as I can. It's time for me to go back."

"What?" Gabriel replied. "Septimus, what's the sense of our crossing if you go back? The citadel has thousands of rooms. How will I find my dad? And what about the torc? Don't you want to get rid of it?"

"Oh, I'll figure it out. Best of luck. Cheers to all!" With that, the man nodded to the children and weaved his way down the path that had brought them there.

"Why is he leaving us?" whispered Pamela.

"Because he's scared." Abby spoke loudly enough for Septimus to hear. "It was his raven who had all the courage."

At this remark, Septimus winced and wheeled around. "*Scared?* How dare you, you obnoxious little imp!" he shouted. "Who do you think you are, with your ridiculous hair, mismatched clothes, and absurd shoes? You have no right to call Septimus Geiger *scared*. Loudmouthed little freak!"

Abby blanched. With every word from Septimus's mouth, she seemed to shrink.

"Abby, don't listen to him!" said Gabriel.

But Abby had stepped away from the group, her face buried in her hands.

"What's happening to us?" Pamela said, her face stricken with worry. "It's that chasm. It really is a chasm of doubt!"

Gabriel turned to everyone. "Listen, you guys, we just need to get across the bridge and we'll be fine."

"I can't and I won't!" replied Septimus.

Desperate, Gabriel approached him. "Whose side are you on?" he cried. "My father's? Or do you want Corax to win?"

"Neither," Septimus replied. "I'm on the side of Septimus Geiger."

"What about good winning over evil?" said Gabriel.

"Right! Don't you care about that?" Pamela agreed.

Septimus shook his head and shuffled a little farther down the narrow trail.

"What are we going to do?" fretted Pamela, looking to Somes.

Somes gently nudged Gabriel. "Wait, he's wearing the torc, isn't he? Why can't he just *wish* himself across the bridge?"

"He's afraid to wish anything," Gabriel replied. "Each wish has a price. He might get across but have an awful surprise at the other end."

Somes thought for another moment. "I have one other idea." He held out the staff to Gabriel. "First, thanks for lending me this."

Gabriel shrugged. "It's really okay, Somes."

Somes glanced back at Septimus. "What if," he began, "what if Septimus took the staff across the bridge. *Confidence.* That's all he needs."

"Give Septimus the staff?" said Pamela doubtfully. "That's the worst idea I've ever heard."

Gabriel considered the narrow stone bridge and the seemingly bottomless chasm beneath it. It seemed a good idea, except for one thing: Somes had spent a lot of time in Septimus's company during this journey. What if this was just a way to get the staff into Septimus's hands? What if Septimus slipped away, as he had before? The more Gabriel thought about it, the more impossible it was to make a decision, and this reminded him of Pamela's remark. *It really is a chasm of doubt!*

But his friends' expectant stares urged Gabriel to make a decision.

"Wait here a moment," he said, and he hurried down the path to catch up with Septimus.

"Septimus!" he cried. "Stop! You're going to cross the bridge."

"But I . . . ," began Septimus.

Gabriel held the staff toward him. "C'mon. Take this."

Septimus peered into Gabriel's eyes. "I'm at the mercy of Corax," he said bitterly. "Why would you trust me with the staff?"

"You said you'd guide me to the citadel," Gabriel reminded him. "Maybe, if you keep one *good* promise, it will free you from him. It's worth a try, isn't it?"

The man's forehead wrinkled, but he seemed touched by Gabriel's optimism. A small amount of trust can sometimes change a soul who is starved of such things. Nervously, Septimus placed his hand upon the staff and gently closed his fingers around it. A delicious tingle of warmth grew in his fingertips. Septimus flinched. He ran his hand along the staff's worn surface and a glow appeared in his sallow cheeks.

His eyes, which had been bloodshot and scared, gained back their prideful resolve.

Septimus surveyed the group, then took a few steps toward Abby.

"My dear," he said. "Please forgive my unkind words. I beg your pardon."

Abby looked up with surprise. "Pardon?"

Septimus planted his foot upon the first step of the bridge and tapped it with the staff. "I'm honored by your trust," he said. "I'll see you all on the other side!" He paused. "That's a promise!"

The moment he uttered the word *promise* the children shared a worried glance.

With his coat billowing behind him, Septimus started across the bridge with broad steps. He never broke his stride or looked back. Soon he was just a speck on the distant mid-point of the bridge. He waved, his snow-white hair bobbing briefly. Then he continued on the downhill part of the span toward the citadel. In a short while they heard him whistle— the signal that the next person should cross.

# ❀ The Crossing ❀

*Steady now,* Somes said to himself. *Just watch your step.*

He felt a sharp, cold breeze from below as he made his way, but he dared not look down. Why was the wind so cold? Wasn't the earth hot in the center? Perhaps it was just fear that ran a chill down his spine. He kept his footsteps steady, pressing forward in short strides along the slender pathway.

*Keep your balance. Concentrate on getting there,* he told himself. *Don't look down.*

Birds were venturing closer. He could hear their cries, but he was still afraid to look at them. They emitted trills of notes that sent flashes of yellow and orange light erupting against the chasm walls.

*Something in the air makes the light do that,* Somes reminded himself. *Keep going. Don't look down.*

A larger bird swooped by, uttering a harsh, sneering squawk. This time, the chasm wall turned vermilion. Somes followed the bird with his eyes, afraid it was a valraven. The bird swiftly disappeared into the darkness. He felt a twist in his stomach, and his knees began to shake. He tried to steady himself.

*I shouldn't have looked down,* he thought.

His knees always shook when his father shouted. *Glasses can't make a dumb kid smart.* Was it true? Was he just a dumb kid? Now his knees were bobbing like pistons. *Stop. Please.* Somes tried to think of something happy, but his mind settled on that bag of peaches and the night Mr. Grindle gave him the black eye. *Don't talk back to me! Idiot!* Then there was the time he fell while running. *Why did you fall down, dummy?* Somes remembered lying on the wet pavement, his nose bleeding, with the boots of his father inches away from his face. His father didn't even help him up; he just called Somes a dummy.

The path was jagged and narrow now; he was in the middle, and each end seemed an eternity away. Somes felt his knees jerking up and down like dribbled basketballs.

*If you just put one foot out,* he told himself, *you can take the next one. Just one step!*

He slid his left foot six inches. *Okay.* He slid the right foot six inches. *Great!*

*I'm not a dummy. I figured out how to get the mausoleum gate open,* he reminded himself.

Left foot. Right foot. *Careful.* Left. Right.

*I'm not stupid. I guessed that the staff would destroy the valraven at the portcullis!*

He began taking longer steps. The bridge path was heading downhill.

*I saved Pamela. And it was my idea to lend Septimus the staff, and guess what? It worked!*

Somes was striding fast now, keeping his eyes on the stone blocks ahead, counting the cracks.

*I solved my own riddle and guessed a few others. Nobody has the right to call me a dummy. Nobody!*

Finally, he looked up. The grand citadel with its thousands of glittering windows towered directly above.

He had arrived.

# ❀ Abby's Turn ❀

Abby set off quickly, thinking that if she could get to the halfway point fast enough, the downhill part would be easy. She had buttoned her four sweaters and pressed her glasses against her face, and she marched at a confident clip.

Moaning and wailing, a breeze from the Chasm of Doubt wrapped her in its taunting, scornful embrace. Abby slowed down and peered from her yellow boot to her purple one.

*I suppose I am kind of a freak,* she thought. *Septimus was right. Sometimes I talk before thinking, and people get upset. I probably shouldn't have solved Mr. Pleshette's crossword puzzle.*

The harsh wind sang again. Abby raised a hand to her many pigtails.

*My hair is ridiculous. Why did I walk out of my house looking like a crazy pincushion?*

A mocking roar rose from the chasm. Abby rubbed her glasses.

*How can anybody stand to be around me? I'm the weirdest. I'm the only freak in my school. It's amazing that anyone takes anything I say seriously.*

The most awful shame enveloped Abby—it turned her stomach over and stole every ounce of her confidence.

*All the things I like to do are weird,* she thought. *If a black cat crosses my path, I have to stop, cross my fingers, and tap the corners of my glasses three times. Who would want to be friends with such a loon? . . . There's no place for me. What will happen when I grow up? I'll be the loneliest person on earth!*

Abby had stopped walking. She stood on the narrowest part of the bridge, unsure which direction she had come from and which direction she was going. *What am I doing here?* Meanwhile, the wind wailed one word in her ears. *Freak!*

She began thinking about her older sister Etta, who was the most normal person she knew. Etta kept her brown hair combed perfectly and let it fall down to her shoulders. Etta liked to fit in. She wore exactly what her friends wore, same colors, same styles. When Abby mixed green with red or stripes with spots, Etta shook her head and pleaded with her to be more normal.

"Why can't you just fit in?" asked Etta.

Abby couldn't explain this to her sister. It was just the way she felt. She had noticed that Etta's friends all looked alike. Once Abby followed Etta when she walked with friends and realized that she couldn't tell them apart from behind. They looked identical. Right then, Abby vowed that she would do her best to look different. *I never want to disappear in a crowd,* she decided.

*Freak!* mocked the wind.

Alone on this solitary pathway, Abby froze with doubt. People were always pulling her pigtails, or laughing at her different-colored boots and shoes. Why couldn't she fit in with everybody else, dress like everyone else, *be* like everyone else? Even grown-ups tilted their heads curiously at her, as if she was a . . .

*Freak!*

As the wind repeated its mocking refrain, Abby realized that she had almost stepped off the bridge. She tottered, hands raised in caution, feeling the most awful dread.

"Oh, stop it, Abby!" she cried. "Stop wishing to be Etta!"

The sound of her own advice surprised her. It was strong and sensible. "You can't trade yourself in for somebody else," she told herself. "There's only one Abby, and you're an original, one-of-a-kind, no-return deal!"

Suddenly, she had an idea. A brilliant idea. She would recite riddles—every riddle she knew—and drown out that teasing, merciless wind.

"What's black and white and red all over?" she shouted. "*A newspaper!* What has six wheels and flies?*" she said, raising her arms to keep her balance. "*A garbage truck!*"

She peered around, looking for the citadel. There it was, with its thousands of beckoning lights. She started marching down the incline, first the yellow boot, then the purple.

"What goes *squeak, bump, squeak, bump? A mouse with a wooden leg!* What do you get when you mix nuts with gravel? *A toothache!*"

It was working. Abby was taking solid steps, arms swinging at her sides.

Somes grinned when he heard Abby reciting riddles across the chasm.

"What's big when you're empty and small when you're full?" she shouted.

He laughed. *"Your appetite!"*

# ❋ The Power of Music ❋

The next figure that tiptoed over the bridge had a violin case over her shoulder.

"Everybody's made it just fine," Gabriel reminded Pamela beforehand. "Don't worry."

The chasm roared as she set out. First, there was the banshee cry of the wind, then a hollow roar emanating from the depths—a hungry, bitter sound, like some vast creature in torment at the bottom of the world.

Pamela tried to think good thoughts. She thought of Somes, who had saved her from the fury of the valraven; she thought of the hug she had given him, and the way he'd carefully hugged her back, as if he'd never been hugged before by anyone. *Poor Somes,* she thought. Then she thought of salty taffy and delicious buttery caramel.

The hollow roar returned, echoing from the depths, deeper and more doubtful.

She remembered her mother yelling at Gabriel: *A few of these and Pamela's beautiful teeth will be ruined. Utterly ruined, thanks to you!* She hadn't brushed her teeth since eating the taffy on the dark staircase. What if they started rotting and falling out? Suddenly, a fragment of rock broke from the slender pathway—leaving a gap in the middle. It looked a little bit like a molar.

Pamela slowed down. "This is ridiculous," she told herself. "I can't be seeing teeth."

She stopped and studied the hole in the path. It seemed to be growing.

"I have to get past this," she told herself.

The wind wailed, and the hollow roar answered from below.

*Wait a second. How long has it been since I've practiced violin?* she wondered. She felt ashamed. She was supposed to be learning Allegro Appassionato, but she couldn't recall a note of it. *Does it begin with a G or an A?* she wondered.

"Have I forgotten everything I've ever learned?" she said, wiggling her toes doubtfully over the edge of the bridge.

She imagined her mother's reaction—the tears and weeping. Her mother was so proud of her musical talent. All those lessons, the sheet music she saved from the fire, and her constant reminders about practicing. It was all for nothing. Suddenly, the view of the citadel turned glittery and liquid and Pamela realized she was weeping for herself.

Her left foot slipped off the crumbling path. She fell to her knees. "Oh, help!" she cried, throwing her arms out to steady herself.

Far away, an echo repeated her words. "Oh, help . . . Oh, help . . . Oh, help!"

*How can I keep going if I've forgotten every song I ever learned?* she wondered.

The citadel was two hundred steps away, but Pamela remained crouched in the middle of the bridge. *Look at me, sitting here on all fours, like a piece of furniture,* she fretted. *Just like that poor writing desk!*

That reminded her of the writing desk's favorite jig.

*How did that tune go?* she wondered.

The rhythm came first, then the melody. *De dum, de de dee, da da dum, dee dee dee!*

Concentrating on the music, Pamela tapped the rhythm on the path with her fingers, then raised her hands and clambered to her feet.

"De dum, de de dee . . . ," she sang, taking a step, then another, keeping time with each step. A distant echo picked up her voice and repeated it, until it seemed that a hundred voices were singing along with her.

The deep, mournful drone from below was no match for her.

Pamela began striding quickly to the jig, and the path started sloping downward as she saw figures waving to her from the citadel.

# ❀ The Last One ❀

The dodo had fallen asleep. Her absurdly shaped bill sank into her chest and she snored while standing. When a cheery whistle echoed across the Chasm of Doubt, she jerked awake, flapped her wings, squinted at Gabriel, and sputtered a fresh welcome. Gabriel had to remind her that he was already signed in.

"That's my friend signaling that it's my turn to cross," he explained.

"Oh, dear," the dodo said. "Be careful!"

After several steps up the incline, Gabriel felt a rush of uncertainty. Would he get across? He focused on the citadel's many windows, hoping to spot his father's silhouette, but saw nothing. Then he noticed a figure at the very top, standing by the parapet. The figure raised his arm; Gabriel was about to wave back when he saw a flock of black birds come swooping from the battlements, as if they had just been released.

Were they ravens or valravens? He slowed down, wondering what to do if they attacked. Within a few seconds, their eyes—glowing unpleasantly—became visible, piercing the darkness.

Should he go forward or retreat? He couldn't decide. "Wait! Think!" he told himself. "If they're flying from the citadel, they obviously don't want me to go that way, so that's the way I should go!"

He broke into a careful jog as the birds came ever nearer. *Coark! Coark! Coark!* they shrieked, swooping at him.

Gabriel fell, belly to the path, just before they reached him. An awful odor of rotting meat filled the air.

The ghouls flew up and around, returning for another attack.

*Caaawwwk!* Gabriel ducked, but a valraven ripped at his ear.

A second valraven attacked from the other direction. Its talons grazed his scalp and a streak of blood rolled down his forehead.

Dazed, bleeding, Gabriel came to a halt at the midpoint of the bridge. *Why did I give Septimus the staff?* he wondered. *It's the one thing I could use right now. What a mistake! Am I going to die because I helped him?*

A large valraven was bearing in, jaundiced eyes glowing, its craggy beak set in a malicious smile.

There was nowhere for Gabriel to go but forward, so he ran forward, arms raised for balance, along the bridge's jagged path. The bird's talons would meet his eyes in moments.

*Pop!*

He was running through a cloud of black feathers; the valraven had disappeared.

Amazed, Gabriel looked ahead and saw Septimus pointing the staff forward with a raised fist. "That'll teach him!" the man cackled.

The children began cheering.

*So*, thought Gabriel, *Septimus has finally chosen a side.*

When he reached the far side, everybody looked giddy and relieved, but no one looked as pleased as Septimus, who grinned with jubilation.

"The pain is gone! Do you know what that means? I can't hear his voice anymore. You were right, my boy. I'm no longer a slave to the Lord of Air and Darkness!"

He pressed the staff into the boy's hands. "Here, lad! A promise is a promise."

At that very moment, there was a cry from the top of the citadel: an unearthly scream of dismay that sent a flock of valravens tumbling and scattering in panic from the battlements.

# ❊ The Strange Reunion ❊

Doves, pigeons, mynahs, and cockatoos perched on ledges; button quail, plover, and sandpipers darted along the passages, with swallows and finches flying overhead. Septimus led them through the great gate at the foot of the bridge, then along a passageway that spiraled up the tower. There were bizarre orange birds that appeared to be feeding the torches on the walls with supplies of twigs and rags.

Septimus led the children through the busy courtyard by the bridge as an uproar emanated from the birds all around them. They looked very excited to see newcomers.

"You'd think they'd never seen people before," said Somes.

"Some probably never have," said Septimus.

"But aren't the prisoners people?" asked Pamela.

"No, mostly ravens," replied Septimus.

"Ravens? Why?" said Gabriel.

"Have you forgotten that ravens are Corax's enemies? Their ancestor Muninn stole the torc from Huginn, first of the valravens."

Gabriel immediately thought of Paladin, and wondered if he was safe.

His thought was interrupted by a dodo who came striding down the spiral corridor. She was slightly pink around the wing feathers, but she had the same reddened eyes and exaggerated smile as her counterpart on the bridge. There was one other difference: a robin stood on her back, reminding Gabriel of a captain at the prow of a ship. The robin's little black eyes settled coldly on the children.

"Septimus!" the dodo said, waddling forward. "You've come back! Welcome, welcome!"

Septimus looked startled; he hadn't expected a friendly greeting after defying Corax.

"We've missed you so," cooed the dodo. "And you've brought friends!"

"I've come to visit Adam Finley," Septimus replied. "Room 1515, I believe?"

"Room 1515? No, I believe Adam Finley is—"

The robin interrupted with a sharp chirp. The dodo immediately changed her answer. "Yes, 1515 it is!" She cocked her head. "Your friends should wait here!"

"I'm coming with you, Septimus," said Gabriel.

The robin tilted its head at Gabriel.

"This is the son of Finley," explained Septimus.

The robin issued another sharp command, and the dodo's expression abruptly turned into a demented grin. "Ah, we've been waiting a very long time for the son of Finley!"

*    *    *

They followed the dodo up the winding corridor. Gabriel felt excited. It was like Christmas morning, when you wake knowing presents are waiting under the tree—but a thousand times better. He had waited three Christmases to see his father.

Septimus was no less hopeful that Adam Finley would know how to remove the necklace festering under his skin. "You know," he told Gabriel, "I dare not think good thoughts for fear of wishing something."

Soon they arrived at a door marked 1515. The numbers were coarse and jagged as if carved by dagger or claw. The robin issued a trill, which seemed to trigger the silver lock to snap open.

"Come, lad," said Septimus as he pulled at the immense door.

Inside, there was a small bed with a sack mattress, a set of shelves with a few books on them, and a desk where a man was seated. He had large, round brown eyes, a prominent nose, and a small mouth. Gabriel recognized his father's features, but he also felt slightly disappointed. Was it possible that he had imagined his father's face being gentler? Nicer? Handsomer? Adam Finley's hair had been brown the last time Gabriel saw him; now it was gray. He had more creases around his eyes than Gabriel recalled, but, again, it couldn't have been easy to live within these four walls, never seeing the sun, the trees, a blue sky, or even his own shadow.

The man raised his head and turned from Septimus to Gabriel.

"Dear me!" he said. "Do I see my son?"

Gabriel rushed forward, tears filling his eyes. He hugged his father, burying his face in Adam Finley's chest.

"Oh, Dad," he said, but sobs interrupted Gabriel's words. He couldn't speak. He couldn't explain all the longing, all the wishing, all the nights he'd fallen asleep hoping his father would return. So instead, he held on tight, eyes clenched shut, waiting for his father's arms to tighten around him and restore the love and warmth that had been missing.

This didn't happen, however. His father clasped him, his hands concealed in the sleeves of his shirt. "Forgive me, I'm very frail," he said in a voice as raspy as a rusty hinge.

"It's okay," Gabriel assured him.

"Adam," said Septimus gruffly. "Apologies for taking so long to come back for you."

Mr. Finley looked at Septimus for a brief, scrutinizing moment. "Septimus, old friend."

Septimus nodded. "Thanks to young Gabriel here, we found the torc and the staff. He's a bright boy, your son. Brave, too. Very brave!"

"We Finleys are all brave," agreed Mr. Finley.

Gabriel smiled.

"Now, may I see the torc?"

Septimus loosened his collar to reveal the burned mark around his neck.

"*That* is the torc?"

Mr. Finley raised his arm to draw back Septimus's collar. A shocking claw with sharp black talons appeared from his sleeve. Swiftly, he drew it back.

Regarding Mr. Finley with fresh scrutiny, Septimus fastened his collar. "Adam, I should think you of all people would know what has happened to me. The torc is buried under my skin. You must know how to remove it."

Mr. Finley looked puzzled for a moment. "I shall consult my books. Why don't you simply *wish* it gone?"

Septimus's eyes flickered at Finley's concealed hand. "Because it might remove my head, too!"

"And where is the staff?"

Gabriel held it toward his father, but Mr. Finley regarded the gnarled piece of wood with skepticism. "This old stick can't be the staff," he said. "Where is the real one?"

Gabriel was about to reply when Septimus cut him off. "I could never fool you Adam," he said with a crafty smile. "Naturally, I put it in safekeeping until I could be sure that you were alive and well. Such a vital tool would be of extraordinary value to Corax."

Mr. Finley rose from his seat. "I'll come with you to get it."

Septimus gave him a sly glance. "Adam? You said you needed to consult your books."

304 GABRIEL FINLEY & the Raven's Riddle

"Ah yes! How silly of me to forget." Frowning, Adam
Finley walked them to his door. "Go, then," he said. "When I
have consulted my books, we shall proceed."

As Gabriel accompanied Septimus back along the corridor, he tried to make sense of the conversation. "Septimus, I don't get it," he said. "You know there is no other
staff."

"Of course not," scoffed Septimus. "And your father
knows this very well, which is why that man was not Adam
Finley! It would have been a grave mistake to give him the
staff."

"Are you sure?"

"Yes, this was a clever masquerade by Corax. I should
have realized when he revealed his talons. Adam's hands are
perfectly normal."


Reunited with Abby, Somes, and Pamela, Septimus explained what had happened.

"The first clue was when he called me 'my old friend.'
The real Adam was very angry with me when I escaped
because I offered to cooperate with Corax. Second,
Adam has seen the staff before; he knows what it looks
like. Our impostor is Corax. All he knows is the torc's
legend. Adam spent years studying the torc's secrets. He
knows its entire history." Septimus's expression crumpled.

"What's to become of me, if I can't be rid of this awful thing?"

"We don't have much time," said Abby. "Corax will be trying to figure out how to get the torc."

"He'll need to ask the real Adam Finley," said Gabriel. "Septimus? Where could my father be?"

## ❈ Where Is Adam Finley? ❈

Paladin and Caruso had been flying in circles around the citadel, peeking in every window for Gabriel's father. In one they saw dozens of what appeared to be metallic ravens dangling from the rafters.

"What are those, Caruso?"

"Corax's wretched cages," said the owl.

Paladin slipped through the bars of the window, and Caruso followed.

A shocking sight lay before them. Each device contained a raven, with round holes for the eyes and rivets along the back and front. A metallic beak with a hinge served as a feeding hole for the desperate prisoner trapped inside.

"Get out, go as far as you can from here!" one caged raven cried.

"Escape!" cried another. "While you're still able!"

"If Corax finds you, he'll lock you up like us!" cried a third.

Overcome by their misery, Paladin cried out to the ravens, "How do I set you free?"

"It's hopeless. Our cages are locked and unlocked only by the song of a robin. And all the robins in the citadel serve Corax."

"I could try to imitate a robin's song," suggested Paladin.

"We've *all* tried. No raven can sing such high notes!"

Caruso fluttered up to examine one of the cages. The raven inside trembled, for the owl's prominent horns and beak were terrifying.

"Diabolical," said Caruso. "Why have you been imprisoned?"

"We have all refused to join Corax," said one of the trapped ravens.

One raven emitted pitiful throks. "Oh, who can help us?"

All the imprisoned ravens began to sway in their cages, uttering pleas for rescue, until the air was filled with such deafening cries that it felt like a madhouse.

Caruso uttered a loud *WHOOOO!*, which instantly silenced the room. "Listen to me!" he bellowed. "Does anyone know where Adam Finley is?"

"He has been moved," said one raven. "I heard the sparrows say that he had been sent down to be hidden from the newcomers."

"Down where?" asked Caruso. "Do you know?"

The raven told him about a room in the lowest depths of the citadel where no other birds dared roam.

It was only a matter of moments before the owl and the

raven were spiraling around the tower in search of this room. They soon found it: a dim cell with the smallest crack of a window.

The man seated inside didn't look very different from Corax, except that his hair was darker, his skin less wrinkled—which made sense, as Adam Finley was ten years younger than his brother. The biggest difference was that this man had warm eyes and his mouth looked poised to smile.

He was holding a candle near a book he was reading, but looked up with surprise when he saw the two birds on the windowsill.

"Well, well!" he said curiously. "A raven and an owl—what an unlikely pair!" He beckoned to them. "Please come in. This is a rare honor."

"I am Paladin, grandson of Baldasarre. My amicus is Gabriel Finley."

"Gabriel?" Mr. Finley jumped from his seat. "Paladin, you say? How is Gabriel? Is he in Aviop—"

"And I am Caruso!" interrupted the owl, bursting through the narrow window like a cork from a bottle. "You saved my life, long ago, with the raven Baldasarre!"

Adam Finley laughed. "Ah, Caruso. Yes, of course I remember. Please, tell me about Gabriel!"

Quickly, Paladin explained how Gabriel had solved the raven's riddle and gotten the torc from the owls. When he described how Septimus had become tormented by the torc,

Mr. Finley didn't seem surprised. "Yes, Septimus was bound to fall under its power," he said. "Corax will want to know how to extract the torc. I imagine he's coming for me now. It would be best to leave immediately."

"We could paravolate," suggested Paladin.

Adam Finley shook his head. "Unfortunately, Paladin, I can paravolate only with my amicus. As Baldasarre has passed on, I cannot fly anywhere."

Finley paced about the room, then examined the locked door. "It's a pity that the robins are so loyal to Corax. If we could simply convince one robin to cooperate and open this lock."

"Leave that to me," said Caruso. He flew up to the windowsill, then balked at the narrow opening. He turned to Mr. Finley. "Lend a shove?" He patted his belly. "I'm an owl, not a dove."

Finley eased the owl gently through the narrow window.

"Much obliged! No more rich food for me. From now on, it's strictly mice and beans!"

Caruso spread his wings and flew up the walls of the tower. His awesome wingspan made him the most formidable bird in the chasm. Others veered away from him in great flocks. Eventually, the great horned owl arrived at the tower's vaulted entrance by the bridge. There, he swooped in, sending terrified little birds scattering in all directions. The owl perched above the courtyard and waited until he spotted a dodo walking down the corridor with a robin chirping commands on her back. In a flash, Caruso swooped, seizing the robin in one of his claws.

Moments later, Adam Finley heard the triumphant hoot of the owl. He peered through the postcard-sized window of his door and saw Caruso hovering in the corridor, holding a protesting robin in one of his daggerlike talons.

The robin was putting on a very brave show. "I'll never open this door! I serve Corax himself! I am a general, do you hear? I fear no one. I'll fight to the death!"

"I have one question for you," replied Caruso, tightening his claws around the robin's bright red breast. "How do you prefer to be eaten? With salt and pepper, or would you like a little *thyme*?"

The robin uttered a high-pitched trill, and the door lock clicked open.

"Oh, very good, Caruso!" said Mr. Finley. "Let's hurry— there's no time to waste!"

# ❊ Septimus finds a friend ❊

The half man, half raven was shedding his disguise as Gabriel's father. With a hoarse cry, he ripped the shirt from his chest. Black feathers burst from skin follicles all over his body, and satin-sinewed wings sprang from his shoulders. He leaped from the battlements of the citadel and flew in a descending spiral to the bottom, throwing smaller birds into tailspins in his wake.

When he alighted at the window of Adam Finley's chamber, he was furious to find its occupant missing. Tearing at the stone window with his talons, he uttered another unearthly cry. The flocks of birds circling aimlessly in the chasm careered in panic, gabbling and shrieking as the furious overlord of Aviopolis calculated his next step.

Meanwhile, Gabriel and his friends had begun a search for Adam Finley. They came to a room filled with dozens of metallic cages swaying from the ceiling, birds weeping and wailing in tight wire mesh, their beaks clipped by tin-plated jaws, eyes peering wildly from small eyeholes. Septimus had seen all this before, so he walked in ahead of the children.

"These chaps have refused to join Corax's side," he explained. Raising his voice, Septimus addressed the ravens. "Look here! Have any of you seen Adam Finley? Anyone?"

The ravens fell silent, save for the squeak of rusty metal.

"Speak up! Are you all stupid? Somebody must know something!" shouted Septimus.

"Maybe the poor things aren't sure whether to trust us," suggested Abby. "I have an idea." She removed her glasses for a second, then recited:

> *"Wherever I swim,*
> *I leave a stain*
> *That people drink.*
> *Do you know my name?"*

In spite of their fear, the ravens couldn't resist a riddle. A round of chatter began to break out among the cages. They were all conferring with each other excitedly. Finally, one raven at the very back spoke up.

"Is it . . . a tea bag?"

"Yes!" Abby laughed.

A chorus of delighted throks broke out, followed by giddy raven laughter.

A second raven spoke. "May we know who seeks Adam Finley?"

"His son," said Gabriel, stepping forward.

After a round of whispers, a third raven spoke. "The starlings have told us that Paladin has found him."

"He has?" Gabriel said, his face brightening into joy. "Can you tell me if he's all right?"

"Adam Finley has escaped!" cheered another raven.

"Beware!" cried another. "The linnets are saying Corax is looking for him all over the citadel!"

"Leave while you're still free!" advised another.

"But do any of you know *where* he is?" asked Gabriel.

"The swallows say he comes this way with Paladin and a friendly owl," said another.

"Very good. Now let's go!" Septimus marched to the door and beckoned to the others.

Gabriel cast a worried glance at the caged ravens. "Wait, Septimus," he said. "There must be something we can do for these poor birds."

"There isn't," said Septimus.

"I think we owe them," added Abby.

Septimus rubbed his scar feverishly. "Look, we don't have much time!"

Pamela nodded. "Corax will be looking for Gabriel's father so he can find out how to get the staff and necklace!"

Somes had tried to pry one of the cages open, but the wire was rigid and strong, and his fingers began to bleed. "They have some strange kind of lock," he said. "There's no keyhole."

"Precisely," Septimus replied. "That's because the locks are sealed with a robin's song."

"A *song*?" said Pamela curiously. She slung the violin case off her shoulder and took out her violin and bow.

"My dear, this is hardly the time for a recital," sputtered Septimus.

"I'm thinking about the robins," she replied. "D'you know that sound they make—it's a *trill*."

"Try it!" said Gabriel.

Pamela drew her bow across the strings, playing a series of trills, but nothing happened.

"Try higher notes," suggested Somes.

Pamela slid her fingers down the fingerboard and drew the bow again. The trills became piercingly high.

Suddenly, a cage sprang open; its raven fluttered free, uttering a delighted *throk!*

Another cage snapped open. The raven jumped to the floor and cackled triumphantly.

Cages popped open all across the room. Ravens jumped from their bindings and flapped their wings, unshackled and ecstatic. In a giddy chorus, the freed birds whistled and throkked with relief.

A raven with speckled markings landed on Pamela's shoulder. It cocked its head at her curiously, eyes dancing with delight. "What rises when the rain comes down?"

Lowering her violin, Pamela paused to think. "Well . . . you raise your umbrella when it rains."

The raven throkked gleefully. "Very good! An umbrella! My name is Specklewing!"

Another raven landed on Abby's shoulder. He had a white streak on his wing and spoke with a wizened voice. "How does the moon smile?"

Abby folded her arms and thought. "Hmm, how does the moon smile? It can only smile one way: that's by *beaming!*" This raven, named Snowtip, uttered a gleeful whistle.

A scruffy bird with a spray of black feathers around his neck landed on Somes's arm. He scrutinized the boy for a moment before speaking.

"I satisfy a hunger, but I am not food. I will not fill your belly, but I will nourish your curiosity. What am I?"

A worried look came over Somes's face, but then he relaxed. "Oh," he said. "The answer is *an answer!*"

The bird, named Hotspur, began a hearty laugh—*CAW! CAW! CAW!*—almost losing his balance on Somes's arm.

"How *touching*, how *sweet!* We're all making friends just before we die!" Septimus cried with impatient sarcasm. At that moment a raven with powdery gray feathers landed on his shoulder.

"Greetings, Septimus," he said in a raspy baritone. "I am Burbage, brother of Crawfin."

The mention of Crawfin startled Septimus. "Burbage? The name rings a bell. Yes, I remember the stories about you," he said, raising an eyebrow curiously. "Weren't you a gem thief? A decent one, as I recall."

Blinking with indignation, the gray raven drew himself up. "Why, how dare you! A 'decent' gem thief? I'm the *best* gem thief there ever was. Even Crawfin would have agreed with that!"

"Of course, of course." A cunning glint appeared in Septimus's eyes. "Listen, my good friend, perhaps we can be of assistance to each other. I happen to be something of a connoisseur of lost objects of great value. It seems to me that we might make an exceptional team if we just put our *minds* together. Why, with my business talents and your unique skill, we could—"

"Septimus? Time to go!" interrupted Gabriel.

With a wink, Septimus beckoned to the raven. "Come," he said.

# ❋ Mutiny of the Robins ❋

The citadel's winding corridor reminded Gabriel of a magic carpet ride at an amusement park; if the stone floor had been smoother, they might have sat down and slid in a spiral all the way to the bottom of the tower. Instead, they walked while birds scrambled, flew, swooped, and squawked ahead of them. Pamela was disappointed when her riddling raven (as well as Abby's and Somes's) took flight to find Adam Finley.

"You can't blame them," Abby reminded her. "This is a big day."

Only Burbage remained with Septimus—it seemed that the two had developed an instant bond and begun conspiring together.

As news of the escape spread through the tower, Gabriel sensed a great surge of joy in the air. It was clear from the squawks, shrieks, and chirps that the Lord of Air and Darkness was losing his grip.

From the bottom of the tower, another group of celebrants wound their way upward—Adam Finley, Paladin, and Caruso. Lapwings and terns darted along the corridors, spreading the news to bobwhites, bluebirds, cardinals, and chickadees.

Only Corax's red-breasted lieutenants—the robins— were upset by the news. These small birds cherished power; they were the jailers; they controlled the locks and rode the backs of larger birds like the dodoes and geese. If there was a chance they might be on the losing side, they were quick to panic.

But when one timid robin began unlocking cages, hoping to win favor with Adam Finley, his friends quickly joined in. As more ravens escaped from their cages, more robins turned against Corax. In a panic, they began trilling at every lock they could find. It wasn't long before hundreds of ravens were celebrating their escapes with gloating throks, filling the passage-ways with chattering, rejoicing, and, of course, riddles.

Soon, the two groups were only a few footsteps apart in the winding corridor. Gabriel heard a tremendous chirping and babbling coming near. A flock of birds fluttered around a man who walked toward Gabriel waving his arms in wel-come. There was no mistaking his eager grin and forthright stride.

"Dad?" said Gabriel.

"Gabriel! At last!"

Gabriel quickly fell into Adam Finley's tight embrace. A great chorus of tweeting, squawking, and honking swirled in joyful eddies around father and son, applauding their reunion.

"I knew you would succeed," Mr. Finley said. "You always had a gift for riddles, Gabriel."

Gabriel felt a flood of memories come back as his father spoke—his deep, warm voice, his boundless enthusiasm.

"I was afraid I'd never find you," Gabriel admitted.

Mr. Finley's eyebrows rose abruptly, as if he had heard an important message in the squawking around him. "We are still in very great danger, Gabriel. You see, the torc—"

They were interrupted by Septimus. "Adam! Old friend!" he cried. "Please, you must help me remove this wretched thing from around my neck at once! Look at this scar."

For the first time, Gabriel's father became stern. "Ah, Septimus," he said. "After leaving me here in prison, you return without an apology, demanding my help?"

Wilting, Septimus dropped to his knees. "My dear fellow, do I get no thanks for bringing your son to you? For saving him from the valravens? To say nothing of coming to free you from the citadel?"

"You old thief, you haven't changed a bit," Adam said. "Well, at least a rapscallion like you knows when luck is on his side."

Septimus assumed a dignified frown. "Rapscallion? Thief? I kept my word. I brought you the torc."

"All right, let's have a look," said Mr. Finley.

Septimus unbuttoned his shirt to reveal the awful burn mark around his neck.

Finley recognized the mark immediately. "Hmm. Well, there's a simple remedy, my friend. To remove the torc, you must make an unselfish wish."

Septimus cocked his head. *"Pardon?"*

"Ask for something that doesn't serve only *your* desire. Be generous. Selfless."

Septimus agonized for a moment, as if Mr. Finley had asked him to speak a forgotten language. "Must I give up such an extraordinary treasure?" he said.

"Freedom has a price, Septimus," said Mr. Finley.

"In that case, I suppose the correct wish," Septimus concluded, "is simply to wish that the torc returns to its place upon the staff."

Instantly, the scar faded from his neck, leaving only a faint blue glow. Then the necklace reappeared upon Gabriel's staff. Its glow vanished as it folded around the wood, resembling a dull trinket again.

"A pity," Septimus muttered. "My brush with the power of gods!" He sighed, wiped his forehead, and buttoned his shirt. "Well, I must be on my way. Business awaits."

"What business is that, Septimus?" asked Mr. Finley.

"Burbage tells me that deep in these caverns there are some rare and valuable . . ." Septimus paused, a secretive look on his face. "Well, it's nothing you need know about. Farewell, lad. Goodbye, Adam!"

"Goodbye!" they answered. And with that, Septimus hurried down the corridor.

"Now, where was I before our interruption?" said Mr. Finley, turning to his son.

"You said I was in very grave danger," replied Gabriel.

"Yes," said Mr. Finley. "Let me explain."

Up and down the citadel corridors, locks were springing open and cages emptying. The robins showed no joy or delight in this task; they were simply determined to be on the winning side. The little jailers were worried about their future. Who would be their leader now? What about their rank, their privileges? Would they still be permitted to ride the dodoes through the corridors? Who would their prisoners be? They wouldn't have minded jailing the valravens, if it came to that; it was all the same to them.

One bold robin, named Snitcher, was still in the grip of the great horned owl, Caruso.

"Oh, mighty victor!" he pleaded. "I have done what you asked. Set me free, as you promised!"

Savoring the thought of a victory snack, Caruso gripped the robin like a precious candy bar. Reminded of his promise, he reluctantly released the bird. Snitcher, however, didn't fly away. He fluttered a short distance from the owl with an expectant stare.

"What are you waiting for?" asked the owl.

"Now that you have conquered Aviopolis," said Snitcher, "I would like to be your lieutenant."

"My what?" Caruso scratched his ear in disbelief.

"I wish to be lieutenant in your army," said the robin. "I will spy for you, lock your prisoners up, and ride your dodoes."

"Ride my dodoes indeed," coughed the owl. "There will be no army, no cages. No dodoes! You are free. Go about your business."

"No army?" gasped Snitcher. "What about my rank? I'm a lieutenant to Corax!"

"Fly away, little bird," said the owl with a sniff. "Feast on worms, and watch that I don't catch you or I will swallow you whole and spit out your bones!"

Snitcher stared at the owl bitterly, then flew off quickly before he was eaten.

# ❊ The Dwarfs' Secret ❊

**M**r. Finley turned the staff slowly in his hand and looked at Gabriel, Abby, Pamela, and Somes. They were sitting in a small room in the citadel, Paladin perched on Gabriel's shoulder. Outside, the joyous chirping and chatter and the exalted throks of freed ravens swooping through the corridors continued.

"Together you have ended Corax's dreams of ruling the world above, and his stranglehold on the world below, by bringing me the torc," Mr. Finley said. "Bravo!"

"Shouldn't we be leaving before Corax finds us?" Paladin replied.

"Yes, my friend," said Mr. Finley. "But first Gabriel must be prepared to defend the torc—something only he can do."

"Defend it?" said Gabriel. "What does that mean?"

"Let me explain," said Mr. Finley. "You see, Gabriel, when the owls gave the torc to you, you may not have realized that you were part of a ceremony. A ritual was being enacted, one that gave you a unique power over the torc."

324   ❦ GABRIEL FINLEY & the Raven's Riddle ❧

"What power is that?" asked Gabriel.

"Let me demonstrate." Rising from his seat, Mr. Finley crossed the small room and gripped the staff with both hands, then nodded at Gabriel.

"Now, from where you sit, take the staff from me."

"I can't reach."

"You don't need to," said Mr. Finley. "It will come."

Confused, Gabriel extended his arm toward the staff.

The staff quivered in Mr. Finley's hands, then began to shake, then zigzag wildly like a trout on a line. Finally, it broke free and zoomed across the room into Gabriel's hand.

"Wow!" Gabriel said. "If I'd known about this, I could have gotten it back from Septimus!"

"Not exactly," said Mr. Finley. "Only when the torc is on the staff can it be summoned by its owner."

"Oh, right; now I remember Ulyssa saying that," said Gabriel.

"But I thought Septimus was its owner," said Somes. "It hung around *his* neck."

"No, Septimus stole it, which is why he was so mistreated by it," said Mr. Finley. "The torc became Gabriel's because of a blood sacrifice."

At this moment, the little robin, Snitcher, flew into the room unnoticed through the narrow window. It had been circling the citadel, hoping to find Adam Finley to pledge its loyalty to him and ensure a better rank than the other robins.

"Blood was shed when the owls gave the torc to Gabriel," said Mr. Finley.

"Oh!" said Gabriel. "You mean when Septimus's ear was bitten?"

"Precisely. According to tradition, the torc changes owners when blood is shed and a riddle is asked that the previous owner cannot answer."

The curious black eyes of the robin widened at this piece of information. It turned its head from Mr. Finley to Gabriel, trying to remember every detail.

"Gabriel made a pun, remember?" Paladin reminded them. "Why is there always something to eat in the desert? Because of the sandwiches there. The owls couldn't answer it."

"So that's how Gabriel became the torc's owner?" said Pamela.

Mr. Finley was about to reply when he noticed the robin.

"Gabriel," he said calmly. "Turn slowly and grab the little fellow behind you."

Gabriel had no sooner turned than the little bird sprang through the narrow window.

"It's only a robin," said Somes. "What does it matter?"

Mr. Finley peered out through the window. "It matters a lot, Somes. Robins are notorious gossips. If Corax learns about the blood sacrifice and the riddle, he can challenge Gabriel for the torc."

"I'll find him!" Paladin promised, and disappeared after the bird.

"I hope so," said Pamela.

"So if Corax wants the torc to serve him," continued Gabriel, "he has to make a blood sacrifice and challenge me with a riddle that I can't answer. It seems too easy."

Finley dusted his hands and sat down. "Easy, yes, but you must understand that the dwarfs who made the torc knew that a granted wish was more often a curse than a blessing."

"How can that be?" asked Pamela.

"People rarely wish wisely," said Mr. Finley. "Instead of asking for good health or a peaceful heart, most usually wish for money, objects, or power, and find misery in return. The dwarfs thought it best if no one could hold on to the torc for very long. So they created this simple way for others to win it."

"But why did they make the staff?" asked Abby.

"Actually, the staff was created by Muninn. He made only two wishes. The first was for a sturdy defense against valravens—a staff that destroys them."

"And the other?" asked Gabriel.

"Well, the valravens kept coming for the torc, and over the years, poor old Muninn became weary of defending himself," explained Mr. Finley. "So he wished himself to some faraway place safe from valravens." He shook his head. "Sadly, he was buried alive in a tomb along with the torc and staff. That's where I found his skeleton, a thousand years later."

"Yuck," said Pamela.

"So you see, no wish is foolproof. Even the torc's owner isn't safe from its mischief," said Mr. Finley. "Now, Gabriel, we must go before your uncle makes it impossible for us to leave."

# ❋ Escape from Aviopolis ❋

Gabriel still felt that something important had been left out of his father's explanation. There wasn't time to ask because Mr. Finley began hurrying everybody out of the room.

"Remember," he said. "If Corax doesn't learn the truth about the torc, he won't be able to take it from Gabriel!"

They joined the immense crowd of creatures hurrying along the corridors of the citadel. These were the flightless birds—bustards, geese, dodoes, and emus. Many seemed unafraid of speaking, which accounted for the noise as they apologized (or complained) when they collided with the children in their frenzy to escape. A deep voice behind Somes said, "Pick your feet up, sonny! We haven't got all day!" Somes turned to see an ornery pelican snapping its bill at him.

As they ran through the bustling hallways, Abby took Gabriel's hand tightly in her own. "What's wrong?" she whispered.

"What if we don't get out in time, and Corax asks me a riddle I can't answer?" he replied. "That's the end of it. He'll have the torc, and we're done for."

Abby squeezed his hand. "Maybe he won't get a chance. Maybe we'll escape before Corax finds us. But if he does . . ." She paused. "Well, you won't have to worry about answering a funny riddle, and those are the hardest."

"Why not?"

"Corax is just a big valraven, and they don't get jokes," she replied.

"Oh, yeah." Gabriel nodded, wishing this was more of a comfort.

There was a massive traffic jam at the entrance to the bridge. Cries of frustration rose from the waddling, flightless penguins, coots, grebes, cassowaries, and kiwis as they jostled and poked their way in front of the dodoes and ostriches, who were making a great fuss to get across first.

"This is crazy," said Pamela. "I can't imagine these silly birds getting across the Chasm of Doubt without forgetting themselves in the middle of the bridge."

"They seem to be moving along just fine," said Abby, looking ahead.

Indeed, the birds kept a surprisingly good pace across the bridge. The confused birds got bumped ahead by the ones behind them. Septimus, of course, had cut in line way ahead of everybody. The children could see him past the halfway point with the raven Burbage sitting on his shoulder.

"I hope your friend Paladin catches that robin," Mr. Finley remarked to Gabriel. "A lot depends on it."

Gabriel peered at the vast cavern, wondering where Paladin might be. His gaze settled on the uppermost battlements of the citadel, where he had first seen the dark figure. "What's Corax planning?" he wondered.

"I don't know, Gabriel," his father replied. "The sooner we cross the bridge, the better."

They were held up, however, as a huge group of penguins scuttled ahead of them.

Pamela sighed. "Well, I'm ready to get home," she said to Somes. "How about you?"

"Home?" His large eyes became sad. "I don't have much of a home to go to."

Before Pamela could answer, Abby let out a cry. "What in the world is that?"

She pointed upward. A churning, billowing black cloud surrounded the top of the citadel tower. Swelling to ominous proportions, it slowly drifted downward. Gabriel recognized the sickly glow coming from thousands of yellow eyes.

Valravens.

Hundreds and hundreds of them. Swirling around each other in eddies and whirls of black feathers, thick with fury and malice, snapping their skeletal beaks and jagged claws, hissing and screaming. Their tattered wings beat the air, stirring up a horrible stench of rancid meat, rot, and death.

When they were overhead, the valravens began darting at the children.

"Quick, Gabriel!" cried Mr. Finley. "Use the staff!"

The moment he spoke, a flurry of valravens converged on Mr. Finley, surrounding him and hissing their fury.

Gabriel pointed his staff at the nearest ones. *Pop! Pop! Pop! Pop! Pop!* Five valravens vanished in an explosion of feathers.

"Quicker!" said Somes. "Look! More are coming!"

Indeed, another cloud descended from the top of the citadel, this one bigger than the first.

"I've never seen so many birds!" added Pamela.

*Pop! Pop! Pop! Pop!* Gabriel spun about, picking them off as fast as he could, but the harpies darted at the children, gagging and screeching like a devilish thunderhead. No matter how many Gabriel destroyed with the staff, they were replaced by twice as many ghouls who were even more determined to keep the children from stepping upon the bridge.

And then it got worse.

"Oh, Gabriel, help!" cried Pamela. A group of valravens clamped their beaks and talons on locks of her hair, pulling at her hood, her sleeves, trying to lift her into the air.

Gabriel pointed the staff at them, destroying twenty in quick pops, but they were swiftly replaced. Pamela fought them off, swinging her violin case until one bird pulled it from her fingers and flew off over the chasm, then clumsily dropped the case when it collided with another bird.

As her precious violin vanished into the darkness, Pamela went limp.

The ghouls took advantage of her distraction by hoisting her up above her friends, then over the chasm. Fearful of falling, Pamela stopped struggling. The valravens swiftly carried her off.

"Can't you do something?" Somes shouted at Gabriel.

"Like *what*?" Gabriel snapped back.

"Make a wish!" suggested Abby. "Wish they were butterflies or something!"

"Butterflies?" Gabriel repeated.

"No!" shouted Mr. Finley. "Butterflies couldn't support Pamela; she'd fall into the abyss!"

"Wish them to vanish, or die!" cried Somes.

"She'll still fall!"

"I don't know what to do!" said Gabriel. In frustration, he looked at his father. "Can't I just wish everyone home?"

"And arrive surrounded by all these valravens? Don't expect magic to be precise—*especially* black magic!" warned Mr. Finley.

Now the attackers swarmed like hornets around Abby.

She tried to defend herself by swinging her backpack at them, but one valraven seized it and flapped away. A second bird attacked the first, and a third pulled the bag in the opposite direction, splitting it down the middle. Viv's candies and several of Abby's colorful bandannas dropped into the chasm and were swiftly snapped up by passing valravens.

One valraven landed on Abby's head and clawed off her spectacles. Abby grabbed them back but found herself rising from the ground, pulled by thirty valravens, their talons tugging at the mesh of her four layers of cardigans.

"Abby!" cried Gabriel, popping off valravens left and right, but the birds were simply replaced by more, who circled Somes next.

Somes put up a brave fight, swinging his fists and kicking as hard as he could. He managed to grab one valraven, swinging it fiercely against the others. After he threw the valraven into the chasm, it swiftly became food for the others. Then Somes felt himself hoisted up.

"Somes, look out!" warned Gabriel.

With claws gripping Somes's sweatshirt, the valravens rose in a flock, but the boy cleverly unzipped himself and slid out. He meant to land upon the bridge but misjudged the distance. Gabriel gasped as Somes dropped below him into the darkness, only to reappear moments later, held aloft by valravens gripping his hair, shirt, jeans, and sneaker laces. It was difficult to know whether he had been saved or preserved for an even worse fate. In either case, he looked as if he was in a lot of pain.

*Why are they taking my friends?* Gabriel wondered.

Mr. Finley seized this moment to speak urgently to Gabriel. "I must tell you something important before the valravens come for you."

"What?"

*"Listen carefully,* Gabriel," said his father. "There is one *other* way to get the torc back if Corax should take it from you. You have to challenge him to a duel."

"A duel? You mean with swords or pistols?" said Gabriel.

"No, nothing like that! The dwarfs dueled with wit and cunning."

"Oh!" Gabriel said. "A duel of riddles?"

"Exactly. If the challenger demands a duel, the torc's power will cease until the duel is won."

"Dad," said Gabriel, "why didn't you tell me this before?"

Mr. Finley looked at his son with tender regret. "Because the duel offers no second chance, Gabriel. The winner claims the torc . . . but the loser forfeits his life. I wanted to be Corax's challenger, but I see now that Corax has plotted carefully. He took your friends for a reason."

"I'm not afraid of him," Gabriel replied.

Mr. Finley looked proudly at Gabriel. "Yes, I realize that. You, Gabriel, are the torc's owner and guardian now." He squeezed his son's shoulder. "One more thing: try not to use wishes for yourself. Remember Muninn's fate—"

Before Mr. Finley could finish, there were screams behind them, and more valravens arrived in a fresh attack. Gabriel tried to disperse them with the staff, but a dozen birds wrenched it free of his grip with triumphant cackles.

Gabriel reached out.

*Zoom!* The staff flew back to his hands. The confused birds squawked and hissed with frustration.

Pleased by this small victory, Gabriel whirled around to help his father, now engulfed by the phantom birds. Suddenly, a great horned owl swooped overhead, snatching and ripping at them, sending feathers and bones in every direction.

"Caruso!" cried Gabriel with relief.

"Ghoulish weather we're having lately, eh?" quipped the owl. "Don't worry about your father, young Finley! I'll take care of him."

This was just as well, because a cluster of valravens had alighted on Gabriel's staff. Although his fingers held on tight, the birds began pulling upward, drawing Gabriel and the staff with them until he found himself dangling far over the chasm.

*What do I do now?* he wondered.

*Never mind about the staff, you can get it later,* said a voice in his head. *Jump!*

*Paladin!* Gabriel replied. *Where are you?*

*Above you. Just jump!*

Gabriel released the torc and staff, which were quickly borne away by two cackling valravens. It was useless to struggle now. Gabriel felt himself drop deep into the chasm. The rock walls became a blur around him. Something was wrong. Where was Paladin? Was this the end? The air turned deathly cold, and as he shivered, his bones suddenly shifted position, and his arms—no, his *wings*—gripped the air!

# ❀ The Unanswerable Riddle ❀

*P*<sub>hew!</sub> gasped Paladin. *You dropped so quickly I lost you for a minute!*

*Glad you found me,* replied Gabriel.

But his relief didn't last long. As he listened to the mocking jabber and squawk of phantom birds echoing throughout the cavern, Gabriel's heart grew heavy with regret at losing both his father and his friends.

It was Paladin who cheered him up. *We'll find them,* the raven assured Gabriel. Together, they veered and looped through the clusters of valravens with almost careless defiance. Cunning, graceful, and swift, Paladin kept his head averted so that the lack of a yellow glow in his eyes wouldn't arouse suspicion; and when a curious valraven did glance at him, Paladin burst into such a convincing fit of hissing and shrieking that the ghoul was dutifully impressed.

Eventually, they spotted a curious grouping of valravens venturing much higher than the others. These creatures were making a course for a place far above the citadel, in the upper caverns of Aviopolis.

Meanwhile, below them, the towering fortress that once imprisoned Adam Finley glittered like a beautiful lantern in the darkness as a few last stragglers made their escape over the slender bridge.

*I hope Caruso and my father escape up the staircase,* thought Gabriel.

The valravens carried three hostages high among the hundreds of simple dwellings carved into the sandstone walls until they arrived, at last, at an ornately sculpted ledge at the very top of Aviopolis. It must have been built by the dwarfs for their own leader; it supported a grand chamber with vaulted ceilings, polished floors, and windows with gold shutters. The brightly lit interior glowed enticingly. One of the window shutters was open, and it was through this opening that the valravens carried their captives.

Gabriel and Paladin landed moments later on the ledge. Padding carefully along the windowsills, they peeked through the shutter slats.

The chamber was full of oddly familiar furniture—cabinets with animal feet, lamps with fringed shades, armchairs and sofas with tasseled pillows. Corax had furnished his lair to resemble the house he'd fled as a boy. Sitting upon a leather quilted bench, the half man, half valraven tapped his taloned fingers impatiently. He wore a black velvet suit like the one in the painting. Poised and powerful, his great silken wings flexed gently behind his shoulders.

*There he is!* said Gabriel. *But I don't remember the wings the last time I saw him.*

*He can probably shift from human form to half human, half valraven for flying,* replied Paladin.

Gabriel tried to pull at the shutters, but they were carved out of stone and alabaster, and impossible to budge.

Abby, Somes, and Pamela stood before Corax. Faces scratched and bruised, clothes rumpled and torn from being wrenched aloft by the sharp talons of their captors, they trembled before the demon.

"It is an honor indeed to meet the valiant friends of my nephew," said Corax.

Bristling, Abby glared at him. "It's not an honor to meet you!"

"There, there," Corax cooed. "I apologize for your rough treatment, but I was afraid you were going to leave without our getting acquainted. I rarely receive visitors here. It's a grand occasion for me. Please have a seat."

"I'll stand," said Pamela, her eyes flashing.

"Me too," said Abby.

Grimly fascinated, Somes looked around the grand chamber. Aching from his struggle against the birds, he chose a very plush sofa and sank into it.

"Nice digs," he remarked with a grunt.

"I'm glad you like it," said Corax. "You'll find that I can be very agreeable to those who tell me what I need to know."

"Like what?" replied Somes.

"I am particularly interested in a necklace called the torc."

"Oh, I know all about that—" said Somes.

"Somes!" said Abby angrily.

The boy shrugged. "I'm just saying that I know what it is."

Corax nodded. "A smart boy. Perhaps you are also aware of its extraordinary properties. Your friend Gabriel, I believe, knows how to use it."

"He's not the only one," said Somes with a trace of irritation—after all, he had saved Pamela from the valraven.

Pamela shot Somes a worried glance.

"Join me," said Corax to the children. "I'm going to change the world. You've all proved yourselves to be remarkable. Be remarkable with me! You deserve more than to go back to those miserable homes of yours. Back to being . . . nobodies. No one will admire you as I do—not your sisters, your mothers or fathers. They can't imagine how special you are!"

When the children didn't reply, Corax continued. "Help me harness the power of the torc. I'll share my victory with you."

He focused his gaze on Abby. "You . . . you're the *unusual* one, the one your sister told to be normal? Now, surely you don't want to go back to that!"

Tears filled Abby's eyes. "I'll never help you," she sobbed. "You're a monster!"

"Then what about you?" Corax said, turning to Pamela. "A gifted musician. What will your mother say when she finds you've lost your violin? When I claim the world above, you can have any instrument you want."

"I wouldn't need one if your awful birds hadn't stolen mine!"

The demon's eyes lingered on the boy the longest. "Well, Somes?" he purred. "Look around. Wouldn't this be nicer than sleeping on the cold floor of a mausoleum? You'll eat well here, and there would be no school if you joined me."

Somes sat up, appearing to give this some consideration. "Join you?" he said. "And do what?"

"Somes!" cried Pamela.

"Please, Somes, don't give yourself up to him!" said Abby.

Corax stepped closer, blocking the girls' imploring looks. "Tell me about the properties of this necklace and share my power," he said. "I'll be fair. I can assure you of that, because most of all, I know how it feels to be betrayed by a father."

Somes looked at Corax with surprise. How could he know?

"Alone. Unloved," Corax continued. "I understand these feelings better than your friends do."

Somes averted his eyes from the girls, then raised his chin stiffly. "If you want the torc, you have to make a blood sacrifice."

"No!" cried Abby in dismay.

Through the slats of the shutter, Gabriel couldn't believe

what he was hearing. He tried to pry the window open again, wedging his fingers under the shutters and pulling until his face dripped with sweat.

*Somes wouldn't tell him, would he?* said Gabriel.

*I think he would,* said Paladin.

*We've got to get through these shutters!*

*And then?* replied Paladin. *There are valravens everywhere.*

Indeed, valravens stood sentry at every window.

Too frustrated to keep still, Gabriel shifted his position, wedging his heels against the slats, trying to shatter them with a swift, well-placed kick, but they were solid as could be.

"Tell me more, Somes," continued Corax, his voice smooth and seductive.

"Somes, please. Don't," begged Pamela.

"I know how to do it," said Somes. "I heard how from Gabriel's father. But I'll need the torc and staff to show you."

"Very good," said Corax, and he raised one of his taloned hands in a signal. Immediately, two valravens fluttered toward him carrying the staff with the torc wrapped around it.

"Oh, no . . . ," murmured Pamela.

Corax turned the staff in his scaly talons, perplexed by the torc's dull appearance. Then, with a cautious glance, he held it out to Somes.

"Proceed."

As Somes's fingers touched the staff, a delicious warmth trickled through them, then up his arm, all the way into his heart. It reminded him of swallowing a steamy barley soup on a bitterly cold day. Warmth, comfort, and sustenance. His aching limbs, his bruises and cuts—they all stopped hurting. He closed his eyes.

"Somes?" said Corax. "I'm waiting."

Somes opened his eyes and stood up from the chair. "Okay," he said. "Like I said, it requires a blood sacrifice from . . ."

He raised the staff at the valravens guarding the windows.

*Pop! Pop! Pop! Pop!* In a blue flash, each bird exploded in a burst of tattered feathers.

"Before you call yourself a hero, I should remind you that I have thousands more where those came from!" hissed Corax.

Somes swung the staff toward Corax, his eyes bright with rebellion. "I wonder what this might do to the *biggest* valraven in the room!" he said. "What do you say we give it a try? You promise all these things, but none of it is real. I can see it in your face. You're a liar. Nothing in you cares about anything but yourself! And you're dumb. I can't believe you just handed me the torc and the staff!"

"You pathetic child," growled Corax, and in a flash, he seized the free end of the staff with his talons.

All the self-assurance Somes felt seemed to drain at Corax's touch. The demon's eyes were fixed on him, his yellow irises glowing brightly. "You're the idiot," he said. "You haven't the intelligence to defy me. It's just as well that I have you here; you and your friends will serve as a fine meal for many valravens to come!"

As Corax scolded him, Somes wilted. He felt his fingers releasing the staff, even as he struggled to hold on to it.

"Don't give in to him, Somes!" Abby cried, grabbing the staff to help.

At that very moment, there was a great crash at one of the shutters as Gabriel finally kicked his way in. He stumbled from the window into the chamber.

The demon spread his wings and wrenched the staff away.

"Stop!" Gabriel cried, and reached out.

The staff left Corax's talons with tremendous force and flew obediently into Gabriel's hands. He trained the staff on Corax while he checked on his friends.

"You guys okay? Abby? Pamela? Somes, you were brilliant!" said Gabriel. "You did exactly the right thing."

"Well, it's my dear nephew again," said Corax, rubbing his stunned claws. "Such perfect timing. You have no idea what a marvelous gift you hold in your hand. Allow me to—"

"Oh, I know how marvelous it is," Gabriel answered. *"To thee I say, resist its lure, devised in evil plot. Around the staff this torc must stay, its wickedness forgot!"*

"Your father has probably told you all kinds of terrible things," Corax said contemptuously. "I'm sure you haven't dared even one little wish! I can show you its virtues."

"You don't need to swallow poison to know it's bad!" snapped Abby.

Ignoring Abby's remark, the demon whispered to Gabriel, "Let me show you how amazing—"

Corax's tone was so creepy and probing that Gabriel felt compelled to interrupt, just to stop him from talking. "I have a wish of my own to make," Gabriel replied. "I wish that the citadel may never lock another prisoner within its walls!"

Gabriel felt scared the moment he finished speaking, for the necklace suddenly flashed brightly upon the staff. Then a distant rumble echoed from below. He and his friends peered through the window of the chamber and saw the citadel, way down in the abyss, glowing from thousands of tiny windows. The bridge was bare now. The prisoners had crossed.

"They're all free," Pamela whispered to Abby.

A loud thunderclap emanated from the bridge.

"Oh, look!" cried Abby, pointing.

A thin line widened in the very center of the bridge, becoming a large crack, and then a piece dropped into the abyss. More sections began falling, one after another, until the entire bridge had vanished. Now that the great citadel was untethered, it moved slightly, as a ship might drift gently from its moorings. A terrible sound, like rock splitting, echoed in the abyss. The enormous tower turned and tipped like a sleeping giant against the chasm wall. The noise was anything but gentle—a thunderous echo rang out as the tower began to crumble against itself, bricks and stones falling, walls collapsing, cracks widening to gaping holes; then the whole fortress sank down with slow, devastating grace.

Corax's eyes glittered bitterly at Gabriel. His talons

gripped the windowsill. His dark satanic wings quivered with anger.

As a cloud of rubble slowly rose from the abyss, the children saw a tiny bird approaching the chamber. It was quite small and caked in powder from the collapsed citadel. After circling the chamber twice, it settled on Corax's shoulder.

The bird shook itself vigorously, revealing a bright red breast. Its malicious black eyes danced at Gabriel, and then it began to chirp quickly into Corax's ear.

*It's that robin!* Gabriel told Paladin.

Paladin took off from Gabriel's shoulder to chase the robin, but Corax closed his other hand protectively around the bird and held him closer to his ear. The robin chirped eagerly, and Corax listened, his angry features slowly calming.

"Well done, my little friend," he said. "You will be rewarded. I wonder what the taste of human flesh will do for a robin?"

"Gabriel, make a wish, quick!" shouted Somes. "Do something to him!"

Gabriel looked at Somes, the same thought on his mind. But what? What to wish? *Try not to use wishes for yourself,* his father had warned.

He could send Corax to the bottom of the earth, but wondered if it was a selfish wish. Might it send him there, too? How do you make an unselfish wish against your enemy?

"Quick, Gabriel!" cried Abby.

The robin had finished its explanation. Corax released the bird, then seized Somes by one arm and drew his talon sharply across his face.

"Aaagh!" Somes clutched his cheek as blood dribbled down his neck.

"*There's* your blood sacrifice!" shouted Corax. He turned to Gabriel. "And here's your riddle!

"What can you make but never give away, break but never repair?"

Gabriel mouthed the riddle to himself. He might have solved it easily in the comfort of his living room, but at this terrifying moment, his mind went blank. He tried to look away from Corax because the demon's eyes seemed to interfere with his concentration. He looked to Abby, but she seemed confused, too. She looked away from Corax and rubbed her spectacles, trying to concentrate.

Now Corax tightened his grip on Somes, ripped the glasses from his face, and pressed two talons to the boy's eyelids. Somes uttered a gasp as his spectacles fell to the floor.

"Time's up, Nephew. Answer now or your friend here goes blind!"

As the demon pressed his claws to Somes's eyes, Gabriel shouted.

"I—I—I give up! I don't know!"

Corax dropped Somes, who fell to his knees.

"What's the answer?" asked Gabriel.

"A *promise*," said Corax. "It can be made or broken, never given away, never repaired." Gleefully, the demon held out one claw.

The staff hesitated in Gabriel's hand, as if reluctant to leave. Then, with a revolted shudder, it zoomed into the grasp of the demon.

"Ha!" Corax shouted. "It's *mine*! And everything I've planned these years shall come to pass. I'll raise a new citadel, and the world above will answer to me alone!"

This should have been a moment for despair. All seemed lost. Everything Gabriel had set out to do had failed. The demon had won. Yet Gabriel felt a surge of confidence. Had the staff delivered an extra helping of self-assurance before it left him?

He turned to Abby, Pamela, and Somes. There was an intense look of admiration and loyalty on their faces. He couldn't have made it this far without their help. And now, well, he felt stronger, just looking at them. They all knew that this demon had to be stopped. In that moment, he realized what he had to do.

For Gabriel, it felt like the task he had been practicing for his whole life.

"I challenge you to a duel!" he cried.

# ❀ The Duel ❀

Corax's mouth opened in disbelief. His cold round eyes darted about the room for the robin, who had disappeared suddenly.

"A duel? There's no such thing!"

"Oh, yes," Gabriel replied, "I can demand a duel."

Corax looked at the other children. They stared back defiantly; even Somes, dabbing his shirtsleeve to the wound on his cheek, picked up his glasses and gave a thumbs-up to Gabriel.

The demon sneered. "Another of your childish pranks, I suppose?"

Ignoring Gabriel, he walked over to the window, shook the staff, and issued his first wish.

"I want my citadel back the way it was!"

Nothing happened.

There was no glow from the torc. No thunder. Not a sound.

Confused, Corax repeated his wish, but the torc didn't even flicker.

"It won't serve you," Gabriel explained. "If I challenge you to a duel, you must accept. When one of us fails to guess the other's riddle, the winner takes the torc and the loser . . ." Gabriel's lips trembled as he tried to finish his sentence. "The loser dies."

Something fluttered frantically to one of the windows. The robin was desperately throwing itself at the shutters, trying to escape.

"You!" Corax pointed a finger at the tattletale robin. "Is this true?"

The robin trembled. Its beady little black eyes darted from Corax to Gabriel and back to Corax. Then it uttered an indignant chirp.

"Useless bird!" murmured Corax, throwing the staff to the ground. "Very well, Nephew, you'll have your duel!"

Somes attempted to pick up the staff, but Corax placed his foot upon it.

There was not a sound in the room as Gabriel prepared his first riddle. Corax waited, flexing his enormous wings impatiently.

*"Every day they say I break,*
*Yet never am I whole.*
*Every day I rise again,*
*Never do I fall."*

Corax narrowed his eyes. He turned to the children, as if expecting that the answer would appear on one of their faces.

Somes quickly looked down, Pamela stared at her shoes, and Abby removed her glasses.

"Something that breaks, something that rises, but never falls." A sneer formed on his mouth. "Quite simple. That would be the *dawn!*"

The children looked disappointed. Abby replaced her glasses and gave Gabriel a determined smile that said *Don't give up!*

Gabriel took a deep breath.

The demon paced for a moment; then, peering out the window, he spoke:

*"A baby hasn't much of me.*
*Old men consult me endlessly.*
*Without me, time's a mystery.*
*What am I?"*

Being careful not to look at Corax, Gabriel repeated the lines in his head. *Without me, time's a mystery.* So it had to do with time. *A baby hasn't much of me.* Could it be a lifetime? But a baby has a lifetime ahead, while an old man has very little that remains. It must be something to do with age. *Old men consult me endlessly.* Well, it couldn't be memory, because anybody can be forgetful. On the other hand, time would be a mystery without the past, present, and future. And babies have almost no past because they've just been born!

"Got it!" said Gabriel. "It's the past!"

The demon arched his wings, then lowered them in obvious disgust.

"Proceed," he said.

The sneer on Corax's lips promised that Gabriel's next question would be infinitely harder. Gabriel looked at Abby. She nodded at him as if to say that this one had to be his best.

Gabriel suddenly remembered something Abby had said before. *Valravens can't laugh.*

It should be something funny.

*Of course,* he thought. *It must be something very funny. Something ridiculous!*

"Are you ready?" asked the demon impatiently.

"Okay, I'm ready," said Gabriel. "What do you call a country where everybody drives a pink automobile?"

The demon frowned and began pacing about the chamber.

"Everybody drives a pink automobile? It doesn't make sense? Why would they . . ."

Minutes ticked by as the demon kept flexing his wings with frustration. Again, he peered at the faces of the children, trying to find the answer. Finally, he scoffed at Gabriel.

"There's no name for such a place!"

"Of course there is," Gabriel replied. "It's a pun."

"A pun . . ." Corax shook his head. "There is no answer!"

"Yes," replied Gabriel. "A pink carnation!"

"*Pink carnation?*" repeated the demon.

"A *pink car* nation," said Gabriel.

*Zing!* The staff flew to his fingers.

Without wasting any time, Gabriel made his wish. It was a simple and sublime wish, a wish that didn't require him to separate his friends from a storm of valravens, and most of all, a wish that served others rather than himself. This was why he knew it would work.

In that instant, a comforting amber glow surrounded Abby, Pamela, and Somes.

"What's happening, Gabriel?" Abby cried. "What did you wish?"

"I'm sending you all back safely!" he cried.

"But what about you? How are you going to get home?"

"Best not to use a wish on myself," he said. "I'll paravolate back with Paladin!"

"Gabriel, I'm sure it's okay if you—" cried Pamela, but she didn't finish her sentence because all three of them vanished in a sudden flash.

The demon stared blankly at the boy and his raven, for although he had lost the torc, he was still standing, intact.

*I thought the loser was supposed to die!* said Paladin.

*That's what my father said,* Gabriel replied. *Unless . . . if one is a valraven, doomed to live forever, there's really no such thing as dying.*

It was a good guess. Corax seemed utterly unaffected by his defeat. His wings beat the air with malicious intensity as he advanced on the boy.

"Congratulations on your *victory.*"

Gabriel raised the staff—he remembered its power against valravens.

"You wouldn't do such a thing to your . . . uncle, would you?"

It should have been easy for Gabriel to point the staff and watch him go *pop!* like every other valraven, but he couldn't. How could he kill his own uncle?

Corax gloated over the boy's hesitation. "What a pathetic hero you've turned out to be."

Boldly, Corax reached forward, tearing the silver necklace from its place on the staff. Then he put the torc on his neck, just as Septimus had, and he made a wish.

"May the torc be *my* body! May its magic be *my* magic! May its power be *my* power!"

Nothing happened for a moment. Then Gabriel noticed something odd about the two ravens' heads at the ends of the necklace. Their eyes began to glow red. And as those little red eyes glowed, Corax began to tremble, then scream. He reached up to the necklace, clawing at it—but to no avail, for the torc remained, fused to his skin. Corax began weeping. Piteous, agonized tears rolled down his cheeks, as if his body was going through some horrible invisible transformation.

Then, quite suddenly, the cries stopped. Corax had vanished. The torc clattered to the floor.

"What happened?" asked Paladin, looking around. "Where is he?"

Gabriel looked at the necklace. The eyes of the raven heads had dimmed again, but he felt leery about picking it up. The dwarfs were right. It was more of a curse than a blessing.

"Wow," said Gabriel. "I think Corax expected the magic to enter him, but instead, he entered the torc. Do you think that's possible?"

Paladin shook his neck feathers. "All I know is, good riddance!"

At that moment something flew over from its hiding place at the shutters. It was Snitcher the robin. Seeing that the boy hadn't picked up the torc, the robin approached it, examining it carefully from every angle. His black eyes darted at Gabriel, then Paladin; then, without waiting another second, he bowed to the necklace, which flopped conveniently onto his neck and shrank to exactly the right size.

"Wait!" Gabriel shouted to the bird.

Ignoring his warning with a triumphant chirp, the robin flew off through the open window with his prize.

"What a stupid bird," said Paladin. "Even a half-wit would think twice after seeing what just happened!"

"The dwarfs were right. Nobody can resist a wish," said Gabriel. "We'd better go after him. The torc belongs back on the staff."

The collapse of the tower had propelled dust in every direction. Thick columns of debris filled the staircase. Uttering a chirp to light its way, the robin weaved through the murky shaft like a spark going up a chimney.

Coughing and gasping as one, Gabriel and Paladin flew blindly after Snitcher. It was a perilous chase in the dark, but the little bird shot ahead with reckless determination.

Eventually, the air in the shaft began to smell fresh and clear. Paladin glimpsed a rectangular opening ahead with a bright, starlit sky. Above them, the gate of the mausoleum hung wide open—a signal, perhaps, that Corax's power over it was gone.

They burst out, seizing every clear breath of cool wintry air with a great sense of relief. Alighting on a patch of frosty grass, Gabriel and Paladin jumped apart and peered past the frosty cemetery stones to see the dim shapes of birds who had escaped Aviopolis. A bustard fluffed his feathers on the ground nearby. Three guinea fowl were cooing bitterly on a tree limb. A fat white ptarmigan dusted herself off as she uttered an embarrassed apology to no one in particular.

Gabriel's thoughts turned to his father. He wondered if he had survived the long walk up the staircase.

As if in answer to his concern, a man's voice called from behind.

"Gabriel!"

# ❀ The Homecoming ❀

Gabriel spun around and saw Mr. Finley approaching with Abby, Somes, and Pamela. They all embraced, breaths billowing in the chilly air, so glad to be reunited. Their expressions soon shifted to astonishment as Gabriel described Corax's last moments.

"And you're sure the robin escaped?" said Mr. Finley.

"I don't know where he is," said Paladin with a downhearted shrug.

"Cheer up, Paladin," Mr. Finley replied. "We made it home, and home has its own rewards!"

Mr. Finley caught Somes's eye after this remark. The boy nodded, as if home had a new meaning after this adventure.

A peach-colored dawn welcomed the group as they followed a path out of the cemetery. They were exhausted from their journey, but their spirits were high. The streets of Brooklyn were empty save for a lone newspaper truck growling past; the city seemed blissfully unaware of the extraordinary danger that had been averted deep underground.

"No one will ever know, will they?" mused Abby.

"I guess not," said Gabriel.

"I hope all these talking birds will be okay," worried Pamela. "I'd bring some of them home, but my mother . . . well, she'll have a hard enough time dealing with the news that I lost my violin."

Abby gave her a sympathetic hug. As they all began to talk about how to explain this adventure to their families, only Somes remained silent, deep in his own thoughts.

"Somes?" Abby said when they came to Gabriel's house. "You don't have to go home; you can stay with me if you want."

"And you're welcome to stay with us," added Mr. Finley.

"No thanks," said Somes.

Abby frowned and reached for his arm. "Somes, are you sure?"

The boy smiled softly at her. "Thanks, but I can take care of myself."

Waving goodbye, Somes continued up the sidewalk toward his house.

Abby gave her farewells and crossed the street. She reached into her coat pocket for her house key, unlocked the door, and entered on tiptoes. It was dark in the hall. Hanging up her dusty coat, she turned the corner into the kitchen and stopped dead.

Her moms and her two sisters were clustered together by

the stove, their hair disheveled, faces haggard and streaked with tears.

"What's going on here?" Abby said.

Her big sister Viv dropped a muffin tin with a loud clatter. "What do you mean, 'What's going on'? We've been worried sick about you!" she cried.

"Where have you been?" cried Etta. "We called the police!"

"And the fire department," said her mom the optometrist.

"And the army," said her other mother. "And the navy."

Abby was pretty sure this last comment was a joke.

"How dare you disappear like that!" cried Viv, smothering Abby with a pair of lobster-claw cooking mitts.

"You'd better explain exactly where you've been," said her mother.

"And have something to eat!" added Etta.

Abby closed her eyes as she nestled in her sister's hug. She felt incredibly glad to be home.

Trudy and Aunt Jaz were bustling about the kitchen when Mr. Finley, Gabriel, and Pamela entered the house. Aunt Jaz let out a tearful cry and rushed forward.

"Adam! . . . You came back!" she cried.

"Yes, Jasmine, I finally did." Mr. Finley laughed and embraced her.

Trudy's mouth opened in alarm when she saw Pamela. "I

thought you were upstairs, asleep!" Then she noticed Paladin perched on Pamela's shoulder. "Shoo, you horrible thing!" she cried. "Get away, get away!"

"C'mon, Mother," said Pamela. "Paladin's my friend."

"How can a blackbird be a friend?"

"Not a blackbird. A *raven*. There's a big difference," Pamela said. "He's very tired and very hungry. We have to feed him."

It was then that Trudy noticed the dust all over Pamela's clothes.

"Goodness, where have you been?"

"I told you before, Mother. Aviopolis."

"No, where have you *really* been?"

"Like I said, far underground. There's a whole city there. We barely made it out alive. I lost my violin."

"Your violin? Oh, my goodness! Not your violin!"

"Mom! I almost died being carried by a swarm of flesh-eating birds!"

"Yes, dear, I'm sure," Trudy replied. "But have you any idea how much that violin was worth? Oh, Pamela, what a tragedy!"

Somes entered his kitchen and discovered the pizza box still sitting on the kitchen table. He warmed a slice in the toaster oven and gobbled it down, catching the melting cheese with his tongue.

Mr. Grindle appeared in the kitchen doorway, his hair in disarray, a frown on his face.

"What are you doing here?"

"This is my home," Somes replied.

"You ran out."

"Yes, I did," said Somes. "But I'm back."

"You expect me to just let you walk in here?"

Somes looked at Mr. Grindle for a long moment. "A father is supposed to take care of his son," he said. "And sons take care of their fathers, too."

The man didn't speak. Somes imagined he might strike him, or he might open the door and tell him to leave. This time, however, Mr. Grindle sat down.

"Any more of that pizza left?" he asked.

Somes nodded and turned the box toward his father.

## ❀ Epilogue ❀

Adam Finley's return was celebrated with an enormous Christmas dinner. Trudy did most of the cooking, but Aunt Jaz insisted on adding some things that she said were Mr. Finley's favorites. This was her excuse to make sure that the meal was full of desserts, and there were many, including Christmas gingerbread cookies in the shape of ravens, a Brooklyn blackout cake, and meringue cookies.

"All this sugar is terribly unhealthy!" complained Trudy.

"If you'd been cooped up in a cell for three years, you'd want a little sugar," Aunt Jaz reminded her.

Trudy was willing to believe that Adam had been imprisoned, but she decided it must have been somewhere in Europe where they punish people severely for parking in the wrong place. She certainly didn't believe in Aviopolis, or that Gabriel had rescued his father. She was most upset when Gabriel described Corax as Adam's jailer.

"Corax, you say? No, I don't believe it. He was a beautiful, misunderstood boy. I'm sure, wherever he is, he's doing great things!" She stared off for a moment with a misty look in her eyes.

Mr. Finley advised Gabriel not to mention Corax to her again. "Some people simply believe what they need to believe, no matter what proof there is to the contrary," he said.

Trudy told Aunt Jaz that Gabriel must have enticed Pamela into a manhole and taken her for a tour of the sewers beneath the city. "That would explain the dust," she said.

Aunt Jaz just laughed.

Pamela kept trying to explain her adventure to her mother; she had her own reason for wanting Trudy to believe ravens could talk and that a person could paravolate. Yet even when she got Paladin to talk in sentences, Trudy insisted it was a trick any parrot could do.

"I won't have you following Gabriel down any manholes again," she told Pamela. "Now that Adam has returned, we shall have to find another place to live. I don't know how we'll afford it. I'm still very upset about your violin!"

Gabriel noticed Pamela's gloom at dinner. "What's wrong?" he asked.

"I love your house," she confessed. "I don't want to go."

"You don't have to," said Mr. Finley, who had been listening. "I've just offered your mom the rooms on the top floor."

"Can we stay, Mother?" said Pamela.

"Well, I'm not sure," she said. "I'm a strong believer in

facts, and this house seems to encourage *untruths.*" Here, she looked sharply at Gabriel. "And there's the matter of the violin."

"Oh, Mother," said Pamela in disappointment.

It was then that the doorbell rang.

Trudy opened it to a white-haired gentleman with a very handsome slate-gray raven perched on his shoulder.

"Greetings, madam. My name is Burbage."

"Yes? What is it?" asked Trudy, puzzled that the man's lips weren't moving.

"It was *I* who spoke, madam," said the gray raven. "Mr. Geiger here has laryngitis, the result of poor nerves and a dusty escape from a perilous abyss!"

Trudy blinked at the bird. "Oh, I . . . What can I do for you?"

"It is not what you can do for me, but what we can do for you, madam."

Septimus Geiger held up a dusty, battered violin case.

"We were crossing a bridge out of Aviopolis—"

"Aviopolis?" Trudy frowned.

"Yes. As we were leaving, this case landed in Mr. Geiger's arms. I believe it belongs to your daughter."

Trudy ran her hands over the dusty exterior. "It landed in his arms?"

"Naturally. He couldn't have caught it any other way," remarked the bird.

Trudy slowly opened the case. The violin was nestled in

black velvet, in perfect condition. She closed it and stared back at the raven.

"How do you like that?" Burbage grumbled to Septimus. "Not even a thank-you!"

Septimus reached into his pocket and produced a white mouse, which he threw into the air. Burbage caught it in his beak and swallowed it whole, which provoked a surprised gasp from Trudy.

Making a flourish with his hand, Septimus disappeared, leaving the gray raven hovering in the air.

"Best regards to Mr. Finley and son!" he said, and flew off over the rooftops.

When Trudy returned to the meal, she looked a little pale.

"Who was at the door?" asked Aunt Jaz.

"Oh, um, a man and a . . ." She frowned and shook her head. "Never mind."


There was one secret that was tormenting Gabriel. He had been waiting for the right time to speak to Mr. Finley about a very tender subject. Late that evening, when everyone was well fed and gone to bed, he crept down from his room and found his father reading in his study.

"Yes, Gabriel?" said Mr. Finley.

Gabriel noticed that his father was sitting in front of the writing desk. Its lid was open, but there was nothing in any of the compartments.

"That will be all," he said to the desk, replacing a book in one compartment.

The writing desk snapped its lid shut and trotted across the room, settling in a corner. Gabriel followed it with his eyes. "It does what you tell it to do?"

"Most of the time," said his father. "But let us talk. What's on your mind?"

"I want to know about my mother," said Gabriel.

Finley gazed kindly at his son. "Of course, Gabriel. I've been waiting for you to ask. Do you remember my saying that the torc was a mischievous device?"

"Yes."

"Well, it may surprise you to know that you owe your existence to it."

"How?"

"If you remember, the raven Muninn made his last wish and was buried alive in a tomb. A thousand years later, I went to Iceland looking for the torc, hoping to keep my brother from finding it. At the same time, your mother came to Iceland to study the mythology of an ash tree known as the Tree of Life. The staff, you see, was made from this remarkable wood. Well, one day we arrived in the same library in Iceland, looking for the same book."

"What a coincidence," said Gabriel.

"More than a coincidence. Dark magic drew us there. You see, the torc craved mischief. It wanted to be discovered."

"Why?"

"Buried for a thousand years in the caverns of Iceland, it was ignored, powerless, and forgotten. Nobody would have wandered there alone to find it. Anyway, your mother and I fell in love in that library. We hiked to the Godafoss—the waterfall of the gods—and found it so beautiful that we took a house nearby.

"We married, and for three years we did our research together and wandered the caverns."

"But how did you ever find the tomb?" asked Gabriel.

"It was just after you were born," said Mr. Finley. "I found an old scroll that suggested that the tomb I was looking for lay in a lower cavern I'd never explored. I'll never forget that day—I left you and your mother, promising to return by nightfall.

"The farther I went, the more I felt a power drawing me in. One can get terribly lost in such caverns. People are always warned to go with a friend in case of an injury. I went alone, and this was part of the torc's mischief. I wandered miles not really knowing where I was going. When I was completely lost and just wanted to go home, I heard voices singing."

"Voices? What kind of voices?" asked Gabriel.

"Beautiful voices, and music that reminded me of home, of my wife and my baby . . ."

Mr. Finley paused and shook his head. "No, that's not true," he said. "It was the kind of music that tricks and confuses, like the siren song that made Ulysses almost go insane on his ship. I followed these voices, tripping, stumbling, until

I fell into a crevasse and gashed my ankle so badly that I could barely walk."

"It was a trap," said Gabriel.

Finley nodded. "At the time I thought it was just an accident, but it was much worse than that. There I lay, crippled and helpless. Those strange voices stopped singing. Now I wondered if I had only imagined them. I crawled out of the crevasse and saw an archway and, beyond it, a riddle carved in the rock in an old Norse language:

*A feast has five guests.*
*Take just one of these guests away,*
*And nobody can eat. Why?*"

Gabriel thought for a moment. "Well, the word *feast* has five letters. If you take the 'e' away, it's a fast. Nobody can eat during a fast."

"Very good," said Mr. Finley. "When I answered the riddle, a small chamber appeared that I had not seen before. I limped into the chamber, and what I saw was astounding."

"What was it?" asked Gabriel.

"A man—no, not a man, a *warrior king*—in his final resting place," said his father. "Surrounded by his weapons, as a great chieftain might have his possessions laid out for a life in the afterworld. A magnificent leather helmet inlaid with garnets and rubies rested on his chest. There were battle-axes and swords with handles of ivory, gold, and bronze and a large shield of leather studded with silver. Beside him lay the skeleton of a raven."

"Muninn?"

Mr. Finley nodded. "I bumped against a cluster of weapons—swords, axes, and javelins—and a stick fell in my way. A dull old stick."

"The staff?" asked Gabriel.

Mr. Finley raised one eyebrow. "At the time, Gabriel, I thought not. It looked to be the least valuable thing in the tomb. My leg was bleeding, so I decided to use it to limp home and clean my wound. In the dim light I didn't even notice the torc wrapped around the top, covered with centuries of dust.

"One fact about dark magic you must understand: it's cunning. It needed someone who could solve the riddle of the tomb to enter. It needed me to find the tomb. And it needed me to take the staff."

"And it needed a blood sacrifice," said Gabriel.

Mr. Finley nodded. "And it made me wish something. As I limped back the way I came, I got lost. My flashlight went dim. Soon I would be trapped in complete darkness. It was that moment when I felt so sorry for myself that I wished simply that I could get home to my family.

"Well, suddenly, the staff trembled in my hand. The next moment, my wound vanished! Then the flashlight started working. So I picked up my stride, sure that I knew my way, and guess what? *I never made a single wrong turn.* Outside the cave, there wasn't a moon, yet I found my way to my car without even thinking about it. I seemed to be on some amazing lucky streak. I couldn't wait to tell your mother.

"I stepped into the house and I could smell the stew she had cooked for dinner. It sat bubbling on the stove, and the table was set. I found you asleep in your crib, calm and contented; there was a pan upon the stove with a loaf of bread that must have just come out of the oven, because it was still steaming. There was ice in the glasses at the table. Your mother must have heard the car pull up. And yet, the moment I walked in that door, she vanished."

"Vanished? How?" said Gabriel.

His father replied with a helpless smile. "I searched the house; wherever she went, she took no shoes or coat, for they were by the door. I called the police. For weeks, they searched for her but found nothing. It became clear to me that the torc took her the moment I would have set eyes upon her."

"*Why?*" asked Gabriel.

"This is the awful thing about dark magic, you see. It takes *whatever matters most to you that you'll forever miss.*"

Gabriel lowered his head sadly. "But all you wanted was to go home."

"Yes. That's the mischief of dark magic."

"Then she's gone forever?"

"Oh, no. I believe that we'll find her. Somewhere out there, the torc must have the answer," his father assured him.

*   *   *

Shivering in the wintry night, a robin perched by the window and listened intently to the conversation within. It had been waiting by the Finley house for weeks, huddling over the chimney, keeping its head close to the window glass, hoping to hear more about the torc.

The silver circle around its neck burned terribly.

# Acknowledgments

I thank my wonderful wife, Terri Seligman, for her enthusiastic support and many readings, and Lola Hagen, my muse and first young reader. Sophie and Brooklyn Hagen asked for stories every morning on the walk to school; there is no better way to learn storytelling. Thanks also to Elizabeth Bogner for her comments on the manuscript and to Noa Scheidlower, who gave me a thumbs-up!

My appreciation also goes to Lee Wade, Rachael Cole, Colleen Fellingham, Tim Terhune, Scott Bakal, Jake Parker, Annie Kelley, and Stephanie Pitts for their super contributions.

Finally, a very warm thanks to my fabulous editor, Anne Schwartz, who asked all the wise, tough, and brilliant questions that made this story as much fun to write as I hope it is to read.